LADY
LAW

Semper Fi!

LADY LAW

BY

KEN FARMER

Cover by K. R. Farmer & Adriana Girolami
Special thanks to Jenna Miller, cover model
for Deputy US Marshal Fiona Miller
Costume by Ravenna Old West
www.RavennaOldWest.com

THE AUTHOR

Ken Farmer – After proudly serving his country as a US Marine, Ken attended Stephen F. Austin State University on a full football scholarship, receiving his Bachelors Degree in Business and Speech & Drama. Ken quickly discovered his love for acting when he starred as a cowboy in a Dairy Queen commercial when he was raising registered Beefmaster cattle and Quarter Horses at his ranch in East Texas. Ken has over 41 years as a professional actor, with memorable roles *Silverado, Friday Night Lights, The Newton Boys* and *Uncommon Valor.* He was the spokesman for Wolf Brand Chili for eight years. Ken was a professional and celebrity Team Penner for over twenty years—twice penning at the National Finals—and participated in the Ben Johnson Pro-Celebrity Rodeos until Ben's death in '96. Ken now lives near Gainesville, TX, where he continues to write novels.

Ken wrote a screenplay back in the '80s, *The Tumbleweed Wagon.* He and his writing partner, Buck Stienke adapted it to a historical fiction western, *THE NATIONS*—a Finalist for the Elmer Kelton Award and winner of the Larmie Award for Best Classic Western - 2016. They released the sequel, *HAUNTED FALLS*—winner of the Laramie Award for Best Action Western, 2013—in June of 2013. *HELL HOLE* was the third in the Bass Reeves saga written by Ken alone. *LADY LAW* is the second novel written by Ken alone.

ISBN-13: - 978-0-9971290-6-9 - Paper
ISBN-10: - 0-9971290-6-9
ISBN-13: - 978-0-9971290-7-6 - E
ISBN-10: - 0-9971290-7-7

Timber Creek Press
Imprint of Timber Creek Productions, LLC
312 N. Commerce St.
Gainesville, Texas

ACKNOWLEDGMENT

The authors gratefully acknowledges T.C. Miller, Fred Shaw, Brad Dennison, Mary Deal, and Doran Ingrham for their invaluable help in proofing and editing this novel.

Published by: Timber Creek Press
timbercreekpresss@yahoo.com
www.timbercreekpress.net
Twitter: @pagact
Facebook Book Page:
www.facebook.com/TimberCreekPress
214-533-4964

DEDICATION

LADY LAW is dedicated to my mom and dad, Robert R. 1908 - 1965 and Johnie Vertis Farmer 1915 - 1974. Rest in Peace.

This novel is a work of fiction…except the parts that aren't. Names, characters, places and incidents are either the products of the author's imaginations or are used fictitiously and sometimes not. Any resemblance to actual persons, living or dead, business establishments, events or locales is entirely coincidental, except where they aren't.

First printing - June 18, 2016

TIMBER CREEK PRESS

CHAPTER ONE

SOLDIER CREEK
CHICKASAW NATION

The water-wrinkled hand reached up out of the muddy river and grabbed an exposed root from a cottonwood tree sticking out of the bank. The weakened man pulled most of his bedraggled body up onto the clay slope with intense effort. The bank bordered Soldier Creek at its confluence with the Red River.

He lay on the shore, half-out of the water, trying to catch his breath for several long moments. It came in ragged, gurgling spurts as he coughed up dirty water tinged with blood and phlegm. Finally, he managed to roll over on his back where he could breathe better—although the breaths were short, irregular and choppy.

He raised his head with some degree of effort, to look down at the hole in his once white shirt. The profuse amount of blood that had leaked from his body had long since washed away after almost ten hours in the river.

The man managed to tear the shirt away from the ragged bullet hole with his left hand. It was no longer bleeding, but he still reached over and grabbed a handful of rotted leaves and red clay, pressed it over the hole and pulled the torn shirt back. He got another fistful, reached under the shirt and mashed it into the second hole just below his collarbone.

He finally regained enough strength after resting for several hours to crawl completely out of the water and up on to the dry, leaf-covered forest floor along the creek. The injured man rested for a while again, and then managed to get to his feet with help from a piece of hickory limb lying beside his leg.

He reached up and pushed the long black matted hair from in front of his ebon eyes and slowly looked around at his surroundings. "Mankiller lives."

SKEANS BOARDING HOUSE
THREE WEEKS LATER

The beautiful, statuesque brunette in a black fitted single-button morning coat—her tiny waist accentuated by a red patterned bustier with a gray underbust—set her carpet bag on the porch and went inside the stately Victorian house. She came back out a few seconds later wearing her black, flat-topped John B. Stetson Gamblers hat, accompanied by a slightly-built shorter man—she turned to him.

"I got my telegram from the Marshals Service in Washington."

Marshal Brushy Bill Roberts looked deep into her steel-gray eyes. "And?"

"They gave me permission to go unattached for as long as I want...It's a new program that actually allows a Deputy US Marshal to roam anywhere in the States they are needed—reporting directly to Washington... with Special Deputy Marshal status."

Bill grinned and pulled out a white envelope from his inside coat pocket and handed it to Fiona.

She glanced at him with a puzzled expression, removed an official-looking document and read it. "Well, congratulations Special Marshal Roberts and welcome to our exclusive club... I suppose we should partner up."

"My thoughts exactly...Special Marshal Miller...So, now what?"

"Well, first, we go to Fort Smith and pay our respects at Judge Parker's funeral with Bass and the others."

A look of pain crossed Bill's face. "I think I'm getting a bit tired of going to funerals."

Fiona nodded. "I know." She paused to allow him to gather himself as she knew he was still experiencing recurrent bouts of depression over the tragic and untimely death of his fiancée, Millie. "After that, we'll see where the wind blows."

"What about home base? We need a regular location to receive our list of trouble spots."

"Don't see anything wrong with Gainesville. We have plenty of friends here to forward notices when we're out and about…There's train service east, west, north and south, plus we have the Rafter S ranch available to rest our horses…and ourselves as the need arises."

"Agreed." Bill pulled out his gold pocket watch, opened the case to see the time. "Train leaves in an hour."

Fiona nodded. "Unusual watch," she said, looking at the filigreed cover.

"Gift from John Chisum when I worked for him over fifteen years ago in New Mexico."

"Nice…You knew Chisum started his cattle empire just twenty miles south of here."

"Didn't know that."

"His 'Big White House'…as it was called…was located in Bolivar and his brand was 'The Long Rail'. The ranch stock was referred to as 'Jinglebob Ear' because of the unique cut on their ears."

"Now, I didn't know that, either."

"I understand he moved his operation to New Mexico in '66."

"Knew that...Just didn't know where he came from."

She grinned. "Now you do...Shall we go?" Fiona bent over to grab her bag, but Bill beat her to it. "Uh, uh, uh...No need to get in the habit of that...Carrying my bag is in the same category as calling me, 'Ma'am'."

"Point taken." He picked up his own bag and they walked out to the street where their horses—his Morgan gelding, Tippy, and her Appaloosa, Diablo—were tethered to upright iron posts with rings on the top. They had already tied on their saddlebags.

They attached their bags to the saddles with the long tie strings and each swung easily aboard.

Bill glanced over at Fiona as they turned their mounts and headed north on Dixon Street. "Interesting silver crucifix you've got hanging around your neck."

She grinned. "As you know, I don't wear much jewelry, but this belonged to my great grandmother in Italy. It's over two hundred years old."

"Beautiful."

PICKENS COUNTY
CHICKASAW NATIONS

The Cherokee renegade stirred around inside the tiny abandoned fisherman's shack he had been holding up in while his wounds healed. He picked up the hickory limb he had used to get to his feet when he crawled out of Soldier Creek four weeks ago—more dead than alive. He looked down at the almost healed holes in his chest and nodded. "Cherokee medicine strong."

He slapped the stick across his palm, and then pushed the rickety door open—it was hanging only by one piece of leather from an old shoe.

Mankiller eased down the creek bank and pulled a narrow leaf from a cat tail. He tied it around his head to keep his long nasty hair from his face, turned and headed off through the woods to the northwest.

The sun was setting as he squatted down in a grove of sweet gum trees and watched the farm house. It was located on a narrow dirt wagon road a little more than two miles south of Oakland.

After two previous farms he had watched, this was the first that didn't have a dog. Only one man—half Chickasaw and half black—his Creek wife and a preteen boy lived there. Mankiller waited with the patience known only to the Indian.

Three hours past dark, a gibbous moon had risen just above the tops of the trees. The last lamp went out inside the house. He got to his feet and stealthily crept toward the back. The Cherokee could make out a two foot diameter stump with a single-bit ax stuck in the top—obviously used for splitting kindling for a wood burning kitchen stove.

Mankiller easily pulled the blade free, checked its edge and dropped the hickory stick to the ground in favor of the ax. Pausing for a moment to make sure there were no sounds coming from inside, he crept up to an open window and quietly crawled through.

There was enough light from the spectral half-moon streaming through the windows, that he could make his way around the dinner table and to an open door. The renegade could see a coal oil lamp with just a hint of a burning wick on a table near a bed. It didn't shed any appreciable light, but there was enough flame that the owners only had to turn the wick up.

He could make out two adult forms on the bed underneath a patchwork quilt. Stepping to the edge, he raised the ax high with both hands and brought it down forcefully on the nearest form, splitting the man's head like a ripe watermelon. The sound of the blade striking his skull was loud enough to wake his wife with a start.

She sat bolt upright wiping blood and brains from her face, saw the outline of Mankiller standing over the bed. The quilt and sheets were already covered in blood from her husband. Her piercing scream split the night for a brief moment and stopped abruptly when the sideways swing of the ax caught her across the throat. The grisly severed head grisly bounced off the headboard and then to the floor on the opposite side of the bed with a thud.

Mankiller saw a double-barrel shotgun leaning against the wall between the night stand and the bed. He turned up the wick on the lamp, picked up the old weapon and checked the chamber—it was loaded.

"Mama?"

He spun around at the sound of the voice and pulled the trigger on the ten gauge. The twelve-year old boy in the doorway was blasted completely back into the other room with most of his face and chest completely obliterated by the full load of double-ought at close range.

"Stinkin' half-breed." The renegade looked at the bloodied body nearest to him on the bed and spat on it.

Opening the drawer in the night stand, he found four shells for the shotgun and slipped them into his pants pocket. He paused, took them back out, placed them and the gun on the blood-soaked bed, and then glanced down at his ragged, filthy pants and shirt.

There was an old three-drawer chifforobe against the near wall. In the top were two pair of blue bib overalls and several chambray shirts, one boiled off-white shirt and a red union suit. Mankiller held the overalls, and then one of the shirts up in the air.

"These do."

Thirty minutes later, Cal Mankiller walked away from the clapboard farm house in clean clothes, a gray slouch hat, the shotgun, five dollars and sixty cents he found in a jar in the kitchen and a flour sack of food stuffs.

The tongues of flames behind him licking out from under the eaves and hungrily consuming the cedar-shingle roof cast an eerie flickering light on the surrounding woods.

"Now, Mankiller find she-devil marshal."

FORT SMITH NATIONAL CEMETERY
FORT SMITH, ARKANSAS

A large number of Deputy United States Marshals, including Bass, Jack McGann, Selden Lindsey, Loss Hart, Fiona Miller and Bill Roberts, gathered in the slow drizzle for the graveside ceremony of Isaac Charles Parker. His interment was taking place at the Fort Smith National Cemetery, so designated by the United States government in 1867 because of the near four hundred Confederate and almost a thousand Union soldiers already buried there—many in unmarked graves.

A number of ladies stood with the Judge's widow, Mary O'Toole Parker, to comfort her as the Reverend W. D. Graham eulogized the great man.

"...Isaac Charles Parker was a man of rare character. In his twenty-one years on the bench, he tried over thirteen thousand cases and seventy-nine men went to meet their maker when they danced on his gallows. To quote the Judge: 'I have ever had the single aim of justice in view. No judge who is influenced by any other consideration is fit for the bench. *Do equal and exact justice*, is my motto, and I have often said to the grand jury, 'Permit no innocent man to be punished, but let no guilty man escape'.

"Many of us who knew and worked with him were well aware of his philosophy. If he had his druthers, he would personally abolish the death penalty. He often said, 'It is not the severity of the punishment that is the deterrent...but the certainty of it'."

He let his gaze drift about over the assemblage, and then continued, "Today, he walks with our Lord and Savior, Jesus Christ...He has gone home...Let us pray."

Bass held an umbrella over Jack as he swung along with his crutches—the carriage was only twenty yards away.

"Be shore not to git that cast wet. Winchester'll have yer hide," commented Bass.

"Think it's already too late...this drizzle is almost heavy enough to swim through...Need to go by his office when we git back to Ardmore anyways...What time is the train supposed to leave?"

"Eleven...We'll make it plenty easy."

"We even have time to change clothes. I feel naked without Romulus and Remus," said Fiona.

"Romulus and Remus?" asked Loss.

"That's what I call my ivory-handled Peacemakers…After the twin brothers supposedly fathered by either Mars or Hercules, raised by a she-wolf and founded the city of Rome in Italy…According to Virgil."

"Virgil who?"

She smiled. "Publius Vergilius Maro, an ancient Roman poet of the Augustan period…A few years before the birth of Jesus Christ."

"That's the only thang you just said that I understood…I know 'bout him. My mama made me go to church with her…They had Bible study fer us younguns…called it Sunday School."

Fiona rolled her eyes and grinned. "And that's a good thing."

"What's a good thing?"

"That they had a school on Sunday to teach you about Jesus, the gospel and basic catechism."

Loss shook his head. "If'n I stay around you much, gonna need a interpreter…It's like listenin' to Bass talk Injun er Judge Parker hand out a sentence."

"Speaking of Sunday…Angie is expectin' everbody to come to the house fer Sunday dinner. Looks like we need to have a meetin' anyways."

"Easy enough, Jack, since we're all taking the same train," responded Brushy Bill.

11

LINN, PICKINS COUNTY
CHICKASAW NATION

Mankiller opened the front door of Ashalintubbi's Mercantile, the only general merchandise store in the small agricultural community. The purloined shotgun was carried loosely in the crook of his right arm and he was wearing the clothes he also stole. He looked like any other Indian farmer in the area, except for his long hair which was tied back at the base of his neck with a leather thong.

It was still early morning and there were only a few other shoppers in the store. A two-inch brass bell attached to the header tinkled when he entered. The store smelled of cedar sawdust floor sweep.

The small, balding storekeep looked up from behind the long glass-topped counter that ran along the east side of the store. "Come right in. I'm Jade Ashalintubbi, what can I get for you today?"

Cal looked closely at the man and finally asked, "Need shells." He held up the shotgun.

"What gauge is she?"

"Not know."

Ashalintubbi's face took on a puzzled expression. "Your gun an' you don't know what the gauge is?"

"Find."

Several of the other customers, a young woman with her seven year old, cotton-headed daughter and a grizzled, white-bearded old timer took notice of the conversation.

The owner shook his head. "Look on the top or side of the receiver. Should say what she is."

"No read."

"Well…" He leaned forward and squinted at the weapon. "…looks to me like a ten gauge." He reached back and grabbed a box of double-ought shotgun shells from a shelf. "See if these here fit."

He broke the gun over and slipped two rounds in the chambers. "Unnn, shells fit." Mankiller looked through the glass top of the counter at the handguns on display. "Meby so you trade for Remington?…Me see."

The storekeep reached in the case, pulled out the 1875 Remington Single Action Army, laid it on the counter and set a box of .44-40 shells beside it. "These go with every handgun I sell… pistol ain't much good without ammunition."

The Cherokee picked up the revolver, pulled the hammer back several times, and then spun the cylinder. "We trade." He opened the box and started putting shells in the nickel-plated pistol.

Jade scratched his chin. "Well, I dunno." He glanced at the shotgun in the crook of Mankiller's arm. "She does have the Treble Wedge-Fast Hammerless feature…but looks a bit worn."

"Not know what is Treble Wedge thing."

"Cocks when you break the barrels over."

"Me know that…Mankiller keep." He held the Remington up.

"Now, ain't said we'd trade yet…Think I'm goin' to have to have a little boot…Say five dollars."

"Said Mankiller keep." He lifted the Greener with his left hand and pulled the rear trigger, blowing the slight-built Chickasaw back into the gun rack and shelves behind him in a spray of red.

The woman and little girl screamed at the earsplitting thunderous report of the ten gauge. He spun around and pulled the front trigger—taking out both of them, spattering blood and brain matter all over the table stacked with bolts of cloth they had just been looking at.

The old man customer picked up a shovel from a nearby bin and charged the Indian through the acrid gunsmoke. "Damn you, redhide bast…"

Mankiller cocked the hammer of the Remington and pulled the trigger on the gun, sending the slug to the middle of the old timer's stomach. The man staggered a couple of steps forward, dropped to his knees, and then fell to his face. The shovel skidded forward to the renegade's feet.

The Cherokee stuffed the box of pistol shells in one of the large back pockets of the bib overalls, and then grabbed the box of shotgun rounds and shoved them in the other. After stuffing all the paper money from the cash register in his front pockets, he glanced around, spied some dark broadcloth suits and grabbed the largest he could see.

As the Indian headed in the direction of the back door, he slung the dirty, tattered old gray fedora from his head, snatched a new black tall-crown, uncreased, cheap hat from a table and tried it on—it was too small. He picked up another, set it squarely on his head—it fit.

Mankiller casually continued his way out the rear of the store just before the town marshal and several of the local citizens burst through the front door responding to the gunfire.

"Good Godamighty," exclaimed Marshal Arlen Cole as he looked around the blood-spattered store with his Colt in his hand. Bile rose up in his throat.

The cloud of gunsmoke was slowly gathering closer to the fourteen foot ceiling.

"Miz Simpson an' her little girl er dead, Marshal," said Carl Anoatubbi, the barber from next door.

"So's pore ol' Jade…Oh, Lawdamercy, his whole face is gone," added Isom Love, a Chickasaw Freedman.

Other town's folk started pouring into Ashalintubbi's Merchantile.

The marshal glanced back over his shoulder, holstered his pistol and started waving his hands. "Out, out, everybody out…Don't need no crowd in here…But leave the door open so's some of this damn stinkin' smoke can drift out.

"Isom, you stand guard and keep the good folks of Linn out. They ain't needful of seein' this."

"Marshal! Ol' Ab's still abreathin'," said Ed Baber, a local farmer that had been passing by and followed them into the store. He knelt down beside the old man and did what he could to stop the bleeding.

"Sam, go fetch Doc Carlisle," ordered Cole to one of the citizens standing just outside the front door with his hands in his overall pockets. "...an' the undertaker."

MCGANN CABIN
ARBUCKLE MOUNTAINS
CHICKASAW NATION

Fiona was bouncing Baby Sarah on her knee and listening to her giggle. She looked up at Bass standing by the native stone fireplace drinking his after-dinner coffee. "Hear tell you got a telegram from Fort Smith."

He nodded. "'Pears that Bill was right...they's changes comin' down the pike." He took a sip from his cup. "Bein' transferred to the Paris office."

"You goin'?" asked Selden.

"Reckon so...this is what I do...Mind I probably cain't do nothin' else...er leastwise don't want to. They's malefactors an' outlaws on the scout jest 'bout most 'ny place you've a mind to look."

"What about applying for a Special Deputy Marshal designation and be a roamer like Bill and me?"

"Pondered on it some, but got a tad bit of a different situation than you an' Bill...Ten kids of my own plus the two I 'dopted, Mame and Hubert. I'm most usually no more'n a day away from the house...don't see as it'd be 'ny difference workin' out of Paris...'Sides it's purty obvious the new judge ain't quite the egalitarian Judge Parker wuz."

"Egaliwhat?" asked Loss.

"Being fair and equal to all concerned," said Fiona.

"Don't understand why ya'll jest cain't talk 'merican."

"It is American...or English to be more exact and for one, it's using one word as opposed to seven...understand?"

Loss shook his head. "No."

Bill grinned at Loss and then continued with the conversation, "Yeah, we heard he's getting rid of all the colored and Indian marshals...How 'bout you, Jack?"

"Well, got me a couple three more months with this here cast." He tapped on the hard plaster with his index finger. "So, reckon I kin still think on it some."

Angie turned around from checking the pies in her stove, popped the dishtowel against her thigh and wagged her finger at him. "There'll be no thinkin' on it, Jack Marmaduke McGann. Ye'll not be traipsin' all over the country chasin' outlaws and other scourge of the earth with Bass way down to Paris...Uncle Winchester has already told ye they want ye to be the town marshal at the Chickasaw capital in Tishomingo with a whole rasher of deputies to back ye up…Now I've had me say."

"She's got a point there, Jack. Fiona and I aren't saddled with a family, so…"

Angie turned to Bill and stamped her foot. "Saddled is it, William Roberts?"

"I didn't mean it the way it sounded. What I meant was we aren't tied down…"

Angie's green eyes burned completely through him.

"The best way to git out of a hole, Marshal Roberts, is to stop diggin'," admonished Bass. "When you've known Angie O'Reilly McGann as long as I have you'll figger it out…That red hair ain't jest fer decoration."

Bill grinned and nodded. "Ah… 'The better part of valor is discretion, in the which better part I have sav'd my life'…More than once. Shakes…"

"Falstaff in Shakespeare's Henry The Fourth, Part one, Scene five," interrupted Fiona. "But, I am glad you quoted it correctly…Most people try to say, discretion is the better part of valor, which is backwards."

"Ya'll er gonna be like two cats in a sack, you work together very long," observed Loss.

"Oh, probably not. I'm kinda like Bass…I've seen her shoot and anybody can shoot like that, I want to stay on the good side of…Figure we compliment one another…She's faster.

"Heck, I never even saw her hands move before those twin Colts of hers roared simultaneously when she nailed Mankiller...Surprised the hell out of him, too...But I'm a better shot."

"Wouldn't count on that," Bass and Fiona glanced at each other when they replied simultaneously.

"Seen her hit three six inch targets at two hundered yards with a Winchester an' it almost sounded like one shot," said Bass.

Bill glanced at Fiona and cocked his head. "Impressive...We'll have to go heads up sometime."

She glanced at him out of the corner of her eye and smiled a little wry grin.

Roberts turned to Lindsey. "What about you, Selden? Got any plans?"

"Think I'll keep on keepin' on...unless they try to transfer me. Bought some land west of Ardmore, been developing it. Gonna take up cattle ranchin' when I retire...If'n I have to do it ahead of schedule...well, that's alright too, already got most of the fencin' in."

"Loss, you ain't said nothin'," commented Bass.

"Well, I'm waitin' on some of Angie's sweet potato pecan pie."

"No, I meant 'bout yer work, marshalin' an' all."

"Oh! Reckon I'll stick with Sel...least fer awhile." He paused. "Howsomever, have been givin' some thought to openin' a restaurant in Ardmore though...of late."

Selden chuckled. "Now, see, Loss. There you go. Thinkin' 'bout doin' somethin' where you'd eat up all the profits."

"Aw, wouldn't do no such a dadburn thang." He stared down at the floor. "Fer one, she wouldn't let me."

Everyone in the room simultaneously asked, "She?"

Loss stared at the floor and scuffed his feet around. "Uh...been writin' Miss Penny Whisman, down to Athens, Texas." He looked up. "Ya'll 'member, from the race thing at Gainesville? She run the Fletcher Davis meat sandwich booth. Called 'em hamburgers...He's her uncle on his wife Ciddy's side...We, uh...been talkin' 'bout openin' a hamburger place in Ardmore...Gonna call it the Loss Penny Restaurant."

§§§

CHAPTER TWO

LINN, PICKINS COUNTY
CHICKASAW NATION

"What do you think, Doc?...Ol' Ab got a chanct?" Town Marshal Arlen Cole squirmed in the ladderback chair as he rolled his hat around and around by the brim.

Doctor Carlisle slowly shook his head as he blotted the old man's forehead and held pressure with a cotton dish towel over the wound. "Gut shot. If he's bleeding internally, there's absolutely nothing I can do to stop it and there's no way he'd survive surgery."

"Think he'll ever regain consciousness?"

"Be a miracle if he does…A bona-fide miracle…Think he's older than me and you put together."

As if on cue, the bearded old-timer moaned, fluttered his eyelids and whispered hoarsely, "Drink."

"I'll get you a little water, Ab," said the doctor as he got to his feet.

His eyes were now fully open. "Whiskey…Need whiskey."

"Don't think that'd be a good idea."

"Been shot in the lights afore…in Lincoln's War. Whiskey done the trick…R…Rye whiskey."

Carlisle looked at Marshal Cole, shrugged and nodded.

"I'll run across the street to Clara's Parlor House. 'Spect she has some." He turned and headed past Isom Love standing guard and out the door.

The doctor grabbed a feather pillow from a table of bed linens, lifted Ab's head and stuffed it underneath. "That better, Ab?"

"Do fer now."

"Gotta be honest with you, Ab. Ain't likely you're gonna make it. No way in hell I know how to stop the bleeding inside."

The old man nodded. "Been there 'fore…Jest needs the whiskey."

He rolled his head slightly to the door to see Marshal Cole enter with a bottle of *Sam Thompson Pure Rye Whiskey*.

"Damn, that's the good stuff, Arlen. I use that in my practice…for medicinal purposes. They been makin' that up on the Monongahela River in Pennsylvania since '44."

The marshal glanced at the doctor and grinned as he handed him the bottle. "Uh, huh."

Doc Carlisle knelt down and held the bottle up to the old timer's lips. "Easy now…just a little."

Ab took a swallow, and then another. He closed his eyes and softly sighed. The doctor put his fingers on the side of his neck.

"I'll be damned. His pulse is stronger." He lifted the cotton towel from the entry wound. "Huh…the bleeding has all but stopped."

Old Ab opened one eye and looked at Carlisle. "Feelin' some better, Doc. Gimme jest another little touch."

He held the bottle for him again as Ab took a third swallow and licked his lips.

"God's own nectar…Did you git 'im?"

"Who?" asked Marshal Cole as he got up from the chair and knelt down beside the old man.

"The Injun what done all this…He shot Jade with his shotgun. Miz Mayweather an' her daughter took to screamin'…He blowed them to perdition with the other barrel." He raised his right hand a little and pointed at the bottle.

Carlisle gave him another little sip.

He sighed and continued, "I didn't see no call fer all that an' so I grabbed up a shovel an' went fer him…an' that's when he shot me…Well sir, felt kindly like I been kicked in the stomach by a mule so I kissed the floor…but I seen his feet shuffle 'round by the counter whilst he put the ammo in his pockets and cleaned out pore ol' Jade's register…"

He took a ragged breath. "'Pears he grabbed some clothes, a new hat an' then perambulated out the back door…purty as you please."

"Could you describe him, Ab?" asked the marshal.

"Shore…Uglest Injun I ever laid eyes on…an' a big scudder, too…Hair wuz long like them renegades wear it…an' he had a big white scar from his left ear to his chin."

"Well, son of a gun," exclaimed the doctor.

"What?" The marshal turned to his left to look at Carlisle.

He had pulled Ab's vest back to cover the dish towel pad over the hole and felt something in the front pocket—a plug of Brown's Mule Chewing Tobacco.

"Look here." The doc held up the half-inch thick plug the size of a deck of playing cards. There was a hole where the slug went completely through it. "I'd say this slowed down the bullet enough that it only penetrated a little into his stomach…This stuff is as hard as a rubber boot heel."

Ab raised his head a little. "That my chaw?"

Carlisle nodded.

"Damnation. Jest bought that this mornin' down to Moore's Drug Emporium an' now it's ruint."

"Well, it saved your life, you old fart…" The marshal took the tobacco from the doctor, stuck his finger through the hole and shook his head. "Think I've seen just about everything now."

The doctor looked about the room at the carnage, nodded again, took a breath and turned to the Chickasaw Freedman standing guard at the door. "Isom, go fetch a litter from my office, would you? There's a couple of them in the back room."

"Yasser." The colored man went out the open door and headed down the street to the doctor's office.

"Oh, say marshal, did hear him say somethin'…Now, don't know if'n he wuz a talkin' 'bout what he did er wuz referencin' his name…but he done said it twict."

"And that was?" questioned the marshal.

"He said, 'Mankiller keep'."

SKEANS BOARDING HOUSE
GAINESVILLE, TEXAS

"See anything of interest?" asked Brushy Bill after he took a sip of his coffee. He was leaning against the hand-carved mantle over the fireplace in the parlor.

Fiona—sitting in the dark green velvet love seat—thumbed through the stack of telegrams from Washington that had arrived while they were at Jack and Angie's. "Nothing that jumps up…Hello. I may have spoken too soon."

"What is it?"

"It's a request from a former Deputy US Marshal for assistance in ferreting out a sophisticated ring of grifters and extortionists up in Garden City, Kansas where he's promoting a prize fight."

"Excuse me, a prize fight?…Don't see your interest."

"Well, for one, it's a three round exhibition rematch between the Great John L. Sullivan and current title holder, Gentleman Jim Corbett."

Bill whistled. "A Sullivan-Corbett rematch? Holy cow!"

"And two, the promoter has gotten word that a syndicate out of New York is going to try to set up a nationwide betting operation…"

"That in itself is not illegal."

"No, but it is if they abscond with the funds while the fight is going on or try to put in a fix…"

"There could be in excess of a million dollars bet on that fight, what with telegraph links from coast to coast now."

"Well, and three, the Latham Company has signed Corbett to an exclusive contract to film the fight with Edison's Kineotscope device to show in those moving picture parlors that are being set up all up and down the east coast…at twenty-two dollars a minute."

"Where there's money being generated, count on mountebanks and malefactors to be drawn to it like flies to honey…who's the promoter that's asking for assistance?"

Fiona got a wry grin on her face. "William Barclay Masterson."

"William Bar...Bat?...Bat Masterson from Dodge City?"

"Among other places, yes," replied Fiona.

"Well, well, this could prove to be interesting...Sounds good to me."

"We can go down to the depot and send him a reply."

"What's the best way to go?"

Fiona placed the flimsies on the coffee table and leaned back. "As I recall, the Gulf and Colorado goes through Wichita...we can switch to the Atchison, Topeka and Santa Fe west to Garden City."

Bill looked down into the crackling fire for a moment. "That means it goes through Dodge City, right?"

She nodded. "Oh, I see where you're going...we get off in Dodge City and ride our horses to Garden City. It's only about fifty miles west...Be a lot less noticeable as horsebackers as opposed to us unloading from the train."

Bill bowed to her. "Right you are, m'lady, right you are."

ARBUCKLE MOUNTAINS
CHICKASAW NATION

The big black 4x2 coal-fired steam locomotive slowed to less than eight miles per hour as it climbed the grade to top the small, but ancient, mountain range. The Gulf and Colorado Railroad would stop briefly in Oklahoma City before continuing on to Wichita, Kansas.

The Arbuckles was one of the oldest mountain ranges in North America. Her once majestic, craggy peaks had eroded down over multiple millennia to just a little over 1400 feet above sea level. Thrust outcroppings of granite laid out in rows stuck up through the prairie grass on the east side of the tracks like they had been planted by some giant farmer.

On the west side, the tracks paralleled the Washita River as she cut through the range toward her rendezvous with the Red on the south.

The big locomotive chugged up the 4% gradient, passing through a rock-cut on the way to the ridge. Immediately after passing through the cut, three masked men sprinted out from behind a large gray boulder and quickly caught up with the red caboose.

The first outlaw jerked the rear door open, rushed inside and slapped the brakeman on the side of the head with his pistol just as the man was getting to his feet from a bunk. He slumped to the floor of the car like a pile of cut string. A rivulet of blood trickled from the split skin over his temple.

Fiona and Bill sat in brown leather facing seats on the east side in the last passenger car near the front. Roberts—in the forward facing seat—was reading a copy of the Gainesville Daily Register he had picked up at the depot when they boarded.

Fiona, facing the rear of the train, looked up from her copy of Harper's Magazine and observed the various rock formations of the folded and faulted formations out her window.

"That's really fascinating the way those rock layers were folded over. Look like some kind of ancient Christmas ribbon candy."

Bill looked up with a puzzled expression on his face. "Excuse me? Did you say Christmas ribbon candy?...Where?"

"I said 'like'...and it was back there in that cut we just passed."

"Oh." He buried his face back in the paper.

She smiled, looked down and turned the page. "Goodness this is lovely."

He looked up again. "What?"

"A poem by Alice Archer Sewall James. Listen...'Nay, lips so sweet, ye must not be so red. Else were all roses for your sake but dead. Would you rob us of summer for your sake? Our pittance of dear Paradise, would take and lock it in the garden of your smile, where our bereavement charmed is awhile? Nay, lips so sweet, ye must not be so red'...We have a problem."

"What? That last line is not part of the poem."

She lowered her voice, "I know...Don't turn around till I give you the word. We just picked up some train robbers...three of them." She surreptitiously glanced up from under the brim of her black gambler's hat. "There's one on each side collecting the passenger's valuables in small flour sacks at the back of the car.

The third is behind and in the center of the aisle with his gun drawn...I got him."

Fiona laid the magazine down across her knees. "Now."

She and Bill simultaneously slowly rose to their feet in the rocking and swaying railroad car.

"You gentlemen have made a grievous error. We're Deputy US Marshals," she said, just loud enough to be heard over the clacking of the wheels.

The man in the back raised his pistol and shouted, "Hell, you say!"

Fiona's .38-40 Colts appeared almost magically in her hands and roared simultaneously. Both rounds impacted the gunman in the center of the chest with audible thuds, not two inches apart. A puzzled look came into the young man's eyes above the blue bandana—they rolled back into his head as his knees buckled. He pitched forward on his face like a falling tree.

The other two dropped the sacks, threw their hands in the air and looked down at their accomplice, dead at their feet between them.

"We give...we give."

"Don't shoot, don't shoot, fer God's sake," said the smaller of the two on the west side. He looked down again as a pale yellow puddle grew around his feet.

Bill glanced over at Fiona, grinned and shook his head. They stepped down the aisle toward the two remaining outlaws. She jerked the mask down from each of the men.

"Marshal Roberts, these are just boys."

"Believe you're right Marshal Miller...Who are you fellers?"

The older of the two replied, "We're Billy Boy and Franklin Norgaard..." He looked at Fiona and frowned. "But yer a woman."

"Just notice that, did you?"

"No, sir...I mean no, Ma'am, it's jest I..." He glanced at his younger brother Franklin. "Uh, we ain't never seen no woman...er lady law afore."

"Yeah, I've heard that too...Well, now you have...Who's that?" She pointed at the body in the aisleway.

"Uh...that's our cousin Clifford. He tol' us this would be like pickin' daisies.

"I do believe he miscalculated." Bill turned to Fiona. "Don't you?"

"It would seem so." She spun around at the sound of the forward door to the car opening behind them—drawing Romulus and Remus again in a blur.

The blue-clad fifty-something conductor literally slid to a stop and threw his hands up until he saw the silver badge on Fiona's red paisley bustier over her white blouse as she pushed the lapel of her black morning coat back with her thumb. He looked at Bill and saw the identical crescent and star federal badge pinned to his gray wool vest.

"Can I put my hands down, Marshals?" His eyes flicked back and forth between the two.

"Unless you've come to rob the passengers too," quipped Fiona.

"Oh, no, Ma'am. I'm the conductor…uh, Marvin Swartzwalter. I was in the next car and heard…"

She grinned and holstered her weapons. Bill still held his Colt Thunderer on the two would-be robbers.

The conductor looked at the body in the floor. "Is he…?"

"As they come," responded Roberts. "Marshal Miller if you'd hand me your set of manacles, I'll cuff these two ne'er-do-wells…my finger's getting a mite tired."

"We'll be good," said Billy Boy.

"Honest Injun," added Franklin.

"Right," mumbled Bill as he started fastening the shackles about their wrists.

"Well, Marvin, they came in the back door. I suspect you need to check on your brakeman, if he was in the caboose."

"Yes, Ma'am. That'd be Arley Needham. He's been brakeman since they opened up this section of the line to Wichita."

Fiona shook her head. "I do wish everyone would quit calling me 'Ma'am…It's Fiona, F. M. or Marshal Miller."

"Yes, Ma…uh, Marshal Miller…You're F.M. Miller?…I didn't know…" stated the conductor.

She held up her hand. "I know. I've heard just about all of them and yes, I am…Now go check on Arley."

The conductor eased by the two outlaws, stepped over the body of Clifford and grabbed the door lever when Fiona interrupted him.

"Marvin, what's the next town?"

"That'd be Wynnewood...Uh, Marshal."

"Better signal the engineer to stop so we can offload these two."

"We were not scheduled to stop, but if...uh, Arley ain't all right, I'll signal the locomotive."

"Appreciate it," said Bill as he pushed the two young men into a seat.

"I'd sit there and be real quiet, boys." He tilted his head toward Fiona, and leaned over closer to them. "You sure don't want to make her mad...They'll be singing your monody."

"Ain't gotta say that but onct, Marshal...Uh, what's a monody?" asked Billy Boy.

"Ode to your life," Roberts said softly over his shoulder as he turned away.

Both the boys eyes got big as saucers.

As the train pulled into the Wynnewood station, Bill turned to Fiona. "I can't believe what you did back there."

"What was that?"

"He had the drop on you...even had the hammer cocked and you still drew and fired before he could pull the trigger. That's twice I've seen you do that. How did you do it? I mean, I'm pretty fast, but I don't think I could come close to you."

"Well, it's pretty simple, really…In the first place, I don't think he'd ever shot anyone before…and two, I read in a medical journal not too long ago about eye to hand coordination."

"And just what does that mean?"

"It takes longer for the eye to perceive movement, send the signal to the hand to pull the trigger than it does for me to pre-plan to draw and fire…almost three times longer…It was no contest. You just have to have the nerve to do it…most don't."

"In other words a planned action is much faster than a reaction?"

"Precisely."

"Ah, but therein lies the rub."

"I believe the quote is: 'To sleep: perchance to dream: aye, there's the rub: For in that sleep of death what dreams may come, when we have shuffled off this mortal coil, must give us pause: there's the respect that makes calamity of so long life.'…But you got the meaning right. You have to have faith and trust that your rounds will fire…that's why I use two guns…Never know when there'll be a misfire."

"I may have to take that philosophy to heart."

Fiona had a wry grin on her face. "Better now than when it's too late."

LADY LAW

SANTA FE DEPOT
WICHITA, KANSAS

Bill and Fiona were leading their horses, Tippy and Diablo down the cleated ramp from the stock car. It was almost two hours until the west bound Santa Fe was due.

"What say we cinch up and give the boys a little ride. They've been cooped up in that car for over ten hours. I imagine they're getting a little sour."

"Good idea, I know I am. Are you familiar with the Wichita area?"

"Been here a time or two when I was working for the Pinkerton Detective Agency. Looks like it's changed some."

"This whole country is changing. I'd say we'd be putting our horses out to pasture and getting one of those newfangled auto-mobiles. Some guy named Henry Ford in Detroit, Michigan, just made one he calls the Quadricycle...Gasoline powered with four bicycle tires...Will do over ten miles an hour."

"Heck, Tippy can beat the hell out of that at a road trot."

"All day?"

"Well, for me, I'll take my horse. He knows what I'm thinking...most of the time."

"You do have a point there, Mister Roberts. You do have a point."

They tightened their cinches, mounted and rode off to an open area near the depot and loped the boys in large circles for fifteen minutes to work the travel kinks out. When the exercise session was finished, they reined toward downtown at a trot—it was a little over a mile.

As they reached the downtown area, Bill noticed a saloon a half-block up ahead.

"How about a beer?...My treat."

Fiona glanced at him from under the brim of her hat. "How much time before the train leaves?"

He pulled out his pocket watch from his vest and snapped the cover open. "Hour and fifteen minutes."

She nodded and they reined in at the Drovers Saloon, dismounted and tied up after letting their horses drink from the trough. They loosened their girths a little, and then stepped up on the sidewalk.

Bill pushed one side of the batwing doors open. "After you, Marshal."

"Thank you, sir."

They stepped inside, waited a moment until their eyes adjusted to the dim light.

"Smells like every other saloon I've ever been in...tobacco smoke, stale beer, vomit and urine," said Fiona.

Bill grinned. "You get used to it."

"Speak for yourself." She followed him to the bar.

The portly, balding bartender with a white towel in his hand, stepped over from where he was drying shot glasses. "What'll it be gents…" He quickly corrected himself when he perceived that one was a female. "Uh, I mean folks."

"Draw me up a cold beer, please…Fiona, what are you having?"

"I think I'll have a glass of Cabernet Sauvignon."

"Only red wine we got is Mer-lot," replied the bartender.

"That'll be fine."

He grabbed a beer mug, filled it from the spigot, blew the excess foam off and set it in front of Bill. Turning around, he picked up the dark bottle of wine, pulled the cork and filled a tea goblet half full. "Ain't got no regular wine glasses, lady."

She smiled. "This will do fine."

"Fifty cents."

Bill dug a Morgan silver dollar out of his vest pocket and laid it on the bar top. The barkeep picked out a couple of quarters from the register, scooped the dollar up and placed the change in its place.

Roberts nodded and put the coins in his pocket. "Much obliged." He raised his mug in Fiona's direction. "To an interesting trip."

"'Heaven send thee good fortune'…Shakespeare's Merry Wives of Windsor."

He nodded and they each took a sip.

"Mmm, good." Bill wiped his upper lip and set the mug on the bar. "How's your wine."

She wrinkled her nose. "Methinks this fruit of the vine has aired just a touch too much...say maybe a month or two...Should have gotten a sour mash."

A dusty working cowboy down the bar shuffled his way to Fiona. "Well, well, what do we have here?...A woman in a man's clothes." He turned to his friends. "What do you boys think 'bout that?"

Bill looked at the man. "I'd suggest you..."

Fiona placed her hand on his arm. "I can handle this."

"Reckon we got a woman in man's clothes or a man tryin' to look like a woman in man's clothes? Which is it?..." He winked at his pals. "How's 'bout you an me go upstairs an' see?"

She looked at him out of the corner of her eye without turning her head. "You know, cowboy, you're interrupting my conversation with my friend here...I strongly advise you to move back to where you were."

"You strongly advise?" He turned again to his friends. "Ya'll hear that? He or she strongly advises...Strongly, mind you...Haw." He seized Fiona's arm and pulled her around to face him.

Quick as a cat, her right hand grabbed his crotch with a grip like a bear trap. She palmed one of her Colts in her left and jabbed it under a nose that gave every appearance of having lost more than one disagreement.

He squealed like a pig under a gate as she slow-walked him backward toward the door—her steel-gray eyes took on a chatoyant shimmer.

"Now you feckless bastard, there's only one reason I don't kill you right here and right now and that's because I'd have to pay for the cleanup."

She continued with her track toward the front. "Just so you know, I'm a Deputy United States Marshal and I don't backwater for any man, much less an ignorant detritus from a dung heap with bad manners." She shoved him backward through the batwing doors.

He stumbled, fell to his knees on the boardwalk with one hand going to his bruised privates. The other tried to stop the bleeding from his nose all the while whimpering like a new born puppy.

Fiona turned and headed back into the saloon, flipping her pistol into its holster and shaking her head. "It's true...stupid does go all the way to the bone." She looked at his associates on the way back to Bill. "Either of you having any?"

There was no reply from the other two cowboys except for a shake of their heads.

"Didn't think so." She sidled back to her spot next to Bill and grinned. "You told me something a while back about an expression a friend of yours you called Big Casino, said often.

"What was that? He said a lotta things."

"Never let 'em get set."

He grinned and flicked his eyes at the bar. "Took the option of ordering you a sour mash while you were taking out the trash."

"It's a gentleman and a scholar you are Brushy Bill Roberts...Well, one out of two isn't bad." She picked up the shot glass and downed the aromatic amber liquid in one swallow.

"Damn, lady. That's hard to do."

She nodded, looked at him out of the corner of her eye and wheezed, "Nothing to it...Let's head back to the station."

He smiled and touched his hat. "Was going to suggest the very same thing...before you have to kill somebody."

"Well, to coin a phrase from Bass, 'Never killed anybody what didn't need killin'." She turned and headed toward the door, commenting to the two cowboys as they passed them assisting their rubber-legged friend back inside. "You boys stay out of trouble now...you hear?"

KEMP, PANOLA COUNTY
CHICKASAW NATION

Cal Mankiller tied up his stolen blood-bay gelding in the alley back of The First Bank of Kemp. He pulled the ten gauge Greener from the boot, walked around the corner to the front and went inside.

There were four customers waiting at the teller windows, a local lawyer at one and three girls from the Bloomfield Academy—an Indian girls' school located three miles northwest of Kemp at another. They were picking up cash for a bazaar their class was holding the following week.

The inside of the bank smelled faintly of fresh lemon scented furniture polish recently used to clean and shine the hand-carved counters and teller windows.

The Cherokee glanced briefly at the customers, raised the shotgun and cocked both hammers. "All on floor...Not say two times."

The lawyer spun around. "Now see here..."

He never finished as Mankiller pulled one of the triggers and blasted him back against the counter where he crumpled to the floor like a wet newspaper.

The girls immediately screamed at the roar of the big gun, and then at the blood that was splattered all over the counter and them as well—he pulled the second trigger.

The three Chickasaw teenagers were standing close enough together that the pattern of the double-ought buckshot caught them all. The impact threw them against the near wall where they collapsed in a bloody pile on top of one another.

The three tellers behind the counter had their hands in the air.

"All money...Now...Put in sack." He pitched a flour sack over the top of the barrier above the counter.

Mankiller reloaded the shotgun while the tellers were nervously emptying their cash drawers. He caught a glimpse out of the corner of his eyes of the baldheaded bank president peeking above the wainscot-high railing that separated his office from the lobby, his eyes wide in fear.

Swinging the muzzle of the double-barreled dispenser of death around, he fired again. The entire top of the portly banker's head disappeared in a cloud of red tinged with gray mist.

Much of the acrid cloud of gunsmoke slowly drifted up toward the fourteen foot tin ceiling. Mankiller looked at the missing half-moon chunk of splintered rail and one inch thick ash paneling where the president's head had been just a few short seconds earlier and almost smiled.

He turned back to the totally panicked tellers, walked toward them and held out his left hand to the nearest. The slight built man in his twenties held the off-white cotton sack toward the renegade—his hand shook so hard he almost dropped the nearly full bag.

Mankiller pulled the other trigger just as he grabbed the money from the man's hand, blasting him back into the other two and almost cutting him in half. Shifting the shotgun to the crook of his left arm, he drew the Remington he took from Ashalintubbi's Mercantile and shot the two men in the head as they tried to get back to their feet.

He pulled a narrow strip of latigo that he sometimes used to tie his hair from the pocket of his black broadcloth coat with the too-short sleeves. The Cherokee looped it around the top of the sack twice, and then smoothly tied a half-hitch knot. Mankiller glanced around at his handiwork with his dispassionate obsidian eyes and sauntered out the back door.

§§§

CHAPTER THREE

DODGE CITY, KANSAS

The boiler of the big black 3x2 locomotive blew off pressure, releasing a huge cloud of steam that billowed out more than twenty feet with a loud hissing sound. White smoke rose out of the straight smokestack of the idle train as some passengers disembarked and still others boarded at the station.

Bill looked out his window as the steam rapidly dissipated. He folded the newspaper he had picked up in Wichita and placed it on his seat.

Fiona and he got to their feet and made their way down the narrow aisleway to the rear door of the passenger car.

The headline of a three-inch column story on the back page he had not gotten to read was:

RASH OF SAVAGE KILLINGS IN SOUTHERN CHICKASAW NATION...LIGHTHORSE BAFFLED

They stepped down the steel stairs to the red-bricked platform and glanced around.

"Well, changed some."

"Been here before, I take it," said Fiona.

"'Bout ten years ago, when I had wandering feet... it was called Hell on the Plains back then."

"Got over that, did you?"

Bill grinned. "Almost...Guess we'll go down and get the boys, and then see if we can buy a pack mule somewhere. I don't relish trying to carry our luggage with us...plus trail supplies."

"How long do you think it will take to get to Garden City?"

"Two days...give or take...Assuming we don't get caught by a storm."

"Storm? What kind of storm?"

"Well, it is fall, so could get a blue norther at anytime...a thunderstorm, or even a twister."

"Twister? Oh, my God...This is tornado alley isn't it?"

"Yeah, but flat as this country is, you can see it coming from a long way off."

Fiona furrowed her brow. "Even at night?"

Bill shook his head. "Well, no, but if you hear a sound like a freight train bearing down on us in the dark...dig a hole."

"Everything looked so flat between here and Wichita."

"Pretty much the same between here and Garden City, too. This is the great prairie and back in the day, millions upon millions of bison wandered about and grazed the grasses...Actually the town was originally called Buffalo City, but there was already a town by that name, so they changed it to Dodge City...after the fort."

"Just as well, I understand the white man almost managed to kill off the buffalo to extinction."

Bill grimaced sadly. "What with the buffalo hunters and the orders from General Sherman to slaughter all the buffalo in order to drive the Indians to reservations, it didn't take too long...By '76 most of the animals were gone and the prairie was littered with bones and skulls."

"That is such a pity, the way the white man came in here, eliminated the native's food source and then stole their land...It was no wonder they went on the warpath...They had to."

They stopped at the livestock car as the hostlers were placing the cleated ramp at the sliding boxcar door. The yardmaster led Fiona's Appaloosa, Diablo, out first, and then Tippy, Robert's chocolate Morgan.

Bill handed him a couple of Liberty silver dollars—they tightened up their cinches and swung into the saddle.

"There a livery around here close, pard?" Bill asked the yardmaster.

He pointed. "Yep, just head on north there on Central Avenue to Front Street, turn left and you'll find Barker's Livery and Wagon Yard 'bout half block past the Long Branch Saloon...or where she used to be."

"What happened?" asked Bill.

"Burnt down in '85 and given that there were another couple dozen saloons, they never rebuilt her...There's the Prairie Hen Saloon right across the street, if you need to wet your whistle, but you'd have to check your guns, though."

He glanced at the ivory-handled Colts under Fiona's unbuttoned morning coat.

"Not in this lifetime," she muttered.

They clucked their horses into a jog trot.

"The legendary Long Branch Saloon, huh?"

"Rowdy a place as you'll ever see...back in the day. Of course things have tamed down a bit."

"Noticed that back in Wichita."

"I know what you're thinking, Marshal Miller...and no, we're not going in to the Prairie Hen. We need to keep our presence in this part of the world a little quiet...Right?... Sure as I'm breathing, you'd get into a hoorah with some cowboy."

"Me?"

"You."

She smiled. "Well, as a student of history, I've come to realize that human nature hasn't changed much over the millennia...but we do always seem to get better weapons."

"Point made."

They dismounted in front of Barker's Livery. A grizzled old-timer in blue bib overalls with a huge chaw in his cheek stepped out of the office—setting his battered old fedora on his head.

He spat a stream of amber juice off to the side and mumbled, "Howdie...Name's Thaddius Barker. What's fer ya today?"

"Need to stall, water and give a bait of grain to the boys here for a couple of hours...check their feet and give them a good brushing, too, " said Bill.

"Shore. Buck a piece." He spat again.

"We're looking to buy a pack mule."

"Funny you should ask. Jest taken one in last week...Now, actually, the feller didn't say nothin' 'bout him bein' a pack mule...He come in aridin' on 'im, but I 'spect he kin carry a pannier er two...First paint mule I ever seen."

"His dam must have been a paint," said Fiona.

"His damn what?"

"No, I mean his mother...How much?"

"Oh, shoulda said so...Twenty dollars'll do."

"Tack go with that?"

He spat into the dirt street again. "You kin have what he come in with…jest a saddle an' bridle."

"Be fine," said Bill.

"We have some shopping to do. Where's the closest mercantile?" asked Fiona.

He pointed in a westerly direction. "Little over a block thataway… Bertram's."

Bill touched the brim of his dark gray Homburg. "Much obliged. Be back in a bit."

They opened the double nine-foot doors to Bertram's Mercantile and looked around. They instantly were hit with the enticing aroma of fresh-ground coffee.

"Well, this place is bigger than May's in Ardmore," said Bill.

Fiona glanced at the clothing section. "Why don't you get our trail supplies… shouldn't take too much for two days…I'll be over here. I've got an idea."

"Due to the unpredictable weather, always better to double up on the food when on the trail."

"Speaking from experience?"

"Actually…yes." He grinned and watched her stroll over to the clothing tables and racks.

Bill approached the twenty-year old, fresh-faced clerk behind the main counter.

"Welcome to Bertram's. How can I help you today? My name's Cletus Bertram."

Roberts pinched his brow. "You the owner?"

The young man grinned. "Oh, no sir. That'd be my daddy. He's makin' sure I learn the business from the ground, or floor up...so to speak. I'm just one of the hired hands."

"Nothing wrong with apprentice work."

"No, sir...Now what can I help you with?"

"Going to be on the trail for a couple of days, need about six cans of beans, two pounds of slab bacon, five pounds of Arbuckle, four pounds of jerky...uh, four cans of peaches and five pounds each of flour and cornmeal...Oh, a pound of salt."

Cletus looked up from his note pad. "Need any utensils?"

"Gracious, glad you said something. Almost forgot...Let me have a coffee pot, two plates and cups...graniteware...couple of knives and forks, a six-inch skillet, a quart pot, box of strike-anywhere matches, two canteens and two full bed rolls...including ground tarps."

The clerk finished his list. "Be a few moments, sir."

"Fine. I'll be over there with that tall lady browsing through the clothing."

"Wife?"

Bill glanced over his shoulder as he walked away. "No."

He worked his way through the tables stacked with bolt after bolt of material until he reached the ready-to-wear. "Find what you're looking for?"

Fiona turned at the sound of his voice and held up a black suit, white shirt with a celluloid collar, black vest and a black string tie. "Your Baptist preacher's outfit."

"My what?"

"I thought we'd go in undercover as a Baptist preacher and his schoolmarm wife...and don't get any ideas."

"Excuse me?"

"Oh, don't have a hissy fit with a tail on it, I'm just kidding. When I answered Mister Masterson..."

"Just call him Bat...he's used to it."

"Right...Anyway, I told him to find a boarding house or something on the outskirts of town. He said he would reserve a room at the same place where he and his wife Emma are staying."

"And you were going to tell me when?"

"What time is it?"

He reached into his vest pocket, pulled his watch halfway out and stopped. "You do that to me all the time."

She flashed a big smile at him. "I know...but you love it or you wouldn't keep falling for it."

"Didn't know he was married."

"He married an actress and singer, Emma Moulton. He met her when he managed and then purchased the Palace Variety Theater in Denver back in '88...He's traveling around the mid west promoting fisticuffs and writing a weekly sports column for George's Weekly...that's a Denver newspaper."

"Bat Masterson writing for a newspaper?"

"Apparently he has an eye to the future."

Bill nodded. "Interesting...Might ought to get us some warm coats. Better to have them and not need them than need them and not have them."

She nodded. "Paraphrased from Second Peter 2:21."

"One day I'm going to come up with a quote that you won't have a clue from whence it came."

"I believe Omar Khayyam said that." She grinned. "I'll get us some coats, too."

Bill and Fiona walked into the big double doors of Barker's Livery. Each carried a large flour sack tied at the throat and their bedrolls under their arms.

The proprietor walked up from back in the barn. "Well, see you folks bought out Bertram's...Got yer horses all took care of. The paloose needed his left front replaced, so I done all four.... Keeps his feet balanced that way, ya see?

Fiona set her bag down. "I really appreciate that. How much for the shoeing? Not good getting on the trail..."

"Yessum, my thoughts too...Jest a dollar. The Morgan's was fine."

"Much obliged...You mind if we use a couple of those empty stalls to change clothes in?" asked Bill.

"Hep yerselves."

"Appreciate it if you'd saddle up that mule while we're changing, I'll loop these flour sacks and hang them on each side of the saddle horn."

The old man nodded. "Oughta work fine."

"He got a name?" Fiona inquired.

"Feller that brung him in jest called him 'Spot'."

"That'll do, I suppose," she replied.

They took their carpet bags into the interior of the livery. She entered the last vacant stall on the right. Roberts took the second from the last on the left.

Fiona set her bag on the oat straw-littered floor and began disrobing, folding her travel clothes and placing them on the top of the stall door.

She took out her white union suit, donned it, and then the rest of her trail duds. Her black wool split-skirt with a single piece doeskin insert on the seat and inner thigh hung down over her pantaloons and tall scalloped black boots.

Fiona pulled her white blouse over her head and slipped her black wool vest on. She buckled her concho-lined black cross-draw holsters with her matched Colt .38-40 Peacemakers about her shapely hips. Finally, she slipped on the long dark brown oiled-canvas coat that served as a top coat as well as a rain slicker.

She might be dressed as a man—except for the ankle length split skirt—but, there was no question she was a woman.

Fiona grabbed her folded clothes from the top of the door and turned to lay them in her carpet bag. She opened the top to place her morning coat inside and jumped back. "Goodness!"

Two blue eyes peaked out of the top of the bag, blinked and a soft meow came out of the mouth of a half-grown solid gray cat.

"Well, and just who are you?"

She squatted down and reached out to pet the kitten on top of its head with her index finger.

The cat rubbed its muzzle and the sides of its lips against her hand and commenced purring. It reached up and grabbed her hand with both paws in a hug and continued nuzzling it.

"My, but you're a real lover, aren't you? That's the loudest purr I've ever heard…What are you doing in my bag?"

As if in answer, it jumped out of the carpet bag up to her right shoulder and butted Fiona's cheek with the top of its head.

"Oh, my," she exclaimed as her eyes began to tear up. "You are so sweet…What am I going to do with you?"

She put all of her clothes in the bag, closed the flap and snapped the catch. "All right, I see I don't have much of a choice."

Heading out into the aisleway, she joined Bill and Thaddius at the front—the cat was still sitting on her shoulder.

"See you found that damn cat…er rather he found you. Been tryin' to git rid of the pesky critter fer couple weeks now.

Carried it a couple miles out of town an' be damned if it didn't beat me back here."

The cat butted Fiona's cheek again.

Barker was holding the mule by a braided cotton rope. "'Pears as though he's taken a shine to you...He don't do nothin' but scratch er try to bite me...Was fixin' to take him out back an' shoot 'im...Hate cats."

"You'll do no such thing." Her steel-gray eyes flashed.

The hostler took a step back from her. "Don't have to git hostile, lady...You take 'im, then...'long with this here mule."

"All right, I will...Does he have a name?" She took the lead rope.

"Naw, jest called him damn cat."

She glanced at the affectionate gray creature sitting comfortably purring and making mash on her shoulder. "Think I'll call you Smoky, how's that?"

He promptly butted her cheek again.

Spot stepped forward and extended his muzzle to the cat, Smoky responded in a like manner—they touched noses.

"Oh, yeah, the mule an' cat seem to be attached. Reckon that's why he wouldn't stay gone...Now I'm rid of both headaches...Makes it a good day." He spat a long stream of the amber juice off to the side and wiped his chin with the sleeve of his shirt.

Fiona grinned and set Smoky on Spot's saddle just behind the two tied together flour sacks. She turned, stabbed her foot in the flat-bottomed, copper-lined stirrup and easily swung up onto Diablo's back. She looked at Bill. "You coming or you going to take a nap?"

He shook his head and grinned. "Just waiting to see if you were through adoptin'."

She nodded at him, dallied the mule's rope around her saddle horn and trotted off. Smoky seemed to be quite at home, sitting in the middle of Spot's saddle.

"Got a damn menagerie," Bill mumbled as he followed behind. "Hey, look there...danged if Spot don't have an amble gait...he's smooth as a baby's butt."

Fiona glanced behind her. "It appears you're right. Smoky likes it," she commented as the cat promptly laid down on the smooth moving mule.

KANSAS PLAINS

A little over a mile out of Dodge City Fiona turned to Bill, riding alongside her and Spot. "Got a trail picked out?"

He nodded. "We'll just follow along the Arkansas River...Runs just south of both Dodge and Garden City."

"That makes it easy."

"And gives us a good water source and wood for a campfire...not to say anything about shelter, should we need it."

"You keep mentioning that."

"Just speaking from experience...just speaking from experience, Ma'am...uh Fiona."

She cut her eyes at him. "Uh, huh."

GAINESVILLE, TEXAS

Cal Mankiller dismounted at the front of Smith Brothers Wagonyard and Corral. A redheaded teenager stepped out of the aisleway of the large barn with a four-tined pitchfork in his hand—he removed his short-billed gray and green baseball cap.

"How do. What can I...Oh, say I 'member you...Fed an' watered yer horse a month er so back...Different horse though. Back in town are ye?

The Cherokee nodded. "Me know you now. Dark then, not see spots on face."

"Yeah." He grinned. "My paw said when I was little, I walked up behind the milk cow while she was eatin' bran an' she farted on me..." He giggled. "Git it?" He rubbed his hand over his freckled face. "You know? She sprayed spots all over my...Uh, never mind."

Mankiller's expression never changed. His cold, black eyes appeared to burn a hole through the young man.

"Well, uh...how kin I help ye?"

"Lookin' for woman marshal...Name Miller."

"A lady marshal?...Oh...shore. That'd be Marshal Fiona Miller...Woowee, a fine figger of a woman, I mean to tell you.

57

A fine figger of a woman…Was undercover here fer awhile trying to catch a killer the paper said…Knows how to ride a horse too…How's come you lookin' fer her?"

His eyes locked on the teenager again. "Where she?"

Even in the cool of the fall afternoon, the young man broke into a sweat. "Uh, well, don't rightly know, 'ceptin' she has a room over to Skeans Boardin' House on Dixon Street."

"Where Dixon Street?…No read."

"Oh, well, shore…Just a minute, I'll go inside an' draw you a map…Ain't too far." He turned and went back inside the barn, happy for a moment at least to be out of the intimidating presence of the big, scar-faced man.

Less than three minutes later, he came out with a lined sheet of paper he had torn out of a Big Chief tablet and handed it to the Indian.

"Kin you make it out?"

Mankiller glanced at it and then to his right down the street, and then nodded. "Uhnnn, me water horse."

"Uh…They's a trough right over there against the corral." He pointed to his left, turned and headed back into the barn mumbling under his breath, "Not so much as a thankee er much obliged."

Mankiller led the blood-bay gelding over to the half-full wooden trough. The grateful horse immersed his muzzle and began to suck up the cool water while the Indian studied the map…

KANSAS PLAINS

Fiona and Bill trotted along the north banks of the Arkansas, tilting their heads forward to shade their eyes from the setting sun already casting long shadows through the scattered trees.

Smoky got to his feet in the middle of Spot's saddle, stretched, and then jumped down to the sandy ground. He loped off to a nearby clump of buffalo grass, scratched himself a shallow hole and did his business.

After quickly covering the spot with sand, he ran after the mule, still maintaining his amble trot, jumped in the air, grabbed the flour sack hanging from the horn on his side and clawed his way back to the seat and calmly took his position again.

"I expect we should find a place to camp for the night, don't you?" asked Bill.

"Sounds good. I believe Smoky had a good idea just then. I need to visit the bushes, too."

"Well, now that you mention it…Uh, oh."

"What?"

"Look to your right."

Fiona looked off to the north and saw a dark purple, almost black line of clouds, just beginning to show above the horizon. "Oh, my."

"That wall is coming pretty fast...See that copse of cottonwoods up ahead near the bank?"

Fiona replied, "I do...Should be a good place between the trees on the north and the river."

They broke into an easy lope and pulled rein just inside the trees.

"If you'll water the horses, I think I see an ideal camp spot. I'll gather some wood for a fire."

There was a five-foot bank of sand where the trees stopped, and then a level sandy area forty-feet wide down to the slow moving river that had it's headwaters in Colorado.

"We can set up below that bank, give us good protection from the north wind...If that's all there is."

"What do you mean," asked Fiona.

"Well, if it's cold with sleet or snow, that's one thing. Just have to hunker down. But, if it's rain...that's something else all together."

"How so?"

He looked back to the north at the ever-growing dark line. "Rain in this country can cause a flash flood in a hurry...We'll have to move above the high water mark."

"Oh, I see your point. Glad you're more familiar with this country than I."

"Being familiar only means you learn to be ready for most anything."

The black cloud was getting closer faster—rolling and churning. The wall was still five or ten miles away when they were hit with the cold outflow, dropping the temperature rapidly.

"Oh, goodness, it's like someone left the gate between here and the north pole down."

Fiona pulled her oilskin long coat tighter about her as she led the animals down to the river.

When she got back to the campsite, Bill had the fire started and was feeding it some larger limbs he gathered from the various piles of deadfall laying around from the last flood.

"Let's jerk their gear and hobble them up in those trees. Be good shelter and they'll have some graze on the winter cheat grass."

"Right." Fiona lifted Smoky from his place in the middle of Spot's saddle, opened her carpet bag, set him inside and closed the flap before she started pulling the tack—he promptly curled up and went to sleep. "I'll take them up to the trees.... I have a little business to take care of."

"What makes you think I don't too?"

"It's a lot easier for you than for me...You can just traipse on down to the water's edge and take care of it...I'll bring some more deadwood for the fire."

"Was hoping somebody would..." He glanced up at the darkening skies that were beginning to get a tinge of green as the temperature continued to fall. "Think we're going to need it…Best dig out those winter coats we bought, too." He pulled his road jacket tighter and flipped up the collar.

Fiona had a good fire going, banked against the shelf of sand, protecting it from the whistling, bitter north wind when Bill walked back up.

"Damnation, that wind cuts right through you like a knife." He reached down and picked up the sheepskin jacket and dark green wool neck scarf she had laid on his saddle. He slipped it over his black broadcloth coat. "Feels like the temperature has dropped thirty degrees or so."

"I expect that's close enough for government work…Coffee'll be ready in just a bit. I'll slice some bacon and fix it with the beans…We can share a can of peaches, too."

"Didn't realize how hungry I'd gotten."

A few hard sleet pebbles mixed with raindrops bounced off the brim of his hat. He glanced up at the boiling greenish-purple clouds almost on top of them. "Uh, oh."

She looked up from stirring the beans in the small skillet. "What?"

"Gonna be sleet and ice instead of snow."

"That's better than rain, don't you think?"

"Yes, but we're going to need more shelter." He pulled his Bowie knife from his belt and stepped over to the vertical river bank next to the fire and started digging into the sand. "Gonna carve us a small cave that will help…Just have to be careful and not dig too deep or it'll cave in on top of us."

"You're just full of all sorts of joyful facts, aren't you?" She held up her hand. "I know…experience."

He glanced over his shoulder at her. "You're gettin' good."

"Not really."

Bill looked back at her again. "How so?"

"Born that way…By the way, you don't see any of those twisters coming, do you?"

He took a peek over the lip of the bank and above the trees at the clouds in the rapidly failing light. "Don't see a wall cloud. That's usually the first sign."

"Usually?"

The sleet and freezing rain got heavier. Fiona looked over at the horses and Spot in the trees. They had already turned their butts to the wind.

"You think the boys will be all right?"

"I expect. There's a right smart of trees and brush between them and the open ground to the north."

"Coffee's ready."

He dragged the last bit of loose sand from the shallow hole in the side of the shelf, brushed his hands off and slipped his knife back in its sheath. "That should do it…. Now to wrap my hands around a hot cup of coffee. They're already stiff from the cold."

"Why didn't you put on your gloves?"

"Got in such a hurry to carve us a shelter, I forgot." He took the blue-speckled graniteware cup from her.

"Then quit whining."

He sniffed of the hot aromatic stout trail brew. "Hmmm, now that I got some coffee, I'm good to go."

A wave of sleet dropped from the clouds, peppering the entire area. Some of the frozen rain drops caught the outer edge of the campfire and sizzled.

"Glad our fire's up against the shelf. Should keep going most of the night. I'll carve another small cave for the extra firewood to keep it dry."

She took a sip of her own coffee. "All the comforts of home."

He grinned. "Wouldn't say that, but like Big Casino used to say, 'any port in the storm'."

They eased over into their shelter—which was just tall enough to sit up in—and nursed their coffee as the sleet and freezing rain pelted down with a fury.

Smoky was contentedly curled up in Fiona's lap.

Their soogans were already spread out underneath the overhang and behind them. They had finished their filling, but meager supper of bacon, beans with hot water corn bread and a dessert of sliced, canned pickled peaches.

Smoky was fastidiously washing his face and paws after sharing their supper. Tomorrow would be another day…

§§§

CHAPTER FOUR

SKEANS BOARDING HOUSE
GAINESVILLE, TEXAS

The dark man-shaped figure in the shadow of the big red oak across the street from the boarding house hadn't moved in over three hours—until now. He turned his head at sound of a horse and wagon coming up the street. The only light, save the gibbous moon, was the lantern Faye Skeans had left burning on the porch.

A green and yellow buckboard pulled by a sorrel mare drew to a stop in front of the Victorian two story house. A man stepped down and tied the lead to the ring on the iron post in the front. He walked around to the other side and helped a woman to the ground—she held a bundle in each arm.

"That was some game with Muenster, wasn't it?" asked Bodie.

"For the life of me, I just don't understand it…Makes no sense that twenty men…"

"Twenty-two."

Annabel frowned at him, and then continued, "Twenty-two men keep runnin' into each other tryin' to put that little ol' funny shaped ball over each other's property line…"

"Goal line."

"Goal line, then…I just don't get the point."

"That is the point, dear…Who can put the ball over the other feller's goal the most times in two hours is the winner."

"Of what?"

"The game."

"The game of what?"

He shook his head. "They call it football."

"But they carry it up and down the field…The only time they touched it with their feet was when one of them kicked it after his group carried it across the other group's property line…"

"Goa…"

"I know…and then I thought the man was mad at the ball because he dropped it on the ground and then kicked it through those sticks poked in the ground."

"That team got two points for that added to the four points they got for carrying it across the line givin' them a total of six points…an' that's how Gainesville won…Don't you see?"

"No." Annabel still seemed confused. "And did you see those three men they carried off that pasture on stretchers? They were out cold...The whole thing is just incomprehensible to me."

"They call it a field."

"Then they should have cleaned off the cow pies before they started." She giggled. "That one...the chubby one...fell face first into a fresh pile...Took him forever to get the green fecal matter out of his eyes...Bless his heart."

"Yeah, gotta admit, now that was funny...Go ahead and take little Bass and Cassie Ann inside, I'll start unloading the groceries," said Bodie.

Annabel pecked his cheek. "I'll tell Faye we're back, I'm sure she'll be tickled to come out and help," she said in her deep Alabama drawl.

"That'll be fine. Looks like we bought out the store. Gonna take at least four er five trips."

"Well, bless your heart, Honey, you know Faye doesn't like to shop more than once or twice a month...That's the way she plans her meals...I swear to goodness, I don't think I've ever seen a more organized woman."

"She's a good person for anyone to pattern themselves after."

Her cerulean eyes snapped. "You watch yourself, Mister Hickman...I'll put a knot on your head Billy Sunday can't remove in a month."

He grinned at his petite blond-headed wife. "Yessum...I know you would."

The ebony eyes from across the street dispassionately watched the woman climb the steps to the porch and tap the bottom of the gingerbread screen door with the toe of her shoe. He saw an older woman with dark-blond hair open the front door, and then the screen door.

"Oh, Annabel, here let me take one of those sweet babies."

"I've got them, Faye, but Bodie could use some help with the groceries."

"Oh, my goodness," she said as she hurried down the red brick walkway to meet him halfway with the first box. "Here, I'll take that...She looked up at the dark moonlit sky, and then to the north. "Norther comin'...I feel a change in the air."

Bodie sniffed. "Do believe you're right, Faye. I'll make sure we have plenty of firewood inside." He glanced off to the north, also. "Bet it gets here before midnight."

The big Cherokee across the street watched the exchange with interest and nodded.

KANSAS PLAINS

"You watch those hands, mister." Fiona elbowed Bill in the ribs.

"Ow...Not my hands."

She sat up in her bedroll and whacked him behind the head. "Not your hands?...That only leaves...Oooo, men." She set

Smoky on top of her blanket, grabbed her tall scalloped-top boots and slipped them on. "It's a good thing my pistols were under the ground tarp."

She rolled out of the tiny cave onto the sleet and ice covered ground. "Goodness gracious," she exclaimed as her foot broke through the crystalline crust. "We must have gotten six inches or more…I'll stoke up the fire and put on some coffee…Unless you're going to sleep in."

"I'm getting up. Smoky's lying on my chest purring and kneading bread."

"He just wants to be fed."

"Now that sounds almost as good as a hot cup of coffee."

Fiona glanced up at the clear, star-studded sky just beginning to gray in the east. "Well, at least the storm has pushed on through to the south."

She brushed away most of the sand they had placed on top of the pile of coals—added some peeled bark from a piece of cottonwood deadfall and blew on it until it burst into a bright yellow flame. "Glad we put that wood in that other hole you dug out or we wouldn't have a fire, coffee or anything."

"Been here before."

"Here?"

"I mean in this situation."

"What was her name?"

"No, that's not what I meant…I meant to say…Oh, never mind." He sat up, forcing Smoky off his chest and pulled his own boots over his socks and tucked his pant legs in the top.

The cat padded over to Fiona and started weaving between her legs, rubbing on her ankles and purring.

"All right, I'll fix you something in a minute."

As if on cue, the feline turned, bounded up the five-foot high bank and disappeared into the trees.

"I think somebody held it as long as they could or else he wanted to go see his buddy…You could go slip the nose bags on the boys and give them a bait of grain while I start breakfast…If you're not too busy."

"Yes, your majesty. Right away your majesty." He grinned and threw a chunk of sleet crust at her, hitting her in the back.

"That gate swings both ways, Marshal Roberts…and don't forget, never mess with the cook."

Fiona slipped on her sheepskin and gloves. She grabbed a few branches, broke them up and placed them in a teepee-like fashion over the tiny flames. In a short time, she had a good cooking fire going and set the coffee pot on a flat river rock close to the heat and sliced the bacon to put in the skillet.

In a few minutes, Bill came back down into camp. "We've got a problem."

"Besides being cold as a well digger's derrière?"

"Someone stole our horses during the storm."

She raised up from where she was squatting by the fire, tending the sizzling bacon. "What?"

"Someone slipped in after the first wave of sleet and ice, cut the hobbles and made off with them. He held up the pieces of severed latigo...Looked to be three, maybe four."

"What about Spot?"

He grinned and shook his head. "Not him. Judging from the torn up ground in his area, he wasn't having any of it. Apparently they wisely left him alone."

"Did you see Smoky anywhere? He headed up that way before you left."

"Oh, yeah...He's sitting on Spot's back, cleaning his paws."

Fiona dished up some of the bacon, stuck it inside a water biscuit she had made last night and grabbed her scarf. She picked up Spot's saddle, bridle and blanket along with her Winchester from under the tarp covering the tack and headed to the trees.

"Where you going?"

"After the horse thieves, of course."

"By yourself?"

She stopped, turned back to him and smiled. "We can't both go... I've seen this ploy before. Some of the thieves steal the horses and when the owners go off looking for them, their pals slip back around and raid the camp...Does that answer your final question?"

"I'll just have some breakfast, then."

"Good idea...They shouldn't be hard to track. I doubt they considered Spot was rideable...Probably thought he was just a pack mule...I'll be back soon..."

"I'm sure you will."

He stomped through the frozen crust over to the fire to the right of their little cave, grabbed his cup, filled it and squatted down. "God help those stupid bastards," he mumbled.

Fiona pulled the empty feed bag from Spot's nose and picked up Smoky from his back. "Don't suppose you'd go back down to camp?"

He gently rubbed the cold tip of her nose with his paw.

"Didn't think so." She fed him some of the bacon from her biscuit, stuffed him inside her sheepskin jacket and rubbed the mule down vigorously with his wool blanket, talking to him all the while.

After making sure all the sleet and ice were removed and his muscles and circulation were stimulated, she folded the blanket with the dry side down and placed it on his back. Lifting the double-rigged Texas A-fork saddle, she set it just at the back of his high withers and pulled a bubble in the blanket underneath the gullet.

After taking the slack out of the latigo, she walked him about in a large circle for a moment to get the hump out of his back, cleaned the ice from his hooves, tightened his cinch again and swung easily into the high-cantle saddle. "All right, let's go...Got to teach some malefactors a lesson."

She squeezed Spot up into his smooth amble and they trotted along, following the tracks to the west.

"Yep, four…two leading the boys and the other two in the front."

After a little over a mile, she pulled the paint mule to a halt. "What's this?" Fiona noticed one of the lead tracks had peeled off to the north. She could clearly see the tracks in the bright white crusty sleet making a big curve back to the east across the flat prairie. "Exactly what I thought…going back to harvest what he can from our camp…Hope Bill is alert."

She reined Spot away from the trail toward the river on her left and eased down the embankment to ride along the edge of the water. Fiona patted him on the neck.

"I'm betting they expect to be followed…by somebody on foot. No need to ride out in the open…That's almost as dumb as riding along the top of a ridgeline or a switchback in our country… but you wouldn't know that."

Spot flicked his long ears back at her. "Or then again, maybe you would."

She looked forward about four hundred yards where the Arkansas River meandered to the south, and then back west and saw a thin plume of smoke rising straight up into the still, subfreezing air on the other side of a clump of willows just around the bend.

"Well, well…Didn't think they'd go too far at night in a storm." Her breath created a fog in the zero cold.

She slowly rode closer to the spiraling tendril of campfire smoke, keeping to the cover of the trees and brush that lined much of the bank of the river.

Fiona dismounted at fifty yards out, checked the loads in her Colts and added a sixth round. She took hold of Spot's lead rope and moved quietly toward the camp, keeping well within the available cover. Being down below the flood line embankment, they were able to stay on sandy river wash.

She looped Spot's lead around the saddle horn with his reins and stepped out from behind the thick clump of junipers. "Good morning, gentlemen...coffee smells good."

The three men gathered around the washtub-size fire—all with cups in their hands—spun around at the sound of Fiona's voice.

"Who the hell are you?" asked the burly man with a full beard.

"Could ask you the same thing."

A younger, thinner, but obviously closely related man, pitched what remained of the thick black brew on the ground and set his cup on a flat river rock next to a battered tin coffee pot. His close-set, dark eyes squinted into the morning sun behind her back. "Why, we're the Zellon brothers...Jest bone pickers, lady...Gatherin' up buffler skulls an' sech...Like some coffee? Believe we got some left."

He grinned, showing three tobacco-stained teeth, and shifted his tan canvas coat away from the six-shooter on his left hip.

"Don't think so...Besides you've made several mistakes."

"Oh... an' that'd be what?" asked the oldest of the three.

"One, you make terrible coffee, judging by the amount of grounds in what you dumped on the sand...Two, you'll never get to that pistol in time…Three, that chocolate Morgan up there by your wagon is a friend of mine's and that 'paloose next to him…belongs to me."

"Why, we found them horses last night, lady. Musta got loose in the storm." The big bearded one glanced at his brothers. "Ain't that right, boys?"

They nodded in agreement.

Fiona grinned. "Well, it's kind of hard for a horse to cut his own hobbles…They don't have thumbs, you see…You know, next to a horse thief, I hate a liar worse than anything…To quote Shakespeare: 'Thou lie out on't, sir, and therefore 'tis not yours. For my part, I do not lie in't, yet it is mine'."

The skinny brother snapped back, "What?…Who the hell is this Shakespeare feller? Sounded like somethin' from the Bible."

"You ain't a callin' us liars, air ye?" The eldest opened his coat also.

"Oh, I actually thought it was fairly obvious…But, let's just say your eyes and mouth don't match."

The beady-eyed youngest Zellon glared at her. "You must not be very bright, lady. We're three guns against one."

The other two started easing to the side, spreading out, trying to get an angle on her and to get the sun out of their eyes.

"Mayhaps we'll have a little fun with you…'fore we plant yer ass in the ground," the thin one said, and then cackled.

"I git first dibs, little brother…she is a might pert, even if a little skinny," said a voice from her far right as the fourth brother stepped out of the brush. "Sorry I wasn't here to welcome you into our camp… I wuz, uh…erectin' a monument up on the bank, in the trees."

Her left hand eased up and undid the loops holding the deer antler buttons, allowing her coat to fall open. Smoky leapt from his place inside to the ground and darted between the legs of the skinny one as Fiona's Peacemakers appeared in her hands faster than the eye could follow. She fired simultaneously in two different directions.

The eldest—nearest the edge of the river—took a round in the middle of his chest knocking him into the shallows on his back. The bearded brother to her near right caught the other at the base of his throat. He collapsed like a wet paper sack—his life's blood spurting out from the wound and staining the sand around his head as he gurgled his last breath.

A piercing squeal made the fourth man on the far right turn to his left as Spot charged from behind the cedars, his ears laid back and teeth bared. The largest of the brothers almost had his gun out of its holster when the mule spun around and launched both back feet.

One caught him in the upper chest like a trip hammer and the other foot under his chin with a sickening snap. The blows knocked him tumbling backward in the air over ten feet with a crushed face and a broken neck. His body came to rest like a rag doll against the base of a six-inch thick willow—he was dead before he hit the ground.

The skinny one in the middle nearest the fire, threw up his hands. "I give...Fer God's sake, I give!" he screamed, and then dropped to his knees.

Fiona stepped forward, holstering her left hand Colt as Smoky padded back from the other side of the man after taking care of his business. He jumped up, grabbed the bottom of her coat, climbed to her shoulder and promptly butted her cheek. "Don't know if you did that on purpose or just needed to relieve yourself, but whatever... thank you for the distraction."

"I'm sorry, we stole yer horses, lady...Honest Injun. The one we used to pull our wagon jest laid down and died on us...We thought you was jest pilgrims."

"Well, you thought wrong, and besides, that's no excuse for stealing...Who was the one that peeled off back there?"

"That was our pa. He figgered he'd see if'n you had anythin' at yer camp if'n you tried to tail us."

A shot echoed from back down the river.

"Sounds like he figured wrong, too."

"How do you know?"

"I'd say that was a .41 caliber...Ever hear of William H. Bonney?...Better known as Billy the Kid?"

"Shore, he got hisself kilt fifteen year or so ago."

She grinned and arched a well-shaped, dark eyebrow. "Did he?"

The young man's eyes grew big as saucers before he finally asked, "What'er you gonna do with me?"

"Nothing...I think by the time you get the rest of your family buried, you'll have learned a good lesson," she admonished.

The surviving member of the Zellon clan shook his head. "It wuz all that damn painted up mule's fault...wouldn't let nobody near 'im. Tol' pa he wuz trouble."

Fiona nodded. "Mules are very intelligent and have an excellent memory. He recognized your brother's voice and retribution was his...Now gather up all of your weapons and throw them into the river."

"Aw, now..."

Her steel-gray eyes hardened into flint. "You can go for a swim and find them after we're gone...that's assuming you don't freeze to death." She turned around, stepped over to Spot and swung easily into the saddle. "Just a word to the wise...Don't ever let me see you again."

She watched him throw the last of the Zellon's guns out into the slow-moving Arkansas before she and Spot rode off back down river toward their camp leading Tippy and Diablo behind.

Fiona dismounted in the area up in the trees where they had hobbled the animals last night and loosened Spot's cinch. "You can come out now," she said while she was tying the horses to saplings.

Bill stepped out from a thick copse of cedars off to the east. "How many?"

"Four."

"Really? Only heard what sounded like your .38-40s once…Maybe going off at the same time."

She nodded. "Spot took out one of them while I shot two at the same time…left the youngest to do the burying and reading…You got the patriarch of the clan I take it?"

"Tried to make him see reason, but we weren't connecting…. He committed suicide."

"Tried to draw, huh?"

"Uh-huh…Made some more coffee. What say we have a cup, and then load up and head west?"

"Sounds good. Think we'll make Garden City by sundown?"

"We should…Is Bat aware…"

"No."

Bill grinned. "Well, this is going to be interesting."

SKEANS BOARDING HOUSE
GAINESVILLE, TEXAS

The Cherokee pulled his gray woolen blanket tighter about him as he lay underneath a thick wisteria bush—the sleet was still lightly peppering down. *Unnn, no one leave house until storm over. Mankiller wait.* He crawled backward out of his hiding place, got to his feet on the opposite side and shook the ice pellets from his blanket.

Without a backward glance, he skulked away in the general direction of the downtown area—only two blocks away—in search of a secluded restaurant.

FULTON'S BOARDING HOUSE
GARDEN CITY, KANSAS

Fiona and Bill left their horses and Spot tied to the iron rings set in the cut limestone curbing in front of the two story Queen Ann house. They climbed the steps to the front porch and Bill twisted the brass knob, ringing the doorbell.

A large, matronly woman with her mouse-brown hair up in a bun opened the front door. "May I help you? I'm Ma Fulton."

"Yes, Ma'am, we'd like to see Mister Masterson," said Bill.

She pushed the green gingerbread screen door open and stepped back. "Do come right in. He and Emma are in the parlor. We were just having some hot cocoa by the fire…Would you like some?"

"That sounds wonderful…We're almost frozen stiff," commented Fiona.

They stomped the ice from their feet on the welcome mat and followed her inside.

"Some folks to see you, Bat."

A dapper, dark-haired, mustachioed man—just beginning to show a thickening around the middle—got to his feet from a burgundy wing-back chair near the roaring fireplace. "How can I be of service?"

Fiona held out her hand. "I'm Marshal F.M. Miller and this is Marshal Brushy Bill Roberts...Please call me Fiona."

The forty-four year old former gunfighter seemed to be taken aback, but only for a moment. "You're?...Well...I was expecting..."

"A man...I know," she interrupted.

"She gets that a lot," commented Bill with a smile.

"I find being a woman is occasionally beneficial in our line of work...the rapscallions and miscreants we have to deal with never expect it and if they do...they underestimate me."

Masterson's dark eyebrows went up.

"I can vouch for that...And believe me she has Bass Reeves' respect...and mine."

Bat's sky blue eyes flashed. "You know Bass Reeves?"

Fiona nodded. "Quite well...We worked together down in Texas and the Nations when we took care of the Tom Story gang. Bass' regular partner, Jack McGann, was laid up with a broken leg...Judge Parker assigned me to Bass." She chuckled. "I think he had the same reaction when the Judge introduced us."

His eyebrows went up again. "Now, I am impressed. There's no finer lawman anywhere than Bass Reeves and trust me, I know more than my share. I couldn't hold his hat...and neither could Wyatt Earp, for that matter."

She nodded and smiled. "He is definitely one of a kind. Just the bare mention of his name in the Nations could cause many an outlaw to get religion...It was truly an education and a privilege to work with him."

"Love to meet him one day."

"It could happen..." Fiona commented.

Ma Fulton interrupted the conversation, "I am so sorry. Where are my manners. Let me take your coats, and then I'll get you some hot cocoa...Goodness me." She stepped forward.

"We need to see to our animals, first, Miz Fulton," said Bill.

"Oh, pshaw, call me Ma...Everyone does."

Bat set his cup on the mantle. "I'll grab my coat and show them the carriage house, Ma...We'll be back soon as we feed and water their horses."

"And our mule...He's been a real hero, so far," commented Fiona. "As well as Smoky."

"Smoky?" Bat questioned.

She unbuttoned her sheepskin and the gray feline jumped to the floor and went immediately to Ma's feet where she stood over near the fireplace and began his weaving pattern accompanied by his extraordinarily loud purr.

"Well, I certainly look forward to hearing that story...Oh, and I'm afraid my manners are also lacking. This is my sweet bride, Emma." said Masterson as he grabbed his long gray top coat and black bowler from the hall tree.

"So happy to meet you. I, too, look forward to some of your stories," said the attractive auburn-haired woman.

Ma Fulton bent down, picked Smoky up and cradled him in her arms. "I'll bet you'd like some warm milk wouldn't you?"

He butted her chin.

Thirty minutes later the trio came back into the house through the back door carrying Fiona and Bill's bags.

"Just set your things in the hallway for now. I'm sure you'd like to warm yourselves by the fire and partake of my special hot chocolate...We've already had supper, but, I'll fix you all some pancakes and sausage in a little bit...Just the thing for a cold winter's evening."

"Sounds wonderful, Ma." Fiona glanced over to see Smoky curled up on an oblong rag rug next to the wood-burning cook stove in the kitchen.

Ma Fulton smiled. "He downed his milk and a little dab of leftover roast beef from lunch and promptly went to sleep there."

She waited until they hung their winter coats and hats on a tree in the hallway, and then handed each of them a white ceramic mug. The steam rose from the hot cocoa as they turned to walk into the parlor.

Bat noticed Fiona's ivory-handled Peacemakers under the flap of her mid-thigh black wool coat. "Nice. May I see one?"

She pulled her left-hand pistol from its holster, flipped it around and offered it to him, butt first.

"You right or left handed?"

She smiled. "Yes, I am."

Bat nodded.

"…It's another thing Bass and I have in common, we're both ambidextrous."

It was Masterson's turn to smile. "I've heard that Bass Reeves doesn't miss."

"Nor does Fiona…With either hand." Bill had a wry grin.

"It's not so much that he doesn't miss…it's that the concept of fear never enters his mind…regardless of the odds," she said.

"That often means more than speed and accuracy."

Bat shucked the five rounds from the Colt and held them in his left hand while he spun the pistol on his finger, stopped it, cocked the hammer and squeezed the trigger in one smooth motion. "Mmm, great balance, smooth…Feather trigger…Nice, very nice. Both the same?"

She nodded. "I call them Romulus and Remus."

"Ah, the twin brothers legend says founded Rome."

"My mother was born in Rome."

He reloaded the five rounds, duplicated her original move and handed the pistol back.

She smoothly spun it, flipped it back into its cross-draw holster and winked at Masterson.

§§§

CHAPTER FIVE

HASTING'S RESTAURANT
GARDEN CITY, KANSAS

Three men, with slicked-back dark hair, sat around a square table with a red and white checkered cotton tablecloth against the back wall of the restaurant. There were cups of black coffee in front of each.

"I'm already tired of dis place," said Depasquale. "Can't get decent food...not even a cannoli."

"Dey even put, eh, how you say?...Meatballs in dere spaghetti...yak," added Grimaldi.

"Where is Lando?" asked Benito.

Ambrogio glanced at the front door. "Dere he is now."

A large round-faced, barrel-chested man wearing a gray herringbone snap-brim longshoreman's cap, worked his way through the other tables. He snatched it from his head, stuffed it in his top coat pocket and pulled out the fourth chair. His left eye was almost swollen shut.

"Dis Corbett didn't want to go along wid de deal, no?" commented Grimaldi.

"You could say dat," said Da Costa.

"I just did."

"Don't cut wise wid me, Celso, me udder eye can see good enough to break yer face wid dis." He held up a ham-like fist.

The smaller man leaned back and held up his own hands, palm open.

"We go to stage two, den…Celso, you an' Lando know what to do," ordered Benito.

The two New York thugs nodded, got to their feet and headed toward the door.

FULTON'S BOARDING HOUSE
GARDEN CITY, KANSAS

"Well, Bat, do you want to fill us in a little more specifically exactly why we're here?" Fiona asked after Ma had fed them her special pancakes with maple syrup and elk sausage.

He sat his after-dinner coffee on the mantle, turned back to the others in the parlor and cleared his throat. "As I mentioned in the telegram, I'm promoting an exhibition three round rematch between John L. Sullivan and Gentleman Jim Corbett...There is a lot more interest in the fight for several reasons. One, there is now a nationwide betting network, vis-a-vis the telegraph and two, it will be the first fight ever recorded on Edison's moving picture system for public exhibition."

Bill had a confused look on his face. "So?...I still don't follow. It sounds like a hellova deal."

"That's the problem...There's potentially a million dollars cash money involved..." He looked over at Fiona. "...as I mentioned, I've gotten word that a criminal organization out of New York is sending some of their men here to...well, ah...make sure that they are on the winning side of the wager."

She cocked her head. "How can they do that...unless they fix the fight somehow?"

"That's exactly what I believe they're planning."

"Do you think that either Sullivan or Corbett are on the take?" asked Bill.

"Not voluntarily...But, in my opinion, if they can arrange for Corbett to lose, then that would set up a third and even more lucrative fight...A title rematch for the Heavyweight Championship of the World currently held by Corbett."

"But, you said you didn't think either man would voluntarily throw the fight," said Fiona.

"I know." Bat turned back to the mantle, picked up his cup, took a sip and made a face. "Damn...Cold."

Emma put down her crocheting and got to her feet from the couch. "I'll freshen it for you, dear."

"Thanks, love. What would I do without you?"

"I shudder to think," she said as she took his cup from him and headed to the kitchen.

"What do you know about this organization...as you called it? Is it one of those New York gangs we've read about...like the Irish?" asked Bill.

"I wish that's all it were. This bunch *controls* the street gangs...They're from the Italian island of Sicily...called the *Mafioso*...means arrogant and fearless...or to bully. They refer to themselves as *La Cosa Nostra*, meaning 'our thing' or 'the family'."

"You mean they have actually organized into a full-fledged crime syndicate and operate in America?" asked Fiona.

Masterson nodded. "The boss is a Giuseppe Morello, born in Corleone, Sicily...he's known as 'Clutch Hand'...He and his brother-in-law, Ignazio Lupo, specialize in counterfeiting and extortion with the support of another Sicilian born American, Vito Cascioferro, in Italian East Harlem...They also have connections to similar Mafia organizations in New Orleans, Cleveland and Chicago."

"And you think they're going to extort Corbett or otherwise threaten him to lose on purpose?"

"I do, Fiona. And since, not only am I promoting the fight, but I'm also the referee...it's possible they might come after me...which really doesn't bother me. I've been known to take care of myself." He got a slight grin on his mustachioed face. "But what does concern me...is they could come after Emma."

"Emma what?" she asked as she came back into the parlor from the kitchen.

He glanced up. "Oh, nothing, sweetheart...I, uh, was just telling Bill and Fiona how I spirited you away from the theatre in Denver."

She handed him his hot coffee and pecked him on the cheek. "Of course you were." She looked him in the eye momentarily, and then continued, "...and I'm so happy you did...Trodding the boards, singing and performing nightly is such a tough existence."

"Oh, I know what you mean, Emma. I only had to do it for a couple of weeks on a case we were working on down in Texas. I was undercover as Starla Marston from New Orleans...Singing and dancing...Ruined two parasols whacking drunk cowboys on the head for trying to be, ah...too familiar, if you know what I mean?"

Fiona and Emma both laughed.

"In the morning, we'll go over and meet with both the Great John L. and Gentleman Jim...I'll introduce you as my assistant." He nodded at Bill and then to Fiona. "...and you as my secretary from Denver…You can borrow Emma's long topcoat."

"I also have a black woolen alpine with a pheasant *aigrette* that I wear with that coat."

"Wonderful…The coat would be perfect to conceal my Colts," commented Fiona.

"What's an *aigrette?*" asked Bill.

"It's French for the plume from the top of a bird's head," replied Emma.

"I knew that."

Fiona grinned. "Of course."

"Mister Sullivan is staying at the Baker Hotel and Corbett rented a vacant farm house just outside of town for his training facility." Bat smiled. "As you may have heard, training is not real high on Sullivan's priority list. He has always counted on his bull rush, mauling tactics to beat his opponent."

"Apparently it didn't work the first time," offered Fiona.

"No, Gentleman Jim uses a new style of fighting…a lot of dancing around, bobbing, weaving, jabbing and killer body shots to wear his opponent down. He knocked the bigger man out cold in the twenty-first round with a flurry of combinations ending with a right to his chin…Changed boxing forever, in my opinion.

"Sullivan was gracious in defeat, saying that if he had to get beat, he was glad it was an American that did it…However, privately, he has always felt Corbett just got in a lucky shot."

"Sounds like it was a number of 'lucky shots'," said Bill.

Bat grinned. "I agree...But it still makes for good prize fighting...John L. thinks he can beat Corbett and that's why I'm promoting the fight."

BAKER HOTEL
GARDEN CITY, KANSAS

Masterson led Fiona and Bill into the half-full plush hotel dining room and toward a table where a thick, broad shouldered man with a dark handlebar mustache sat. The table was piled with several stacks of pancakes, a platter of steaks, a second platter of fried eggs and a large pitcher of sweetmilk—all within easy reach of the big man. The room was permeated with the strong morning smells of fresh hot coffee and sizzling bacon.

"Good mornin', Sully, I want you to meet my assistant, Bill Roberts and my secretary, Fiona Miller from Denver," Bat said as they walked up.

John L. got to his feet, wiping his mouth and mustache with his napkin and addressed Fiona first. "Well, well, mornin', darlin'..." He turned to Masterson. "You, too, Bat...and what'd you say this little fella's name was?" He indicated five foot eight Roberts.

"Bill," replied Bat.

He wrapped his giant paw around Brushy Bill's hand, rubbed the tips of his fingers together as he crunched down on the much smaller man's appendage. "Nice to meetcha."

"You too, Mister Sullivan," Bill managed to grit out through the pain until John L. grinned and released his hand.

"Have a seat, have a seat...Would ye be havin' breakfast?"

"We've already eaten at Ma's boarding house, thank you," replied Bat. "We just came by to say hello..."

Sullivan gazed appreciatively at Fiona's attractive face. "Pity...a real pity."

"...and to ask if you've seen any city folks around where you've been training at the high school gymnasium?...You know, New York, Chicago types?"

The bull of a man shook his head, and then grinned. "You know me, Bat, don't pay much attention to the leaf peepers when I'm workin' over my sparrin' partners." He winked at Fiona. "...Most of the time."

"Good...Well, we're going on out to see Jim."

"Tell him I'm lookin' forward to tomorrow." He looked at Fiona again. "Sure you won't stay and maybe have some coffee...or somethin'?"

She batted her eyes. "Oh, thank you so much Mister Sullivan. Maybe some other time."

He bowed, took her right hand and lightly brushed her fingers with his lips. "I look forward to it, pretty lady...and just call me John." The thick-necked man flashed a grin reminiscent of Teddy Roosevelt.

Fiona smiled back and tilted her head at him before they turned and walked back toward the exit.

BARTON RANCH

Masterson flicked the reins over the rump of the sorrel pulling the Stanhope buggy. "Come on up there, Sally."

The high-stepping American Standardbred mare crunched through the re-frozen crust of yesterday's sleet pulling the two-seated carriage down the well-traveled dirt ranch road. Fiona sat beside Bat in the front seat while Bill rode alongside on Tippy.

The Barton ranch was some two miles west of Garden City and one mile north of the Arkansas River. It was bisected by Kiowa Creek. There were traces of early winter wheat sticking up through the sleet on both sides of the road.

Fiona took a deep breath. "I do so love it out in the country. The air is so much cleaner than in towns."

Bat nodded. "I'm afraid we'd best enjoy it while we can."

"Oh?"

"When you get within fifty miles of Denver, you can already see a brown haze forming over the city...Smoke from the factories and of course from the many fireplaces. Being nestled up against the Rockies in a natural bowl, pollution flows up the side of the mountain, and then rolls back down on top of the city in a never-ending cycle….The result of the industrial revolution."

"Newton's Third Law," stated Fiona.

"Beg pardon?" asked Bat.

"For every action there's an opposite and equal reaction."

"I don't…Ah, yes, I see," Masterson commented. "I do believe you're right."

"She usually is," said Bill.

Twenty minutes later, they drove through the gate into the headquarters.

"What's going on here?" said Bat as he took note of the obvious chaos.

One of Corbett's entourage ran up and grabbed the horse's lead rope and led her over to a hitching post. "Shore glad you got here, Mister Masterson."

"What is it, Buster?" He asked the colored ringman.

"Somebody kilt Heywood."

"What?" asked Bat.

"Who's Heywood?" whispered Fiona.

"Corbett's corner trainer." He turned back to Buster. "When?"

"Last night…late. Found him jest a bit ago out behind the barn where we gots the ring set up…He was done stiff."

"How?" asked Masterson.

"Choked to death...Had a piana wire 'round his throat."

"Garrote," said Fiona.

"No'm, definitely piana wire...Kilt his little dog, Buddy, too...bashed his head in with somethin'."

Fiona grimaced and nodded.

"Have they moved the body?"

"Yasser, Mister Masterson. He be inside the barn on a table next to the ring."

"Damn," said Bill. "So much for a clean crime scene."

"Let's go back there anyway. Sometimes you never know what you'll find....Bass taught me that," said Fiona.

Buster led the three around the melee going on inside the barn to where the body was found. The sleet and ice was trampled and slushy—there were many footprints.

"Yep, that's what I was afraid of. Looks like a herd of cattle has been through here."

"There's where the body was...See the melted impression in the sleet, Bill?" indicated Fiona. "And over there is his little dog...Poor baby." She pointed at the small brown and white wire-haired terrier with bloodstained sleet and ice around its head.

"Yessum, that's Buddy. Heywood never goes anywheres without him....They wuz best pals," said Buster.

"But look there….A set of footprints facing the dog and away from Heywood's body. Whoever it was, braced his feet and swung some type of club," said Bill.

Fiona knelt down almost three feet from the little dog's body and studied the tracks. "Brogans…Heels worn on the back outside."

"Meaning?" asked Bat.

She looked up at the dapper ex-lawman. "Walks like a duck…splayfooted. Plus whoever made these was a really big man…See the depth of the track? Well over two hundred and fifty pounds."

"How'd you know about the wear pattern on his shoes?" asked Bat.

She winked at him. "Bass, of course."

"Of course."

"Should be easy to track him through this crusty sleet." Bill started moving away from the barn toward Kiowa Creek.

Bat and Fiona spread out and paralleled him.

"Eureka!" exclaimed Fiona. "Another set of tracks joined him…much smaller man, also wearing brogans…My bet is it's Heywood's killer…Big man took care of the dog, little man was the assassin."

They followed the tracks down to a copse of willow trees near the bank of the creek.

"Not familiar with riding," observed Bill.

"How so?" asked Bat.

"See how both men hopped around trying to get their foot in the stirrup…Horses were circling because they knew their riders were amateurs."

Fiona added her view, "Look how close the horses tracks are?…The men were scared and were holding a tight rein on the animals, abusing their mouths…making them dance."

"So to speak," said Bill.

"You two have it all over me. Most of my law enforcement days were spent in town…Didn't get a lot of experience tracking someone on the trail."

"Most of the town work back in the Nations was done by Lighthorse and Sheriffs. Our job was to chase down outlaws on the scout," added Fiona as she pointed. "Don't see any sense in following these tracks any further."

"How so?" asked Masterson.

"Another thing Bass taught us was to think like the evildoers…Anticipate where the tracks were going to lead and meet them there. They're headed back to town."

"Well, let's go see Corbett, then," said Bat.

Masterson and the two undercover marshals approached Gentleman Jim next to the rope ring that had been erected in the center of the barn. The six-foot-one, trim boxing champion was in his monogrammed white cotton training robe. His hair was perfectly coifed in a full-grown pompadour and, unusual for the time, he was clean shaven.

After Bat made the introductions, he asked that they move over to the side of the open area to talk privately.

"Sure sorry to hear about Heywood, Jim. It's a real pity. Do you know if anyone saw anything or anybody?"

Corbett shook his head in resignation and said through gritted teeth, "I think we both know who did this, Bat. After I decked that bear of a man…think his name was Lando Da Costa…for offering me ten thousand dollars to throw the fight, he said it wasn't over…I'll not tolerate any blackguards and rapscallions from the east side of New York to push James John Corbett around…You know that."

"So they go after your team." Bat saw Buster enter the barn from the back and walk over to them.

He was carrying something brown and white in his arms—it was Heywood's dog. "Mister Masterson…" He looked down at the furry creature as it raised its blood-smeared head and licked Buster's hand. "Buddy woke up…He woke up. Reckon he wuz jest stunned…Still cain't stand good."

"Ohhh." Fiona took out a handkerchief and started gently wiping the blood from the large lump on his head. She took him from Buster, opened her long wool coat and slipped the pup inside, next to Smoky. "This will warm you up." The cat licked the ice crystals from the long white whiskers on the little dog's muzzle.

LADY LAW

"This keeps up and we'll have to find you a bigger coat," said Bill.

She looked down at the dog and cat nuzzling each other. "Can't help it. I have this predilection for anything that can't take care of itself...especially furry creatures."

"That's very admirable, Miz Miller," said Corbett. "Very admirable, indeed...Heywood loved that little fellow." He turned to Masterson. "What do you suggest we do, Bat?"

Masterson thought for a moment. "You go on about your training, Jim...I think I have an idea." He glanced over at Fiona and Bill.

SKEANS BOARDING HOUSE
GAINESVILLE, TEXAS

The ominous figure stood in the shadow of the large red oak tree catty corner from the Victorian-style white house. From his vantage point, he could see the clothesline between the back of the house and the carriage house.

There were large, thick evergreen hedges on both sides of the one acre lot, but the back was open to the alleyway to allow access to the carriage house and stable.

The Cherokee surveyed the yard on the south side with a similar style two-story house in the center. The north side was bordered by Church Street. All the streets outside of the downtown area were still packed dirt and subject to the vagaries of the weather.

His obsidian eyes watched as Faye carried a basket of wet wash out to the wire clothesline. She set it on the ground and began hanging the garments and bed linens with one piece wooden clothespins from a red polka dot square cloth bag hooked to the line.

There was still traces of sleet crust on the dead grass lawns and the street in front of and to the side—as well as the alleyway—and all were muddy from the melting frozen precipitation.

"Unnh, no good. No hide tracks." He looked up at the clear blue sky and the bright sunshine. "Be dry by-and-by soon…Mankiller wait."

FULTON'S BOARDING HOUSE
GARDEN CITY, KANSAS

Fiona opened her coat and allowed Smoky to jump down and run to his spot on the rug near Ma's stove. She carefully lifted the injured dog out and placed him also on the rug next to the cat.

"Ohhh, who is that?" asked Ma.

"That's Buddy. The men that killed Mister Corbett's ringman tried to kill him too. Knocked him in the head with something…I suspect he has a concussion. He's still a bit woozy."

"Sweet baby. I'll fix both of them some warm milk…Put a little honey in his. I'll wash that dried blood from his head too."

Ma knelt down and scratched him under the chin. Buddy closed his eyes and raised his head.

"I think he likes that, Ma," said Fiona.

"I know he does. I lost my little Percy just last month…Cocker Spaniel. I'd had him for fifteen years. Broke my heart when he finally crossed the rainbow bridge…" She looked up at Fiona. "Do you think that maybe I could take him off your hands? He'd have a good home."

Fiona stepped over and gave Ma a hug as she got to her feet. "Oh, goodness, I was hoping you'd say something like that. I was wondering what I was going to do…I couldn't leave him out there…What with him losing his master."

"Consider it done, then." She curtly nodded and turned around to get the milk from the icebox and pour some into a pan.

"Ma, is that coffee I smell?" asked Bill.

She smiled. "It is and it's been on since you all left this morning. I would surmise it's getting a mite thick and strong by now."

Bill and Bat looked at each other.

"Just the way we like it," said Masterson.

Fiona sat on the dark green love seat to the right side of the roaring fireplace—Bill and Bat occupied the matching burgundy velvet wingback Thomas Chippendales on the other. Each was nursing a steaming mug of Ma's coffee.

Bill blew across the top of the cup and took a sip. His face puckered up and he closed one eye. "She was right, it is a little on the stout side."

Ma entered the parlor from the kitchen with a small green cut-glass bowl. She removed the lid, took a pinch of the coarse pink crystals inside and sprinkled it over each of their cups.

"What's that?" asked Fiona.

"Imported Himalayan salt…It'll take the bitter out." She handed each a spoon. "Give it a stir."

Bill stirred the black liquid briefly and laid his spoon on a doily on the coffee table. He licked the edge of the cup and took another sip. His eyes went wide and he looked up at the matronly proprietress. "I would not have believed it."

"Trick my grandmother from the old country taught me…Beats throwing it out in the yard."

"Unless you're trying to kill weeds," mumbled Bill.

"I have to remember this, thank you, Ma," said Fiona. She glanced over at Bat. "Now, Mister Masterson, what was this idea you mentioned?"

He sipped from his cup, looked up at the marshals and grinned. "Well, you do realize this is still the old west?"

They nodded.

"We noticed that back in Dodge," said Fiona.

"I don't think our visitors from New York actually understand what that means."

BUFFALO GAP SALOON
GARDEN CITY, KANSAS

The popular local watering hole rapidly filled up after sunset. Town residents as well as farmers and cowboys from the surrounding area drifted in. Cigar and cigarette smoke gathered at the top of the fourteen foot ceiling.

Several individuals stood in close proximity to the three wood-burning potbellied stoves that were strategically located around the fifty foot square establishment. The aroma of the burning hickory permeated the air.

The Buffalo Gap served dinner plus had pickled quail eggs in gallon jars scattered along the thirty foot bar on the east side of the room. Some patrons were eating, some playing faro or poker and some just drinking.

Five of the Morello crime syndicate—sometimes known as 'Wiseguys'—sat at a round table near the back of the room. There were two more standing at the bar when Bat, Bill and Fiona entered the double nine foot doors at the entrance.

They stood quietly at the front door for a moment until their eyes adjusted to the dim light, and then they spread out, allowing at least three feet between them. Bat was in the center, Bill on his left and Fiona, his right, nearest the bar.

Bat carried his 1885 nickel plated, custom-made .45 caliber Colt SAA in reverse draw on his left side. The hammer was specially constructed to be exceptionally fast on release. He was dressed in his usual attire, a natty dark three-piece suit and black bowler.

Brushy Bill was dressed similarly and carried his Colt .41 caliber birdshead Thunderer on his right hip under his black morning coat.

Fiona was wearing a single button black morning coat over her dark gray split skirt and red paisley bustier. A black Stetson Gambler's hat sat forward on her head, its shadow stopping just above her steel-gray eyes—long raven hair was draped over her left shoulder in a soft curl. Her twin ivory-grip .38-40 Peacemakers in cross-draw, were partially obscured by the long coat.

They stepped forward in a line toward the New Yorker's table and stopped fifteen feet away. The room became deathly quiet as the wiseguys looked up.

"Youse guys lookin' fer us?" asked Depasquale.

"You could say that," said Bat.

"Den I'd say youse found us," chimed in Ambrogio Sciortino. "What'd youse want?"

"We want you out of this town…now."

"Says who?" asked Benito Alaimo.

"Says Bat Masterson."

If the room was quiet before, every breath was now being held.

The smallest man at the table glanced over at the first speaker. "I think I'm scared, is youse, paisano?"

"I'm shakin' in my shoes, Celso." His gaze shifted to Fiona. "Youse bring a chippy to hold yer coats?" He looked at the others and laughed. "What do they call youse girlie, Florence Nightengale?" He laughed again and was joined by the others.

She grinned a tight smile. "Oh, some call me one thing and some call me another...But mostly they call me Deputy United States Marshal Fiona Miller...One of you bastards killed Corbett's man and hurt his dog...and this just isn't going to be you little bunch of ophidian's day."

"What'd she call us," asked Benito.

"Snakes," replied Bill.

They hadn't noticed the big man, Lando Da Costa leaning against the bar. He slid over behind Fiona, wrapped his arms around her in a reverse bear hug and lifted her off her feet.

"I thought I killed de little mutt." His garlic breath wafted across her face as he licked her cheek.

"That really would have made me mad, I like that dog," Fiona calmly said as she slipped her hands—which were already pinned to her side—against the grips of Romulus and Remus, eared back the hammers with her little pinky, and then squeezed both triggers with her ring fingers.

Her cross-draw, open-bottom holsters were already canted to the rear and the .38-40 caliber bullets went completely through both of Da Costa's huge feet and into the pine plank floor.

The big man screamed, released Fiona and fell heavily to his back trying to grab both of his bleeding feet.

She dropped to the floor and spun in a tight circle, drawing her pistols at the same time. Her right hand gun drilled the second man at the bar in the throat as he was drawing a .32-20 revolver from his waist while her left sent a round into the middle of Depasquale's chest before he could squeeze his trigger.

Ambrogio drew his Russian made Nagant M1895 seven-shot double-action revolver from a shoulder holster and started pulling the trigger. He got off three wild shots before Brushy Bill put a round through the middle of his forehead.

Benito pulled a sawed-off, pistol grip, double barrel shotgun from his overcoat, raised it toward Fiona when Bat delivered a .45 round to the center of his misshapen nose, blowing the back of his head completely off.

Both barrels discharged, blasting twin holes in the tin ceiling overhead as he staggered backward and caught two more rounds from Fiona as he fell. Even though they weren't necessary. He was dead before he hit the floor.

The barrels of four guns centered on the survivor, Celso Grimaldi, as he dropped his thirty-eight revolver to the floor with a clatter and fell to his knees with his hands over his head.

"*Mi arrendo...Mi arrendo*," he blubbered as a yellow puddle grew around his knees.

"What's that mean?" Bat asked Fiona.

"I surrender."

The round-faced Irish bartender raised up from behind the bar and looked around at the carnage. "Holy Mary, Mother of God," he whispered.

Bat stepped over to Celso and leaned down over him. "You get your skinny ass and that big bastard over there on the next train east and tell your boss in New York that Bat Masterson said stay the hell out of his business...And this was just a sample of Old West justice...*Comprendo?*"

Grimaldi nodded rapidly. "*Capire.*"

§§§

CHAPTER SIX

SKEANS BOARDING HOUSE
GAINESVILLE, TEXAS

"Not a cloud anywhere. I'll bet it gets to seventy again today…I can get the rest of the laundry done." Faye pulled the light yellow cotton curtain aside and looked up at the bright blue sky.

"That's Texas for you. Get six inches of sleet and four days later it's dry as a bone and shirtsleeve weather," commented Bodie as he poured himself a cup of coffee.

"It's a good thing. The linen closet was getting a little thin."

"Make you a deal…after you get the unmentionables and diapers hung, I'll help you with the bed sheets…How's that?"

"Oh, wonderful. They're so hard to hang and keep from dragging the ground...They're ready to run through the wringer in the wash room, I just have to put a couple of capfuls of Mrs. Stewart's Bluing in the rinse water."

Bodie took a sip of coffee. "I'll crank 'em through soon as I finish my coffee."

She smiled. "Don't know what I'd do without you and Annabel."

Faye had three of the wooden clothespins in her mouth and a diaper in each hand. She draped the corner of the thick white cotton squares over the line, slipped a clothespin over it, pulled up the other corner and secured it, too, and then did the second—overlapping the corners.

She reached down to the wicker basket to pick up several more when she was startled by a voice behind her and a steel-like grip on her upper arm.

"You come."

Faye turned, focused on the stranger's black expressionless eyes and the long white scar from his left ear to the point of his chin—a cold chill ran down her back. "You're hurting me...let go."

"You come," he repeated and started pulling her toward a buckboard in the alleyway behind the carriage house.

She screamed and tried to pull away from the big Cherokee just as Bodie came out of the back door with the full basket of wet linens.

"Hey! Hey! What the hell do you think you're doing?"

He couldn't see the Remington revolver in the Indian's other hand until it was pointed it at him and a ball of fire blossomed from the barrel. Bodie felt a heavy thump to his chest and a stinging, burning sensation.

Faye screamed.

He dropped the basket, looked down at the circle of blood spreading out from the finger-sized hole just above the second button of his white shirt. His knees buckled and he tumbled the rest of the way down the steps from the back door and lay still.

Faye screamed again as Annabel rushed out the screen door in response to the shot, just in time to see her husband crumple to the ground.

"Bodie!" She fairly flew down the steps and fell to her knees on the damp ground, sobbing beside his motionless body. "Oh, my darlin'! My darlin!" She held his head in her arms.

"Woman!"

Annabel's tear-streaked face looked up at the man holding the pistol pointed at her in one hand and his other arm wrapped around Faye.

"You tell *Ageyv Txvsgina*, me trade woman…for her…Mankiller not wait long. When moon next rises from lair, she come to iron bridge that crosses Hommá River or…woman dies."

Faye flailed ineffectually at the Cherokee's chest and face with her tiny fists. Mankiller swung his pistol against the side of her head with a sharp crack. She went limp in his arm. He slung her over his shoulder and disappeared behind the carriage house…

WELLMAN'S CLINIC
GAINESVILLE, TEXAS

A wan-faced Annabel sat in a straight-back chair in the waiting room of Doctor Wellman's clinic twisting her damp linen handkerchief in her hands—there were deep dark circles under her eyes and her cheeks were sunken.

Francis Ann Durbin had her arm wrapped around Annabel's shoulders comforting her. Her husband, acting town marshal Walt Durbin and her father, Tom Sullivant, paced the room, nearly bumping into each other on each pass.

"I wish you two would sit down."

Walt looked at her. "Frandarlin', that's my best friend in there…Cain't sit still…I'd blow up."

"I know…" She looked up as Doctor Wellman entered from the operating room.

The ladies shot to their feet.

"Is he…" Annabel started, and then brought her hanky to her mouth.

The doctor pulled down his surgical mask, stepped over and took both her shoulders in his hands. She looked up at his exhausted face with searching eyes.

He pressed his lips together, and then nodded. "I got the bullet out…His guardian angel must have been close by. It missed his aorta by less than the thickness of a piece of newspaper. That's why it took me four hours, plus all the bone shards from his sternum I had to remove…the slightest slip…"

"Will he?…"

"I don't know, Annabel…I just don't know. He's comatose, but that's probably a good thing. If he survives the next forty-eight to seventy-two hours…he's got a chance…lost a lot of blood…All we can do now is wait."

She nodded slowly, looked up at him, and then at the others. "And pray." Annabel knelt down, bowed her head and clasped her hands against her bosom.

Francis, Walt and Tom knelt down beside her, joined hands and bowed their heads, too. Doctor Wellman dropped to his knees and took the grieving woman's hand in his.

Annabel tried to pray aloud, but her voice wouldn't let her.

Walt was able to clear the lump in his own throat and took over. "Our gracious Heavenly Father, I ain't none too good at this. Guess I don't do it near often enough…But, Lord, that man in there is my friend. Now, I reckon if you need a good friend, too...then he's yours to take. You won't find a better one...but he's got a young wife and two beautiful babies that are gonna need his guidance...He's a real special fella..." His voice cracked, and then he continued, "...but I reckon you already know that.

"We're just askin' that you hold off takin' him home, if you would, Lord...I know we ain't got no right askin'...no right atall, but we are anyways. There's not a soul in this room he wouldn't give his life for and I feel the same about him...so if it be thy will, I hope you can see your way clear to pass your blessin' on him.

"Lord, you know Bodie's tougher'n boot leather, but right now he needs some help...Your help.We humbly beseech thee. We ask this in Jesus' Holy name...Amen."

The 'Amen' was echoed by the others around the room just as the outside door burst open to admit Deputy US Marshals Selden Lindsey and Loss Hart from Ardmore, IT. The two law officers immediately snatched their hats off when they perceived they had interrupted a prayer.

Hart was still hobbled from the double-ought shot from Doe Lee's shotgun that caught his foot up in the Nations—he used a handmade hickory cane to help him get around.

Walt and the others got to their feet.

"Selden, Loss. Ya'll got here in good time," said Walt as he stuck out his hand.

"We lucked out. There was a work train headed south. We flashed our badges and hooked a ride. Had to ride on a flat bed and hold our horses reins. Wadn't no problem...Is Bodie..."

"Let's step outside and I'll fill you in with what I know...Doc just came out of surgery an' we wuz sayin' a prayer. The next few days'll be the tellin' of the tale."

The three lawman stepped out to the front yard of the clinic.

"Who done it? I mean who took Faye and shot Bodie?" asked Loss when they had closed the door.

"Well, based on the description Annabel give us...It was Cal Mankiller."

"I thought that renegade was dead? Didn't Fiona put a couple balls in him?" exclaimed Selden.

"She did and he fell into the river, but apparently he survived," said Walt.

Loss looked over at Selden. "Well, I think that solves a mystery."

Lindsey nodded.

"What mystery?" asked Walt.

"There's been a rash of killin's, rapes and burnin's all along the north side of the Red...Men, women and even children...We've been investigatin', but been comin' up empty-handed," said Selden.

"All them crimes fits right into that killer's mo-dus-op-eran-di."

114

"Damn, Loss, where'd you learn them big words?" asked Selden.

He grinned and ducked his head. "My Penny's been makin' me study. Says I need to be more edgacated if I'm gonna be a bidiness man."

Selden just shook his head. "How's come he took Miss Faye?"

"Well, that's the thing. Best we could git outa Annabel was that he wanted to trade for *Ageyv Tvs-gina* or something like that at the next full moon. But I got no idea in hell what or who *Ageyv Tvs-gina* is."

Selden's jaw set as he looked back at Walt. "That's Cherokee for She Devil...He wants Fiona." He exhaled sharply. "Is there a meetin' place?"

Walt nodded. "Middle of the railroad bridge crossin' the Red. Fiona's not there when the moon rises...Faye dies."

Loss slammed his hat to the ground. "That evil son of a bitch will do it too...an' enjoy it."

FULTON'S BOARDING HOUSE
GARDEN CITY, KANSAS

Bat, Fiona, Bill and Emma Masterson sat around the parlor, enjoying the roaring fire and coffee.

"Well, it's been quiet around the training camps since that little worm and man mountain got on the train. Kinda funny to watch Da Costa hobble aboard with those crutches and both feet wrapped up," said Bat.

"I should have killed him anyway…Would have if he'd had a gun," commented Fiona.

"He wasn't armed?" asked Bill in surprise.

She shook her head. "All he had was a sawed-off baseball bat in a pouch inside his coat."

"I suspect he was what they call on the East Side, an enforcer…Breaks knee caps of the longshoremen that don't want to go along with the union."

"I don't think he'll be breaking any knee caps for a good long…"

Fiona was interrupted by the ring of the brass twist-bell at the front door.

"I'll get it," said Bat as he set his cup on the coffee table and headed to the foyer.

They could hear his baritone voice telling someone to come on in.

He led a tall, lanky, redheaded teenage boy inside with a too-small Western Union jacket on. The young man snatched his short-billed baseball cap from his head.

"Got a telegram for Marshal Miller." He held it out toward Bill standing near the mantle.

"That's Marshal Miller over there, son." He pointed to Fiona sitting in one of the wingback chairs.

"We did everything we could...Scoured up and down the bank all the way past Big Mineral to Harris Creek."

"Should have gone further...to the other side." She turned and looked at him sitting across from her. "It's apparent that's what he did...someway. I told you I had a bad feeling that day."

"Yeah, your intuition...What do you want to do?"

"Well, first thing is to check on Bodie in Wellman's clinic, and then go see Annabel." She turned her head back out the window. "Then we put on our trail duds and go tracking...We have four days until the full moon. I intend to make it count...With God as my witness, that maleficent bastard is going to pay...And I'll see that it's not quick...you can count on that. 'I will do such things...What they are, yet I know not: but they shall be the terrors of the earth'."

"Uh, huh...from King Lear, Act 2 - scene 4, as I recall."

All the time she was staring out the window and talking to Bill, Fiona absentmindedly rubbed under Smoky's chin.

"You're gonna rub all the hair off, you keep doing that."

"Oh, I didn't realize I was even doing it. Thanks." She looked down at the gray head sticking out of her coat. The cat looked back up at her and butted her hand. "Looks like he wasn't done yet."

"Why didn't you leave him with Ma? She would have loved to keep him."

Fiona shook her head. "Tried, but he wasn't having any of it. Every time I picked up my bag, he would jump in. He knew we were leaving…Just so you know, people don't own cats…It's the other way around. Besides I think she had plenty to do, nursing Buddy back to health."

"Hate it we couldn't stay for the fight this weekend…But I think Bat has it well in hand…Did you ever see anybody more calm and collected than him in a gunfight?"

She looked across at him. "Yes…Bass Reeves."

"Ah…Correct."

LOVE COUNTY
CHICKASAW NATION

Mankiller led the other horse up the sandy bank out of the water on the Nation's side of the Red at Brown's Crossing.

A bloody and battered Faye Skeans slumped in the saddle, her hands tied to the saddle horn with rawhide thongs—her head bobbed loosely with each step.

The Cherokee had abandoned the wagon at a small house in the woods off a ranch road next to Summit Creek in north Cooke County. He previously picketed two stolen horses close to the water on some graze. After jerking a resistive Faye out of the wagon and to the ground, he raped, beat and kicked her into unconsciousness before tying her in the saddle of a lanky bay gelding.

She painfully lifted her head as she regained some degree of consciousness and tried to look around. Both eyes were black and almost swollen shut—everything was a blur. Her day dress had one sleeve torn off and was now dirty, bloodstained and tattered.

Faye tried to mumble through her split and puffy lips. "Why?"

The Indian didn't even turn in his saddle. "Woman no talk...Mankiller beat again."

He reined the horses to the left and walked them down a long abandoned logging road through the woods that paralleled the river bottom to the west. The renegade carried his ten gauge shotgun across his lap, just behind the shoulders of his saddle.

A little over a mile from the Red River Ferry Road, an old man stepped out of the woods on the north side of the trail just six feet away. He had six large fox squirrels and one cottontail hanging from his belt and a 410 shotgun over his shoulder.

"Howdy, neighbor..." he started speaking until he saw Faye behind him. "What happened to..."

He never got another word out before the Indian swung his shotgun around and blew the old hunter's head from his shoulders.

Faye jumped at the sound and began to scream.

"Shut up, woman," Mankiller commanded as he dismounted.

He stepped over to the body, checked his parfleche pouch for money or other valuables, slipped the carry strap over his head, and then removed the squirrels and hung them from his saddle horn. After dragging the body off into the brush, he remounted and continued west at the same pace.

The Cherokee drew rein at the edge of the right-of-way for the Gulf and Colorado Railroad. He heard the chuffing of a locomotive heading southbound, turned the horses into a copse of cedars and waited for the passenger train to pass. Mankiller was startled as he saw Fiona's face in the window of one of the cars as it passed his hiding place—then he almost smiled. "*Ageyv Tsvsgina,*" he hissed.

WELLMAN'S CLINIC
GAINESVILLE, TEXAS

Bill and Fiona rode directly from the depot to the clinic to check on Bodie. Tying their horses and the pack mule, they entered his private room. It was Walt Durbin's shift to sit with the comatose man. Doctor Wellman wanted him watched twenty-four hours of the day until he regained consciousness—under the assumption that he did.

Walt got to his feet, hugged Fiona and shook Bill's hand.

"How is he?"

"No change, Fiona. But at least he's still breathin'...slow, but reg'lar."

"We moved Annabel and the babies out to the ranch. She needed help with the twins...not to say nothin' about the support from friends...She's takin' this real hard."

She shook her head, her mouth tight. "It's all my fault...I wasn't good enough."

"That's not so, Fiona...I saw both those hits to his chest. I called 'em kill shots too," said Bill. "It's just some fluke of evil he survived."

"Figured ya'll would come by here first so I brought the case histories Lindsey and Loss brought down of the crime spree across the southern portion of the Chickasaw Nation." He handed Fiona the bulky manila envelope.

She took it, moved to a nearby chair. "A lot more here than we read in the paper." She glanced at the unconscious Bodie as she did.

Fiona removed several of the documents and began to read. "My God in heaven." She shook her head as she started with the family massacre in Oakland. Tears began to flow as she continued to Lynn in Pickens County and Kemp in Panola County and on to the others.

She finally spoke, "No question, it's him...Evil, evil, wicked son of a bitch...Trailed the bastard long enough to know his every habit...He's a hard one to track."

"Well, we do have an advantage."

"What's that?"

"We know he took Faye away with a wagon. Bet anything he headed north, back across the river. He knows the territory…The fact he's not by himself…"

"True…but it is some rugged and wild country. Chances are he switched to horseback somewhere along the way."

"Why don't ya'll come out to the ranch? Got plenty room," offered Walt.

They both nodded.

"Good idea. Need to talk with Annabel too. We'll go by the boarding house first and get rid of these city duds and be right out…Then we hit the trail," replied Fiona as she petted Smoky. "Bet you'll be glad to get out of this coat too, won't you." The gray cat stretched up and butted her chin.

"See you picked up a passenger," said Durbin.

"Other way around." She smiled. "Name's Smoky."

"Woulda never guessed."

RAFTER S RANCH

Fiona, Walt and Bill leading Spot, jog-trotted their horses through the gate at the ranch. A short stub of a man from southern Louisiana, Little John Boutté, met them at the front of the rambling two-story ranch headquarters.

"Marshal Fiona, Marshal Bill, how ya'll are?…You too, Walt, uh, Marshal Durbin. 'Course jest see'd you this mornin'," he greeted them in his Cajun drawl. He looked over at the painted mule. "Woo-law, ain't never seen a cat ridin' a mule, no."

"That's Spot and Smoky. They're pals."

"Well, see there you is…Takes all kinds, yeah it do." He unbuckled the bags from Spot's saddle. Smoky cocked his head and watched him. "He be payin' special attention to my untrappin', ain't he?"

Fiona grinned. "He's just making sure you're doing it right, Little John. He has been known to swat people pulling things off out of order."

"Well, now, that's good to know…Be…the cat, uh, Smoky, goin' off to the barn wiff him?"

"Oh, yeah. He knows we're stayin' here a spell. He'll make himself a place in Spot's stall."

After he had removed everything that was going into the house and set them on the porch, Boutté stepped back and looked the animal over. "Ain't but the second painted-up mule I ever seen, yeah it is. The other, he be a some smart animal, he was…I guarontee."

"Well, that one is too…and has a good memory. Some bad guys we encountered, could attest to that. He helped me out when I was in a tight," Fiona said.

Tom Sullivant, the owner of the Rafter S stepped out on the big wrap-around porch smoking a rosewood pipe and letting the screen door slam behind him. "Well, ya'll made it just in time for a bite of lunch. "Annabel and Fran are fixin' to go in to sit with Bodie, this afternoon…My shift is tonight…Maybe Annabel can fill ya'll in, first hand."

"Be bringin' the carriage over soon's I turns these critters loose in the paddock. Got's to feeds and throws 'em some hay, Mister Tom. Cain't have 'em goin' hongry, no."

The rotund, balding owner nodded. "Be fine, Little John, be fine…Ya'll come on in. Sing Loo'll whip up some sandwiches from the leftover pot roast."

"Mmm, roast beef on his fresh-baked bread with a slather of mustard sounds great," said Bill as he swung down and untied his soogan and saddlebags from behind his cantle.

"I'll say," Fiona added while she also removed her gear.

"I heard Bodie shout an' then the shot. I ran from the kitchen just in time to see my sweet husband tumble down the steps to the ground." Annabel used her linen hanky and dabbed the tears that were flowing down her cheeks again."

"Take your time, Annabel," said Fiona.

The petite blonde twisted in her chair at the dining table and nodded slowly. "I rushed down the steps and held his head in my arms. That's when that abomination told me about the next full moon and tradin' Faye for…for you and then he hit her with his gun." She paused and took a deep breath. "He carried her out to the alleyway and threw her in the back of a green buckboard."

"Did you see what kind of horse was pulling the wagon?" asked Bill.

Annabel shook her head. "I could only see the back end of the wagon. The rest was blocked by the carriage house." She sniffed her running nose.

Bill and Fiona finished their roast beef sandwiches and ice tea and got to their feet. She gave Annabel a hug.

"We'll find her and that evil man."

Annabel looked up at the taller woman with her tear-streaked face. "But...he wants you!"

Fiona gave Annabel a wry smile. "He can have me...but he's not going to like it one bit, I can assure you. Heraclitus once said, 'A man's character is his fate'." She turned to Bill. "You ready to go, Marshal?"

"Waitin' on you, m'lady."

"Then you must be backing up." She grinned.

SKEANS BOARDING HOUSE

Fiona knelt down underneath the clothesline in the back yard. "Notice the chunk knocked out of the heel of Mankiller's right brogan?"

Bill bent over for a closer look at the track in the soft ground and pointed. "Yeah, soles almost worn through, too. Not that way when we tracked him before…Chances are these shoes were stolen…probably from one of the farms he robbed."

"I'd say."

Roberts rose to his feet. "What a piece of work is a man."

"I don't think even Hamlet would describe this creature as a 'man'…More in the realm of a 'monster'."

§§§

CHAPTER SEVEN

SMITH BROTHERS LIVERY
GAINESVILLE, TEXAS

Fiona and Bill dismounted in front of Smith Brothers Wagonyard and Corral.

"Figured we'd lose the tracks once they got to California Street," said Bill.

Fiona nodded. "Uh, huh, too much traffic. We'll check all the other wagonyards and livery stables and then do an arc on the northbound roads about a half-mile out of town."

"Northbound?"

"If there's one thing I've learned about that renegade, it's that he prefers to keep to an area he knows...and that's the Nations."

A tall, lanky redheaded teen sauntered out of the livery barn, wiping his hands on a red paisley bandana. "Afternoon. Hep you folks?" He noticed the federal badge affixed to Bill's gray vest, and then Fiona's pinned to her blue patterned velveteen bustier. "Oh, Marshals...Say, hey, you'd be Marshal Miller, wouldn't you, Ma'am?"

"I wouldn't make it a habit of calling her that, son," cautioned Bill.

"Huh?"

"I am. We're looking for a big Cherokee...Renegade...Has long hair and..."

"A big white scar runnin' from his left ear to his chin?" He traced his finger along his face.

"That's him." Bill nodded. "Seen him, I take it."

"Oh, yessir, twict. He come by back in the summer 'fore the big race, then again not too long 'fore the sleet storm." He glanced at Fiona. "Was alookin' fer you, Ma'am."

"Marshal will do...So it's safe to assume you told him how to find me."

"Yesssum...Even drawed him map over to Miss Faye's...Was that alright?"

"Doesn't matter much now," Bill mumbled.

"Know anyone around here with a green buckboard?"

"Uh, huh…Harley Smart, jest north of town has one. Got stole last week…I painted it fer 'im an' put a brand new wheel rim an' hub on the…"

She interrupted. "Left rear…Correct?"

NORTH COOKE COUNTY

Weaver Street changed to Weaver Road after it left the city limits of Gainesville. Fiona and Bill started their arc at Taylor Road and had ridden cross-country to the west, crossing all the northbound country roads.

She raised her hand and they pulled their horses to a halt.

"See something?"

Fiona nodded, dismounted in the roadway, dropped to one knee and studied a wagon track. "New rim." She stepped over to the off track. "Yep, the same as over on Dixon Street. This is our boy." She stuck her toe in the stirrup, her split riding skirt allowed her to swing easily into the saddle.

They reined their mounts to the north toward the Red seven miles away.

Four miles out of town, the tracks pulled off the lightly traveled Weaver Road to the east onto an even less used small farm road and headed into the timber that filled the Red River valley.

They followed the tracks as the tiny road snaked around some of the thicker trees and brush.

131

"Believe that's a shack through the woods yonder," said Bill. "I can see the wagon, too."

Fiona nodded. "Bet he's not there, though. Not his style to light anywhere for very long and the tracks we've been following are at least a day old."

"Still a good idea to err on the side of caution, don't you think?"

"I do, Marshal Roberts, I do indeed."

They dismounted, drew their pistols and crept toward the shack.

"No smoke," observed Bill.

"Not good...Uh, oh," she said as they got close enough to see the entire wagon. "The horse is dead. Probably shot...Still in his traces."

Bill stepped up on the rickety porch, stood to the side of the door and pushed it open with the barrel of his Colt. He listened and could only hear the whimpering of a child that rapidly escalated into a wail—and then became two, then three. He brushed the flies from his face that came out of the open door and looked inside.

"What is it?" Fiona asked from the steps.

Bill staggered back, grabbed a porch post, leaned over and spewed vomit over the ground. "Oh, God...oh God in Heaven." He vomited again.

She quickly stepped to the open doorway and went inside. What met her eyes, brought back memories of some paintings inspired by Dante's Inferno. She slowly slumped to her knees and covered her mouth.

The eviscerated, scalped bodies of a man and a woman lay sprawled on the blood-soaked floor. Their intestines were unceremoniously piled in the middle of the dining table with a candle stuck in the top.

Green blowflies filled the room. A three month old baby fretted in a crib near a wall while a one year old and a two year old toddler sat crying underneath the table—all were covered in blood and flies.

"Help me, Bill, help me," Fiona managed to croak out, choking back her own bile rising in her throat.

She holstered her Peacemaker, grabbed the baby—bloody blanket and all—from the crib and made her way through the swarms of insects to the door. "Get the other two," she was able to bark at him as she went down the steps.

Bill wiped his chin on the sleeve of his coat, took a deep breath, and stepped inside, waving the buzzing creatures away.

Fiona carried the child toward a rock-encased hand-dug well almost thirty feet from the house and laid it on the ground.

She dropped the wooden draw bucket over the side, listened to it splash at the bottom and gave it time to fill half up before pulling it back to the top.

Roberts came back out the front door with a filthy, screaming child under each arm and made his way to the well. He set them beside the baby on the ground.

"Go back inside and see if you can find some towels or something we can use to clean these babies with." They even have flies inside their mouths and nostrils.

Bill had a blank look on his face and just stood there. She slapped him sharply across the face. "Now, Bill! Now!"

He shook his head, blinked and spun on his heel back inside.

In a couple of short moments, he came back out with an armload of towels and a clean patchwork quilt. "Found these inside a linen trunk over by the parent's bed."

"Now I need a wash pan and some soap."

He nodded took another deep breath and headed back inside.

Thirty minutes later, they had the children cleaned up and in fresh clothing Bill had brought back out on his third trip.

"These babies haven't eaten or had anything to drink since sometime yesterday, judging from the condition of the bodies and the flies....See how dehydrated they are?" Fiona rocked the baby in her arms. "We've got to get them to town and to Wellman's clinic quick as we can...I'll carry the baby, you have the other two...Let's see if we can get the toddlers to at least drink some water."

"I saw a couple cans of evaporated milk and a clean nursing bottle on the counter."

She looked at him and cocked her head. "Well?"

He nodded. "Did I ever tell you how much I hated flies...almost as much as snakes."

"I have something I hate more than those put together...Calvin Mankiller."

After feeding all three babies some evaporated milk mixed with a little water, Fiona and Bill road-trotted their horses back down Weaver Road toward town. She carried the swaddled baby on her hip while Bill held the one year old in his left arm and the toddler sat in the saddle in front of him. The rhythmic motion of his horse at the fast trot had thankfully put all three sound asleep.

WELLMAN'S CLINIC
GAINESVILLE, TEXAS

It only took a little over forty-five minutes to cover the six miles back to town and to Wellman's Clinic.

"You realize Mankiller set that up just for us, don't you?"

Fiona nodded as she also pulled rein and dismounted carefully, not waking the baby girl in her arm. "I know...He knew we'd be tracking him. That's why he didn't murder these babies. It wasn't because of any scruples on his part, I assure you. He knew we'd have to break off the hunt to take care of them."

Bill looked up at the churning purple skies. "Plus I think he knew a rainstorm was coming like most Indians do."

She nodded. "Wash out any tracks...He's a devious bastard."

"Among other things."

"The big thing I'm afraid of though is he has no intention of bringing Faye to the meeting alive."

Fiona looked sharply at him. "You think?"

"Stake my badge on it."

Annabel and Francis Ann had heard them trot up and came out the front door of the clinic along with Doctor Wellman.

"The Hancock children?...What in the world?" He started to step forward, but the ladies beat him. Annabel grabbed the three month old and Fran took the one year old from Bill. "How..."

"Later, inside, Doc," Fiona said. "I think the older children are still in a state of shock."

Bill watched as Annabel and Fran carried the other two siblings inside the clinic. He dismounted and eased the still sleeping toddler from the saddle.

"Let's take them to the nursery in the back," said the doctor.

Wellman's nurse came out the front.

"Martha, make three beds ready...extra blankets," he said as he cradled the two year old in his arms.

The matronly woman in a starched white uniform turned around and headed back inside. "Right away, Doctor."

"Well, Doc, that's pretty much the story," said Bill as he finished telling about finding the children as they sat in the doctor's office.

Wellman got to his feet. "Guess I best go out there. Got to do death certificates on Nathan and Katie."

"Not much need, based on how we found them…I'd say just the undertaker. He's more equipped to handle the…ah, situation."

He sat back down in his swivel chair behind his desk. "I suppose you're right, Fiona…it's just hard to fathom there are actually human beings like that snake of a renegade."

"Considering what we saw…I don't know if I'd put him in the human classification," offered Bill.

Wellman nodded. "I need to get word to Sue Land, she usually knows who's wet nursin' around here…plus, got to find a family to foster the two boys after I watch them for a day or so."

"How's Bodie doing?" asked Fiona.

He paused, pursed his lips, shook his head and glanced at the door to make sure it was closed and Hickman's wife couldn't hear. "Not good. His breathin' is starting to get a little ragged and labored…think his lungs are collecting fluid…If he gets pneumonia…well, I think you know what his chances are…Need to send a telegram to Doctor Ashalatubbi for a consultation. He has a lot more experience with this type of wound from working in Lincoln's war as a young physician."

Roberts got to his feet. "I can do both, Doc. Just tell me how to find Sue…Have to get our horses over to Pap Clark's Livery for shelter from the storm anyway before it hits…Looks like it's going to be one of those kind that'll be with us for a day or so."

"Kill two birds with one stone. The Western Union operator knows her and can get a messenger out to her house plus send the telegram up to Ardmore."

The thunder rolled ominously overhead. Bill looked up and got to his feet.

"Guess I better get moving." He turned and headed to the door.

Forty minutes later, Bill ducked back in the front, shaking the rain from his hat. He pulled his oiled mustard yellow *poncho* over his head—it was the style worn mostly in New Mexico and Arizona—and hung both on a coat rack beside the door. "Dang, it's coming down cats and dogs out there."

Then he noticed Fiona was by herself in the front waiting room sitting at the end of the dark green couch along the far wall. Her head was on the padded arm and her body was shaking with sobs.

"Fiona, what happened. Did Bodie…"

Her tear-streaked face looked up and she shook her head. "No…I was just thinking about what you said when we got here and I know you're right. If Faye's not already dead…she will be soon and it's all my fault…He's toying with me." She leaned back against the couch. "I think all we'll find at the bridge is a mutilated body."

She buried her face in her hands and sobbed again. "Why, why?"

The front door of the clinic banged open behind Bill and a dark hulk of a man in a brown slicker carrying what appeared to be a body wrapped in a soaking wet gray wool blanket stood in the opening—a yellow and black spotted dog beside him shook the water from his fur.

Fiona jumped to her feet. "Bass!"

Doctor Wellman burst in from the hall door at the sound. "What's goin' on?...Bass, what is it." He quickly strode forward and peeled back the sopping blanket and looked down on the battered face. "My God! Faye!"

He felt of her carotid artery. "Back here, quickly." Wellman spun on his heel. "Martha! Prepare a bed...Now."

Fiona moved with Bill over to the door and closed it behind the legendary marshal against the driving rain. "How? Where?"

"Later. Pore thang's jest barely hangin' on," Bass said as he followed the doctor down the hall to a room. The dog followed.

"Glad I added this wing of beds last year," Wellman commented as he led the procession into a small room next to Bodies'.

Annabel and Francis were already on their feet at hearing the commotion and looked out the door of Bodie's room.

"Who is it?" asked Fran.

139

"Faye," the doctor said over his shoulder as he ushered Bass into the room.

Annabel put her hand to her mouth. "Oh, thank you sweet Jesus."

"Put her there, Bass." He pointed at the bed Martha was standing beside. "Ladies, my nurse could use some help gettin' those wet things off her so I can do an examination. Bass, you and Bill can leave, if you would? It's a little crowded in here."

A flash of lightening followed by a loud clap of thunder from the storm punctuated his statement as the smell of ozone permeated the small clinic.

"Yasser, no problem. Got's to see to my horse anyways. He don't like lightening much."

After Bass and Bill had taken Flash down Pecan Street to Clark's Livery, they sat in the clinic's kitchen warming up on hot coffee. Fiona came in the open doorway.

"Somebody make a fresh pot?

"Brand new," answered Bill.

"They ran me out too after we got Faye in bed. Doctor Wellman said he had never seen so many contusions and scrapes on a person…She has three broken ribs and had been violated several times." Fiona wiped a tear that had started running down her cheek."

Bill filled a white porcelain mug with the fragrant steaming brew. "Bass was just starting to tell how he found her."

"This I have to hear." She took the cup, looked over at Bass' Catahoula Leopard dog curled up next to the stove, and then walked over and hugged the big man's neck and whispered in his ear, "Thank you."

Fiona took a seat at the small kitchen table, took a sip of her coffee, set back in her chair and waited for Bass to commence.

"Well, first off, it was Buttercup what actually found her…"

"Buttercup?" questioned Bill.

Bass glanced over at his dog, now sound asleep.

"Oh."

"See, Walt sent a telegram fillin' me in on the details. So I takes the train down to Marietta…Taken me near two days to git there."

"But, how on earth did you pick up his trail?" questioned Fiona.

He blew across the surface of his coffee, licked the edge of the cup, took a sip, and then continued, "'Member how I tol' you once that sometimes you jest gotta go where the miscreant is a gonna be rather than try to tail 'em?"

She nodded.

"Well, 'course livin' with the Cherokees fer a spell helped some too…Know how they thank."

"What about Mankiller?" asked Fiona.

"Gonna get there, jest gimme time…See, figured he'd stay fair close to the bridge, thinkin' he could bushwhack you when you showed up fer the exchange…of which they wadn't gonna be one."

"That's what we thought, too," said Bill glancing over at Fiona.

Bass nodded. "Well, wind was out of the north, so's me and Buttercup sweep along the sand dunes on the Nations side of the Red tills we catch a scent of smoke."

"How'd you know that was them?" asked Bill.

"Would you let him tell the story?" Fiona snapped.

Bass grinned. "It's alright…Didn't. But, see, Injuns have they own smell, jest as black and white folk does…an' Chinee an Mescan, too, fer that matter…Well, Buttercup, he perks up and growls low down…he don't much care fer Injuns he don't know an' then leads us to the north.

"I finally catch a whiff of Injun mixed with white, an' reckon that narrowed it down to a fare-thee-well. So's I puts on my knee-high Apache moccasins, ground ties Flash, an' me an' Buttercup slips up through the woods towards where the smell was a comin' from."

Bass paused and took a long sip from his coffee, rolled the warm cup back and forth between his big hands, and then set it down on the table.

Bill got to his feet, grabbed the pot from the stove and refilled Reeves mug.

"Thankee kindly…We ease up to this little camp. They's a hat-sized fire agoin in front of a juniper leanto…but no

Mankiller. Reckon he was a off a walk huntin'. I seen two horses hobbled on some grass nearby and so I cuts 'em loose an' they takes off.

"Then I seen Faye ahangin' by her wrists like a gutted deer from a big ol' oak limb off at the edge of the camp...Mind he wad't wantin' her to run off whilst he was a huntin'.

"Oh, my God," exclaimed Fiona.

"I knowed Buttercup would warn me if'n he heard er smelled him a comin' back...I gots me a good smeller, but, ain't nothin' like his."

Buttercup looked up at the sound of his name from his spot on a braided rag rug in front of the stove, scratched an ear with a hind foot and laid his head back down.

"We move into the little camp an' I grabs Mankiller's blanket from his leanto, cut Faye down...she was unconscious an' barely breathin'...wraps her up an' carries her to where Flash was...Thought it best to git her to some help rather than stay around and try to git the Injun.

We was headed back this away when the storm broke...Knowed we needed to git across the river 'fore it started risin', so we hurried ever chanct we got...an' you know the rest."

Doctor Wellman entered the kitchen. "I do hope there's some of that left...Actually, I hope there's a lot left."

"Absolutely," said Bill. "Want anything in it?"

He shook his head. "No, don't want to ruin it."

Roberts smiled, got to his feet and grabbed another mug from the cabinet.

"Just barely run it over. I need all the help I can get…been a rough day."

"How's Faye?" asked Fiona.

He took a deep breath. "She's going to be all right…with time. Plus lots of rest, plenty of fluids and care…Can't say about her mind yet…Faye's still terrified. Being with that animal for three days…"

"Calling him an animal is disparaging to God's creatures."

He glanced up at Fiona over his coffee and nodded.

There was a tap on the door jam and a Western Union messenger came in. "Telegram for Doctor Wellman," he said as he reached inside his slicker.

"Right here, son." He pulled a coin purse from a pocket in his white smock, extracted a fifty-cent piece and handed it to the young man.

"Thank you, sir…Will there be an answer?"

Wellman didn't say anything until he finished scanning the yellow flimsy. He looked up and nodded. "Will meet you at the station in the morning. Stop. Wellman."

"Yessir, git this right out. Sorry about dripping water on your floor, sir."

"It's all right, son."

The teenage messenger spun about and headed back to the front.

The doctor looked up at Bill and Fiona. "Winchester's coming in on the morning train…I asked for his help."

"I'll get a buggy and pick him up for you Doc, if you like?"

"That would be wonderful, Bill.

Roberts glanced over at Bass and Fiona. "What say we check in on Bodie and Faye, and then head over to the boarding house and get some rest…Think we're going to need it.

PICKENS COUNTY
CHICKASAW NATION

Cal Mankiller examined the cut ends of the rawhide thongs still hanging from the limb where he had left Faye Skeans. He spat on the ground. "Paugh."

He dropped to a knee and closely looked at what was left of the moccasin tracks after the rain under the spot where she hung. "Big man…walks like Indian…Nation Indians no longer wear moccasins…Meby Comanch er Apache." He stepped over and picked up the cut hobbles, looked at them and slung them up into a nearby pecan tree.

He spied some other tracks. "Dog." The furious renegade trailed the moccasin tracks into the surrounding woods where they disappeared in the thick layer of soft wet leaves.

He roared at the bare treetops and threw the three fox squirrels he had attached to his belt into the brush. The big Cherokee stomped in a circle twice and kicked what was left of the soaked small fire. Then he turned his wrath on his juniper leanto after seeing his only blanket was missing and tore it asunder.

The cold rain began anew. He roared again.

WELLMAN'S CLINIC
GAINESVILLE, TEXAS

Fiona, Bill and Bass entered Faye's room—she was awake, propped up against several pillows. There was a wooden tray across her lap with a small bowl of bone broth she was slowly sipping from. Her face was swollen and ranged in color from black to yellow. Faye's upper and lower lips were split and puffy.

She looked up as the trio stepped inside. "Oh, thank ya'll for comin'…Bass, you've come a long way."

"It was Bass that found you and brought you in here, Faye," said Fiona.

She brought her hands to her face. "But, how…"

Bass knelt down beside her bed and took her right hand in both of his, being careful of her bandaged wrists. "You're my friend, Faye. I knowed I could find you when nobody else could…That's what friends 're for." A tear rolled down his chocolate cheek.

Faye lifted her hand from his and brushed the tear away with the back of her fingers. "Of course. Thank you so much,

Bass…He was a vile, dreadful, dreadful excuse for a man. I've never wanted anyone dead in my life…But, now I do…He…he…"

"We know, Faye…we know," interrupted Fiona placing her hand on her shoulder. "…and he's going to pay…I promise."

Wellman entered. "All right, folks, time to go. She needs her rest. Come see her tomorrow."

They bid Faye their adieus and stepped next door to look in on Bodie.

He was still comatose as they entered. Annabel and Fran started to get to their feet, but Fiona held out her hand for them to stay seated.

"We're just looking in. We checked on Faye and are going over to the boarding house…Can we bring you anything?"

"That's so sweet, Fiona bless your heart…I would love a book. Faye has a wonderful library," said Annabel.

"I'd love one too. I'm sure the roads are too bad to go back out to the ranch, and Walt won't relieve us until six," added Fran. "So I expect we'll be stayin' at the boardin' house tonight, too."

"Anything in particular?" Fiona asked Annabel.

"I saw *The Scarlet Letter* by Nathaniel Hawthorne on one of the shelves. I've only read it once."

"Fran?"

Annabel looked at her friend. "How about *Northanger Abbey* by Jane Austen? It's there too. Have you read that?"

"Oh, goodness, no, I haven't."

"I'll bring those back over," said Bill.

"We're going to rest up a while until the rain stops." She looked up at the ceiling and listened to the rain steadily drumming like millions of fingers again on the standing-seam metal roof of the clinic. "Assuming it ever does...Bill is picking Doctor Ashalatubbi up at the depot in the morning in a buggy to bring him over here. Doctor Wellman wants him to take a look at Bodie," said Fiona.

"I just love him. He's amazing. If anybody can help my Bodie, it's *Anompoli Lawa*."

"*Anompoli Lawa*?" asked Francis.

"That's Doctor Winchester Ashalatubbi's tribal name...It means...He who talks to many. He's the Chickasaw shaman and also a trained medical doctor."

SKEANS BOARDING HOUSE

Later that evening, Fiona, Bill, Bass, Annabel and Francis sat around the big dining table enjoying the chicken and dumplings Fiona had made when she got back to the house.

"Mighty fine dumplins, Fiona, mighty fine."

"Would you like some more, Bass?"

"Yessum, I shorely would." He passed his plate down to Fiona and she ladled some more into the big man's plate."

"I need to take a plate to Walt at the clinic," said Fran.

"I'll run a basket over to him…You don't need to be getting out anymore today…considering your condition." Bill grinned.

"I'll fill a Mason jar with chicken and dumplins, wrap some fresh biscuits, and put in a big slice of apple pie, plus another jar of tea," said Fiona. "Are you going to be able to go with us after Mankiller, Bass?"

He shook his head and sopped up some juice with half a biscuit, popped it in his mouth and swallowed. "That new marshal at Paris done give me a stack of warrants to serve and Jack's got another month or so 'fore the cast comes off…I'd best be gittin' on back…but, warrants be damned, I had to come see 'bout Faye…I'll be a catchin' the east bound train of the mornin'."

"I guess Bill and I will be starting from scratch. Doubt there'll be any sign left leaving that camp where you found Faye."

"Meby, meby not…"

"How do you mean?" asked Fiona.

Bass wiped his mouth and mustache with his napkin. "Well, 'member I tol' ya'll I put on my knee-high Apache moccasins when I slipped up to his camp?

Fiona and Bill nodded.

"I 'spect that even after the rain, they's some tracks left since I didn't bother to be none to careful" He grinned. "…an' if'n I'm right, that's gonna confuse him a right smart."

"I don't understand," said Bill.

Bass grinned. "See, Injuns from the civilized tribes in the Nations don't wears moccasins no more...But the Apache, Comanche, Arapaho, Pawnee, Kiowas an' even the Delawares over in the Territory still do...I believes he's a gonna head west an' lick his wounds fer a spell...They's plenty places to hide in the Wichitas."

§§§

CHAPTER EIGHT

KATY DEPOT
GAINESVILLE, TEXAS

The big black 4x4x2 locomotive released pressure from her boilers on both sides, creating huge clouds of steam enveloping the platform—a plum of white smoke drifted up from her straight stack. People waiting to board and those waiting on disembarking travelers backed away. The heavy drizzle that fell between intermittent thundershowers quickly dissipated the hot vapors.

Marshal Roberts—holding a black umbrella over his head—searched the faces of the passengers stepping down from the cars for Doctor Ashalatubbi. Finally, he spied the white-haired practitioner looking around for a friendly face.

"Winchester!" he shouted and waved.

Ashalatubbi looked down the platform, saw Bill and nodded at him. He was carrying a carpet bag and his black leather physician's valise as he headed Bill's way.

"Good to see you, Doc, let me take one of those." He took the proffered carpet bag and shook the physician's hand. "You just missed seeing Bass. He boarded the east bound about thirty minutes ago…He came down and found Faye."

"You don't say? Look forward to hearing that story…Sorry to have missed him."

"Tell you on the way to the clinic…buggy's this way."

WELLMAN'S CLINIC
GAINESVILLE, TEXAS

"Go on inside, Doc, I have to take the horse and buggy back to Clark's Livery. Join ya'll in just a while," Bill said as he pulled the bay mare to a halt at the front. "You'll probably find Annabel, Walt Durbin's very pregnant wife, Francis Ann, and Fiona…Walt may have dropped by, even though it was his shift last night."

"Know Annabel well…Marshal Miller by reputation and wasn't able to make Walt and Francis Ann's wedding, so we've

152

never actually met," Winchester said as he grabbed his bags and stepped down.

"She's a case all right...Fits Walt perfectly. Reminds me a bit of Angie."

Doctor Ashalatubbi smiled, ducked his head against the heavy drizzle that was fast becoming a steady rain and hurried to the front door. He entered and removed his tall-crowned, uncreased black hat with the Chickasaw traditional Red Hawk tail feather stuck in the beaded band encircling the base of the crown.

He spied a wooden hall tree just inside the door, shook the water from his hat and hung it on a side hook, followed immediately by his long wool top coat.

"Winchester!"

He turned at the sound to see Doctor Wellman enter the waiting room from the hallway.

"Thought I heard the door close...Good to see you, my friend."

They shook hands and slapped each other's shoulders.

"Not to cut things short, Bill, but from your telegram, you've got a critically ill patient who's also a good friend of mine we need to take a look at."

He frowned. "We do indeed...and he's not gettin' any better."

"If you'll take my bags, I assume your kitchen is still in the same place…I need to wash up from the trip. Do you happen to have an extra clinic smock?"

"I do. Look in the tall cabinet after you wash, you'll find several starched and ironed ones. Should fit fine…Looks like you've put on a pound or so since I saw you last." He grinned and patted Winchester's tummy.

"Earned every inch, my friend…every inch."

Wellman chuckled as he picked up Ashalatubbi's bags. "Bodie's in the second room on the right when you come out of the kitchen."

Five minutes later, *Anompoli Lawa*—wearing one of Wellman's white starched smocks—opened the door to Bodie's room.

Annabel, Walt, Fiona and Francis were indeed there, along with Doctor Wellman. Winchester's bag sat on a small table next to the bed.

"Doctor Ashalatubbi, so good to see you. Bless your heart for comin' down from Ardmore," said Annabel as she gave the elder Chickasaw a hug.

"Good to see you too, Annabel…just wish it were under different circumstances."

He and Annabel glanced over at Bodie.

"Well, let's get to it, shall we?" He stepped over to his valise, opened it and took out a six inch long ivory-colored device with a small brass cup on one end.

"What's that, Winchester?" asked Wellman.

"It's a custom-made stethoscope made of elk antler. Had one of our tribal artisans hollow it out, carve this bulbous ear piece to fit my ear canal..." He pointed at the small round knob on the end opposite from the brass cup. "...and attach this brass listening cup on the other end. The density of the elk antler enhances the sound picked up by the cup and sends it to my ear...I find it far superior to those we can get from the medical supply houses."

"Interesting," commented Wellman.

Winchester stepped over to Bodie's bed and pulled back the covers. "Scissors, please." He held out his hand for Wellman's nurse, Martha, to place them in his palm.

He cut the cotton bandages along the side of Bodie's chest and peeled them back exposing the angry red wound in his sternum. Winchester turned to the nurse. "We'll want to clean this when I'm done. I brought a healing salve with me."

"Yes, Doctor."

He bent over and placed the brass cup on the upper left side of Bodie's chest, and then put his ear against the hollowed out knob. He moved down halfway and listened again. Then he moved to the bottom of his chest for a moment. He repeated the procedure on the right side, and then raised up and put the stethoscope in a pocket of his smock.

Ashalatubbi frowned and slowly nodded. "No question. Lungs are filling with fluid." He turned and saw Marshal

Roberts standing in the open doorway. "Bill, need you and Walt to raise him up. Martha, I want three pillows behind him…We have to get his upper body propped up at a forty or forty-five degree angle. It will slow down the collection of fluid in his lungs."

He reached into his bag and removed a black doeskin leather pouch tied with a narrow strip of latigo. After untying the bundle, he unrolled it on the top of the small table. There were ten small brown stoppered vials. Winchester removed one from the bottom row and pulled the cork.

Martha, Bill and Walt had Bodie propped up against the mass of pillows behind his back.

"Martha, I need a small funnel."

"Right away, sir." She hustled out the door and in less than a minute, came back with a tiny metal funnel.

"Thank you."

Wellman handed a small box toward *Anompoli Lawa*. He looked at it with a puzzled expression.

"The latest thing. Rubber gloves from Goodyear. They started making them last year," Wellman said as he opened the box.

"Ah, very good. I've read about them. Will help in keeping the corruption at a minimum." He slipped the formfitting off-white gloves over each hand. "Very good, indeed." He flexed his fingers, and then removed eight of the bottles from their holders and set them on the table top.

"What are those, Winchester?" asked Wellman.

"Special tribal oils and tinctures. Some have been used in the Muskeegian culture for many hundreds of years...This is oil of peppermint." He held up the others one at a time. "Skunk cabbage oil, creosote bush oil, pleurisy root tincture, wormwood oil, cypress oil and one I import from Australia...eucalyptus oil. This last one here is balsam fir needle oil...known for the last two thousand years or so as The Balm of Gilead...All will work together to enhance Bodie's breathing and help clear the collection of fluid in the bottom of his lungs...He needs more air if he is to heal."

"Amazing. I need a set of those oils," said Wellman.

"I make most of them myself, except for the eucalyptus oil. I will prepare a set and send it down...Or I can just leave this set with you, I have more back in my office."

He started to drip the various oils and tinctures into the first vial he had removed—it was an empty one. After carefully counting the drops from each bottle, Winchester, corked them and replaced each in their respective pockets. He replaced the cork in the newly filled vile and shook it vigorously. "Now I need a surgical mask."

Wellman removed one from a pocket of his smock and handed it to Winchester. The Chickasaw shaman leaned forward, placed it over Bodie's nose and mouth and tied it behind his head.

"Now watch, children." He took the newly concocted mixture and slowly dripped five drops in a small circle on the thick white cotton just under the comatose ranger's nose. "Do this every two hours," he said as he handed the vial to Wellman, and then gave him a small leather drawstring pouch. "When he wakes up, start him on this."

"What is it, Doctor," asked Annabel.

"Skunk cabbage and pleurisy root tea."

"Oh."

"It's doesn't have the most pleasant aroma, but it will give his immune system a boost."

"You said when…" said Annabel.

"I did. I surmise he'll awaken sometime this evening."

"How can you tell?" asked Fiona.

"You *pindah-lickyoee*, as the Apache call you, or white-eyes, refer to me as a shaman or medicine man…but I just wear this medicine pouch around my neck for show." He grinned and winked at her. "I could shake a dried gourd over him, chant some mumbo-jumbo and dance around, if you like?"

"Would it do any good?"

"No."

She looked at the small pouch hanging around his neck by a leather thong that was similar to the tea pouch except it was heavily beaded. "What all's in that, if you don't mind my asking?"

"Oh, some asafetida, hawk bones, polished cowrie shell, some dried mushrooms and a small tin of Garrett's Snuff."

"Oh, look, he's breathing better already," Annabel exclaimed as she stepped over to the bed and took Bodie's limp hand in hers.

"I know," replied Winchester. "It doesn't take long for aroma of those oils to open his bronchial tubes up."

He reached back in his valise and took out a round tin about the size of a Mason jar lid, popped the top and took a finger-full of the thick whitish salve. He smeared it around the wound in Bodie's chest, starting out as far as the bruising extended and worked his way to the angry red scabbed-over hole. "Bandage him back up when I'm done, Martha…Change his dressing no more than every three days and reapply." He gave her the tin.

"As you wish, Doctor," she replied.

"Let me guess," said Wellman. "It's that turpentine and hog tallow salve of yours…another tribal remedy?"

Ashalatubbi shook his head. "Got it from Jack's wife, Angie…It's an old Irish cure."

"How does it work?" asked Fran.

"Don't have a clue…and really don't care. All I know is it works miracles on wounds of all types…How's Faye?"

"Improving…It's just going to take some time. I'll probably let her go home day after tomorrow," said Wellman.

"And the children Bill told me about on the way from the depot?"

He smiled. "That's the thing about children, they're very resilient. A local lady, Sue Land, took them into her home…A much better environment than this clinic for them. Her younger sister is going to wet-nurse the baby along with her own."

"Very good…Well, I'm hungry. Any chance of getting something to eat?" He pulled off his rubber gloves.

SKEANS BOARDING HOUSE

Fiona served everyone sitting around the kitchen table smoked ham sandwiches and some potato salad she had whipped up.

"Outstanding lunch, Fiona, my dear, outstanding," commented Winchester.

"Thank you, Doctor. I was glad Faye had some hams hanging out in the smokehouse. That made it very easy…I'm sure Annabel and Fran will like some, too."

"I'll take a basket back over. I have to get back to the office anyway," said Walt. He turned to Fiona. "That story you and Bill told earlier about Bass finding Faye…You mentioned he said he put on his tall Apache moccasins…Where on earth did he get a pair of those? They're pretty unique for the Nations."

She grinned. "That's another story all together."

"Well?"

Fiona took a sip of her tea, dabbed her mouth with a napkin and leaned back in the chair. "When Bass and I were riding together, he told me about trailing a bank robber west to the

Oklahoma Territory and into the Wichita Mountains, which is part of the Apache reservation…There aren't near as many towns in the Territory as there are in the Nations and those that are there are scattered far and wide."

"That's true enough," added Winchester.

Fiona continued, "He said he met an Apache War Chief, *Shoz-Dijiji*, or Black Bear…Now, truthfully, he wasn't actually an Indian…He was a white man who had been captured by the Apache as an infant and raised by Geronimo. He preferred living with the tribe, even after he found out he was white…Anyway, Bass noticed his moccasins came all the way to his knees and asked about them."

"I have heard of the great war chief, *Shoz-Dijiji*," said Winchester. "He talked his adoptive father, Geronimo, into surrendering, knowing the Bedonkohe band of the Chiricahua Apache faced complete annihilation at the hands of General Nelson Miles troops if they continued to fight."

Fiona nodded. "They were transferred to a reservation near Fort Sill in '84 which included the Caddo, Comanche, and Grady counties…Bass and Black Bear ran across each other in the Wichita Mountains in Comanche County and he asked about the tall footwear.

Shoz-Dijiji showed him how they protected his legs from thorny brush and snake bite, and then taught Bass how to make them…Preferably from buffalo or elk hide because it's tougher than deer…They actually go all the way to mid-thigh, but are traditionally folded over to just below the knee and laced with thong…They're only two pieces of leather, the sole and the top."

"That's when you made your set?" asked Bill.

"No…Bass made them and gave them to me for a present." She grinned. "…Said I made too much noise walking through the woods in my boots. They're handy when you're tracking down bad guys…Like Epictetus said, 'One should not moor a ship with one anchor, or our life with one hope'."

"Gotta make me a pair…we're a bit short on elk in this part of the country, though. Maybe I can find some mule or horse hide at the local tannery."

"When are you going after the Cherokee?" asked Doctor Ashalatubbi.

"Looks like the weather is trying to clear from the west, so I'd say tomorrow." She looked at Bill. "That all right with you, partner?"

"I'm ready when you are. I'll ride down to the hide plant and see about some skin and make mine tonight…sans beading, though. Not too handy at that."

Winchester smiled. "It's a definite skill."

He held up his very ornate medicine pouch. "If you come through the Arbuckle area, I'll see about some of our ladies dressing them up for you…If you like."

LADY LAW

ANADARKO
OKLAHOMA TERRITORY

The Cherokee renegade walked the buckskin gelding he had stolen from a horse ranch just outside of Pike, back in the Chickasaw Nation, down the middle of the street. He had been unable to catch the horses Bass had cut loose and stole the buckskin after murdering the white ranch owner, his Chickasaw wife and replenishing his supplies before burning their house.

Anadarko was named for the Nadarko Indians, a branch of the Caddo. The US government had made a clerical error when they established a Post Office in 1873 and added an 'A' in front of the name—it stuck.

Unlike the Nations, there were saloons in number throughout the Territory. Mankiller pulled rein in front of the Sandbar Saloon. It was so named because back of the building was built on thick cypress stilts out over the south bank of the Washita River. The water way was known as the Oakdale River back to the west.

The owner, a Caddo named *Kiwat Lesh*—normally referred to as Big Dog by his patrons because of his size—had been known to take unruly or drunk customers and throw them out the back door into the shallow waters of the river to sober up.

The renegade pushed open the batwing doors at the front, allowed his eyes to adjust to the dim light, and sauntered toward the handmade hickory bar.

A huge man, well over six feet five inches with his long black hair pulled back in a single thick braid behind his head looked up from drying a beer mug. "What'll it be?"

"Beer."

"You look Seminole," he said as he filled the glass he had been drying.

"Paugh." He spat on the sawdust floor. "Cherokee."

"Never seen a Cherokee with long hair before."

His cold obsidian eyes glared at the big man. "Have now." He turned to observe the ten other customers in the room—two of whom were US cavalry troopers. One was a private and the other, a bit older, a corporal.

"Just what we need in this country, another damn redhide," mumbled the corporal.

Mankiller drew up to his full six foot three height as he stared at the man down the bar. "Little white man say somethin'?"

The stumpy five-eight soldier shrugged his shoulders. "Didn't say nothin'."

The big barkeep laid his hand on Mankiller's forearm and whispered, "Don't need no trouble with the Army in here, friend."

The renegade stared for a moment longer at the corporal, and then turned back to his beer. "Long knife needs watch what say. Mankiller no like."

"Mankiller? Heard of you...I'm Caddo. Named *Kiwat Lesh*. Most just call me Big Dog." He leaned closer. "On the run from the Nations, are you?"

"Big Dog ask many questions."

The two soldiers finished their beers, glanced briefly at the Cherokee, and then headed toward the front and out.

"Part of running a saloon...you know?" He grinned.

Mankiller didn't.

A local cowboy leaning against the bar on the other side of where the two soldiers had been standing, spoke up, "Them blue-bellies might be a tad shy on guts, but I ain't...Had enough of you stinkin' redskins hoggin' all the good land and the best water holes around here...Need to finish what the army started."

He turned to face the Cherokee and pulled his tan canvas jacket back from his Smith and Wesson Russian revolver he carried in a cross-draw.

"White man no want see sun tomorrow?" Mankiller said without turning to look at the cowboy.

He laughed. "I'm only interested in seein' another dead Injun...If'n yer packin', I suggest you slick it out...er die where you stand, heathen."

The renegade slowly turned and faced the other man.

The bartender laid his towel on the bar. "Now look, boys, let's not have any trouble."

"No trouble," said Mankiller.

"The hell you say." The cowboy reached for the butt of his pistol, but he never cleared leather as a ten inch Bowie imbedded itself almost to the cross guard in the center of his stomach with an audible *thunk*.

He looked down in amazement at the bone handle protruding two inches above his hand that still grasped the grip of his gun.

The cowboy mumbled, and then looked back up at Mankiller, "How in hell?"

His knees buckled, his eyes rolled back up in his head and he collapsed forward on his face like a sack of wet grain. Three inches of the razor sharp steel blade showed out of his back.

Mankiller rolled him over with his foot, jerked his knife free, wiped the blood on the cowboy's once blue boiled shirt and replaced it in the deerskin sheath stuck in his gunbelt on the right side.

"*Tor-v hv-tke* no see tomorrow."

"What's *tor-v hv-tke*?" asked *Lesh*.

"Cherokee for white eyes," replied Mankiller.

"The Apache word is *pindah-lickyoee*."

"Same, same."

Big Dog yelled at his swamper back in the kitchen. "Jessie, get out here. Got a mess to clean up. A tall, skinny colored man in an apron stuck his head out of the swinging door.

"Yassa, boss. I'sa comin'."

He shuffled out and around the bar, stopping when he saw the body on the floor. "Oh, lawdy, lawdy."

Jessie bent over, grabbed the cowboys heels and dragged him toward the back door, leaving a wide swath in the sawdust.

"You're not the only person around here on the dodge…See them two fellers over yonder at that table?" said *Lesh*.

"Me see."

"Been watchin' you since you come in."

"Mankiller know." He took a long swig of his beer.

"Renegade outcasts from the Prairie Band of the Potawatomi Nation in Kansas. Not wanted here in Oklahoma Territory or over in the Nations…yet."

"Why you tell this?"

He shrugged his shoulders. "Just thought you might like to meet some other…uh, fellers like yourself is all."

"They full bloods?"

"Far as I know."

Mankiller grabbed his beer and walked over to their table. "*Osiyo*, I am called Calvin Mankiller or *Inoli*, Black Fox in Cherokee."

"*Bozho nikan*, I am known as *Michicaba Pokagon* or Snapping Turtle. This Billy *Maumksuck*…Big Foot. We are Potawatomi." He held his hand to his chest, and then swept it toward the Cherokee, palm down. "You sit. We talk."

PICKENS COUNTY
CHICKASAW NATION

Fiona and Bill carefully walked around the perimeter of Mankiller's former camp where Bass found Faye. Smoky had jumped down from Spot's saddle and was nosing around the damp ashes of the former campfire looking for a suitable spot to leave his deposit.

"Well, six inches of rain can play havoc with sign," said Bill.

"Except that we know he was here and the grass still shows evidence of trampling by the horses on the west side. When Bass cut the hobbles, they would have gone in the opposite direction from him and the camp, which would be to the northwest…Now, I'm betting that because Mankiller stole them in the first place…"

"He wouldn't be able to catch them even if he did find them."

"Exactly," Fiona commented. "The nearest settlement where he could steal other horses and get supplies is Pike…I'd say some twelve miles to the northwest and across Walnut Bayou."

"We should be able to get there by late afternoon. The town marshal there is an old friend named Carson Waters. We worked for the Pinkerton Agency together a while back."

Near sundown, Bill and Fiona with Spot in tow, walked their tired horses down the single main street that ran through the small hamlet of Pike. There was one rooming house, a restaurant, general store, a combination town marshal's office and post office, and a livery, along with several other assorted small retail stores.

They eased up to the water trough between two hitching rails in front of a sign hanging over the boardwalk that read: Marshal/Post Office. They allowed the horses and mule to drink. Smoky jumped down from Spot's back, and then up to the two-inch wide edge of the wooden trough where he perched while he lapped up the cool water.

"Looks like everyone was thirsty," commented Bill as he dismounted and loosened Tippy's cinch.

Fiona followed suit. "I could use a cup of coffee myself."

The plank door of the marshal's office opened and a stocky middle-aged man with a dark brown Buffalo Bill type mustache and goatee, stepped out onto the boardwalk. "Well, as I live and breathe, Brushy Bill Roberts, or should I say, Deputy US Marshal Roberts...How are you, ol' son?"

The two old friends shook hands and pounded each other's back—trail dust flew from Bill's coat in a big cloud.

"Carson, want you to meet my partner, Marshal F.M. Miller. Goes by Fiona...and if you value your life, don't call her 'Ma'am'...Pard, this is the feller I told you about, Carson Waters...A good man to have watching your back."

She stuck out her hand. "Sheriff, it's indeed a pleasure."

He quickly doffed his hat and grabbed her proffered hand. "Yes, Ma'am…uh." He quickly glanced at Bill and then back to her. "Uh, Marshal Miller…Heard tell of you."

"Thank you…Fiona will do." She flashed her even white teeth at him.

He blushed and ducked his head.

"That restaurant serve anything worth eating, Carson?"

"Betty Mae will make you want to shoot yer grandma, Bill. Let's take your stock down to Hayden's, and then go grab a bite. What say? Kinda hungry my own self."

"Thought you'd never ask," said Fiona as she pulled Diablo away from the water.

They led the animals the block and a half down to Hayden's Livery.

Carson shouted down the wide aisleway of the big barn. "Haystack! You in there? Got some customers out here."

A long tall, skinny as a rail man in his late fifties, stepped out of one of the stalls holding a four-prong pitchfork.

"Don't have to shout, I ain't deaf…leastwise not yet." He spat a long stream of tobacco juice off to his right. "Whatcha got here, Carson? Some wayward vagabonds?"

He whipped off his battered dark gray fedora and revealed a thick mat of straw-colored hair that stuck out in all directions. "Howdo, Ma'am." He spotted her badge pinned to her burgundy vest. "Uh, Marshal." He glanced over at Bill and nodded. "Marshal." He turned to Waters. "Am I in trouble, Carson?"

"Only if you don't take care of their stock, you old coot." He grinned. "This is Marshal Miller and Marshal Roberts."

"A lady law, well, I never…"

"Now you have," commented Fiona. "We'll be spending the night in your fair city…I'm assuming you can take care of our stock?"

"That's what I'm here fer. Fifty cents a head, brushin' an' oats included."

"Give them an extra bait of grain, old timer, if you would," said Bill.

Haystack spat again. "Be an extry twenty-five cents…an' I ain't old…jest look it.

Fiona hid a smile. "Don't worry about the cat."

He looked over at the gray feline sitting in the middle of Spot's saddle, washing his face.

"Was wonderin' if he needed a stall of his own with a bowl of milk."

"No, he'll bed down with the mule. Might like the milk though," she said. "Is that extra?"

"Naw, I'll throw that in…like cats. Got a cow out back I gotta milk anyhoo…What's his name?"

"Smoky."

"Woulda never guessed."

Bill and Fiona undid their gear from Spot's saddle.

"We'll be back in the morning," said Roberts.

"I'm takin' 'em down to Betty Mae's fer somethin' to eat fer supper then over to Miss Ruby's fer a room."

"You'll enjoy both, Marshals."

They nodded, turned and headed back down the street toward the restaurant.

"Kinda glad ya'll showed up, Bill."

"How so?"

"It's normally a pretty quiet area around here."

"Normally?" asked Fiona.

Carson nodded and frowned. "Had three sets of killin's in the last four days in the area...Ain't normal, ain't normal atall."

§§§

CHAPTER NINE

BETTY MAE'S CAFE
PIKE, PICKENS COUNTY, IT

Betty Mae Kennedy brought out three plates heaped with big chunks of honey baked ham, cut corn, creamed new potatoes, boiled cabbage, a big pan of hot buttermilk biscuits and a bowl of redeye gravy. Her restaurant was almost full with evening customers.

"What did I tell you?" said Carson. "It's a wonder I don't weigh three hundred pounds."

"Oh, go on with ye blarney, Carson Waters." The attractive redheaded owner swatted him with the dishtowel she had draped over her shoulder. "I'll bring back the coffee pot. It's lookin' like ye be needin' a refill."

"I think that Irish lass has the eye for you, Carson," commented Bill as he opened a biscuit and spooned some redeye gravy on each half.

"Aw, Bill…" He blushed again.

"I think she's lovely. Reminds me of Angie."

"Angie?" asked Carson.

"Jack McGann's wife," said Fiona.

"Jack got married? I'll be danged and double rectified…Guess if'n he took the plunge, there's hope fer me yet."

"I think he chased her till she caught him." Fiona winked.

When they had finished their plates, Bill wiped his mouth with his napkin and took a sip of coffee. "Now what was this you mentioned on the way down here about some murders?"

"Well, it started last week right after the rain. Millard Histree and his mulatto wife were found murdered and scalped at their horse ranch. Their house was burned to the ground. Couldn't tell how many or even if any of their horses were stole, but a neighbor said he thought a buckskin geldin' was missin'." He paused while Betty Mae refilled their cups.

"Got a peach cobbler be out of me oven in just a wee bit."

"Sounds good, Betty Mae…Love your cobbler, uh, huh," said Waters.

"Ye are a bit partial to me pecan pie, too." She winked at him, turned and headed back to the kitchen with that sashay known only to women.

"My, my, that is choice," he said as he watched her walk away. He finally turned back to a grinning Bill and Fiona and took a breath. "Anyways, 'bout a day later, 'tween here an' Orr, Bob Butler and his Chickasaw wife were also butchered and scalped. Their eight year old daughter and ten year old boy had their throats cut an' were just layin' out in the yard…Burned their house and barns too…Killed their dog. He raped the little girl…" His voice broke a little. "A eight year old girl an' the animal raped her."

"My God," whispered Fiona.

"Almost the same thing happened to the Farquhars…Wealthy, his wife Fannie an' their three year old daughter…"

"Let me guess, they were half Chickasaw," interrupted Fiona.

He glanced over at her and nodded. "How did you know?"

"Because I know who's committing these heinous crimes…Calvin Mankiller…Cherokee renegade. He hates anyone not full-blood Indian. We've been on his trail for a while …Thought I killed him once, but somehow he survived…He's a mad dog."

"What direction was the Farquhar place?" asked Bill.

"Northwest of here, just past Orr."

Bill looked over at Fiona. "Straight shot toward the Wichita Mountains."

"If that's where he's goin' he'll have to swing north toward Anadarko so he can go around Fort Sill," commented Carson. "They frown on anybody crossin' through the military reservation."

WELLMAN'S CLINIC
GAINESVILLE, TEXAS

Annabel slowly rocked in the slat-backed rocker next to Bodie's bed. The kerosene lamp over her shoulder on his night stand cast an orange glow on the book she was reading. She was about a third of the way through *The Scarlet Letter* by Nathaniel Hawthorne.

Fran had stayed at the boarding house with a mild case of pregnancy nausea.

"Who would a feller have to kill to get a drink of water around here?" came the slightly muffled voice to her left.

She jumped, dropping the book to the floor and quickly glanced over at her husband. His deep blue-green eyes blinked above the white surgical mask.

"What's this mask for?" he mumbled.

"Bodie!" Annabel got to her feet and pulled the mask down from his face. "You're awake!" She kissed him all over his face.

"And thirsty."

She filled a glass three-quarters full with water from a white ceramic pitcher. Placing her left hand behind his head, she held the glass to his lips and allowed him to drink.

"Slowly, Honey, slowly. You don't want to choke."

He nodded, took a couple of more sips and leaned back against his pillows. "Never knew water could taste so good...My tongue is thick...Feels like a worn saddle pad that's grown hair."

He smacked his lips a couple of times and rubbed his tongue against the bottom of his front teeth.

The door burst open and Doctors Wellman and Ashalatubbi rushed in. They had been having a cup of coffee in the kitchen just across the hall and heard him talking.

"Guess you were right, Winchester," said Wellman.

The Chickasaw medicine man pulled his elk antler stethoscope from his pocket. Winchester held it against Bodie's chest over the bandages in several places and nodded. "Much better." He turned to Wellman. "We'll need to keep using the oils on the mask at least another day...maybe more."

"How long have I been out?"

"A little over three days, my darling," said Annabel.

"Damn, no wonder I'm hungry."

"You can have some bone broth and skunk cabbage tea," said Winchester.

"Broth? I need somethin' more than that...and what's that odor?" He sniffed at the surgical mask under his chin. "Smells kinda like pine and peppermint."

"Magic," replied Ashalatubbi.

"Huh?"

"Tell you later. Broth and tea is all you get for a couple of days...You lost a lot of blood."

"Feel like I been kicked in the chest by a mule." Bodie looked down at the white bandages.

"A .44 caliber mule," said Wellman.

He wrinkled his forehead and looked at the doctor for a moment "Oh, yeah. Mankiller...All I 'member is the flash..." His eyes went wide. "What happened to Faye? Is she all right? Last I saw, she was..."

"I'm right here," she said as she came through the door in a pale green chenille robe.

"Whoa, what happened?" Bodie asked as he looked at her bruised face.

"She can tell you later, right now you need to drink some more water, have your broth and rest," said Winchester.

"Rest? I've been restin' for three days, you said." He started to rise up from his pillows. "Ahhhh..." Bodie collapsed back. "Bad idea."

"Uh, huh." Wellman turned to his nurse who had entered the room. "Martha, Mister Hickman needs a bowl of your bone broth."

She grinned from ear to ear. "With pleasure...Be right back."

LADY LAW

WASHITA RIVER, OT

Snapping Turtle, Big Foot and Black Fox rode down the steep banks of an arroyo that led to a southern bend of the Washita. Their horses' tails dragged across the packed sand as they partially slid down to the flat bottom.

Five men got to their feet from around a dry wood, smokeless campfire built against the far wall of the steep-sided gulch.

"Uhhh, good camp. No see," said the Cherokee.

The three Indians dismounted at some willow trees near the camp and tied their horses.

Michicaba introduced Mankiller to the other five. There were two Apache—*Juh* and *Kuruk*; two Comanche—*Nacoma* and *Kadar*; and one Kiowa—White Horse—all full blood.

"*Inoli* sit. We have coffee." Juh gestured at a log they had dragged up.

Mankiller nodded, sat down, pulled out his makings built a roll-your-own. He bent over, grabbed a burning twig from the fire, lit his smoke, took a long drag and blew a cloud over his head. "Black Fox happy to join great warriors of the People."

He gave the cigarette to Mamksuck, who drew a puff and passed it on. After the quirley made the rounds, *Kuruk* handed what was left back to Mankiller who took a final drag and threw the butt into the campfire.

"We are brothers," said *Juh*. "We eat, then plan raid on white eyes."

179

NORTH PICKINS COUNTY

Fiona and Bill circled the northwest side of Wealthy and Fannie Farquhar's farm, carefully cutting for sign of the Cherokee.

They had been on the trail since daybreak, after having breakfast at Betty Mae's with Marshal Waters—the sun was now almost overhead.

"Hold it." Fiona held up her hand, handed Spot's lead rope to Bill, and dismounted to study a very clear set of tracks. "Single set leading northwest...Not in a hurry." She walked a twenty foot circle from one side of the road to the other. "Don't see any tracks coming in from this direction."

"Good thing there was no rain since that last deluge." Bill looked back over his shoulder at the burned-out remains of the farmhouse and barns. "What with all the tracks back there of neighbors and the law collecting the bodies and all, it was smart thinking to move out several hundred yards."

She nodded. "Bass always said, 'Cut for sign where you can see it'...Ah, bar shoe, left front, fairly new. My guess is because of a quarter crack in the hoof wall...What's the next town in this direction?"

Bill unfolded the map Carson had given them. "Duncan. About twenty-five miles or so...Chisholm Trail passed just to the east. A Scotsman, William Duncan, established a trading post about 1890 at the junction of the north-south Chisholm

Trail and the east-west military trail between Fort Arbuckle and Fort Sill."

"How big is the town now?"

"I think about a thousand people."

"Too big, he'll go around it. He doesn't like places where there'll be Lighthorse…I'm betting he'll stick fairly close to the old cattle trail and go east, then back north. That'll take him around Fort Sill, too."

Bill nodded, looked at the map once again, folded it and put it back in his coat pocket. "I'd say let's cut over, head to Rush Springs, cross the Chicago, Rock Island and Pacific Railway and then head on northwest…There's no settlements west of the railroad until you get to Anadarko."

Smoky launched himself from Spot's back and disappeared into the brush in a flash. In less than a minute, he reappeared with a prairie dog hanging limply from his mouth. He jumped back up in the saddle, laid his prize down and looked at Fiona as if to say, "I was hungry."

She looked at Bill. "I think he has a good idea. What do you say we find a spot to stop for a bit and have a bite of lunch."

"Thought you'd never bring it up."

They reined down toward Stinking Creek, found an open area with some grass for the horses near the full running creek and set up a small camp. Bill built a hat-sized fire and put on the coffee to boil while Fiona broke out some hot water pan cornbread hand-sized patties and jerky from their poke.

After letting the coffee come to boil twice, Bill announced it was ready and filled their cups with the stout trail brew.

"There you are Marshal," he said as he handed it to her in return for a warmed-over corn dodger she had placed on a flat rock next to the fire and a piece of peppered jerky.

Fiona tore off a piece of the tough, spicy dried meat, chewed for a moment, and then washed it down with a sip of the hot coffee. "You never talk much about your time in New Mexico…I kinda sense there's a story there."

Bill studied the surface of the dark coffee in his blue speckled graniteware cup for a moment, and then looked up. "I suppose you could say that…I did some things I'm not too proud of." He paused. "Guess you could say I was a different person back then…I worked for John Chisum and then for a man named John Henry Tunstall…He was like a father to me."

He took a sip of his coffee. "The Lincoln County Sheriff ordered him killed and I guess I kinda went off the deep end…Joined a group called the Regulators. We were deputized by Justice of the Peace, 'Squire' John Wilson…and went after Sheriff Brady and his deputies…killin' him and five of his men. It was called the Lincoln County War…Lasted five days." Bill stared into the fire for a moment.

"We, the Regulators, were declared outlaws and warrants were issued for our arrest…Well, I rode the owlhoot trail for about three years till in '81 I tired of runnin', faked my death, changed my name and left the state."

"That's when you went to Kansas?"

He shook his head. "Decided to go to Mexico." He laughed. "Lived with the Yaqui Indians for about two years…Then I drifted up to Kansas…Worked for Buffalo Bill in his Wild West show for a year or so ridin' bucking stock and doing some trick shooting…Then, because I had some experience…" Bill grinned and cleared his throat. "I, uh, got a job with the Anti-Horse Thief Association from '85 to '89."

"When did you go to work for Judge Parker?"

"In '90…He originally hired me to investigate the rash of train robberies…There were something on the order of one every three or four days. I determined that it wasn't organized to any extent…basically just random."

"Then the judge hooked you up with Bass last year?"

Bill nodded. "You know the rest."

"What was your real name?"

He smiled. "Well, I was born Henry McCarty in New York. My father died and my mother married a man named William Henry Harrison Antrim…so, I guess you could say I've had several names.

"Killed a man in Arizona…actually it was an accident. We were playin' cards in a saloon and he called me a pimp and I called him a son of a bitch and…well, it went downhill from there to fisticuffs…We struggled over my gun. It went off, shooting him in the stomach. He died the next day. As luck would have it, they arrested me anyway. But, I escaped from jail, stole a horse, fled to New Mexico and changed my name again."

"To?"

He ducked his head. "That one I'll have to keep under my hat, if you don't mind...May tell you one day, but just not right now. That fellow still has a warrant out for him."

"I understand." Fiona glanced at him out of the corner of her eye. *Not that I need you to tell me who you really are.* She pitched the remains of her coffee in the fire and got to her feet. "Guess we should hit the trail. How far is it to the railroad?"

"Well, with a by-guess and a by-golly, I'd say fifty or sixty miles...We should get to Velma by nightfall...Oh, by the way, as the legal hounds say, *quid pro quo,* when we stop for the night."

"*Quid pro quo?*"

"Your story...How you came to be a deputy marshal and all that."

"Ah...Fair enough."

CHICKASHA, IT

"Give all money...Now!" ordered *Juh* as he waved his pistol around the lobby of the Chickasha Merchants Bank, finally coming to rest on the first teller.

Mankiller, both Comanches, *Kadar* and *Nacoma*, and the Potawatamie, Billy *Maumsuck* covered the five customers and two tellers.

The Kiowa, *Tsen-tainte*, or White Horse, the other Apache, *Kuruk* and *Michicaba Pokagon* stood guard outside with the horses.

A portly, balding man with thick gray mutton-chop whiskers strode out of his office at the side of the teller's counter. "What's all this then?" he boomed.

Mankiller swung his ten gauge and fired the left barrel, point blank, at the bank president, almost cutting him in half.

A woman customer screamed and he used the right barrel on her, spraying blood all over two of the other customers and the side wall.

Juh and *Kadar* both glared at Black Fox, rushed up to the two barred teller windows and shoved white flour sacks across the counter.

"Fill," both said at the same time.

Nacoma and *Maumsuck* each shot the nearest customer while the Cherokee reloaded his shotgun and took out the last person standing. He was a stooped gray-haired old man with a cane.

The terrified bank employees emptied their drawers into the bags, threw them over the top of the partition to the two Indians on the other side, and then both dropped to the floor behind the counter for cover. Thick choking clouds of acrid, sour gunsmoke hung like a pall in the air of the lobby.

Juh turned to the others. "We go." He headed to the tall double doors at the front of the bank and burst outside, gun at the ready.

185

Chickasha's citizens on the boardwalks and in the street were running, seeking cover in stores, alleyways or diving behind water troughs.

The three mounted renegades holding the other horses fired at the ducking and dodging townsfolk and in the air while *Juh*, Mankiller, *Kadar, Nacoma* and *Maumsuck* swung into their saddles.

The gang turned their mounts and with war whoops and gunfire, spurred down the middle of the empty street toward the west side of town. They headed in the general direction of their hideout on the Washita River in Oklahoma Territory.

Juh turned in the saddle to the Cherokee riding beside him after they had slowed to a trot a couple of miles out of town. "*Inoli* fool to shoot fat banker. Tell all in town bank being robbed."

"He was white eyes...needed killin'."

The Apache grunted. "We scatter, hide tracks, meet back at arroyo tomorrow...Then go to Wichitas. Have better hideout there. No track Indian over rock."

VELMA, IT

The sun was at dark thirty when Bill and Fiona trotted into the small, one main street town leading Spot. They spied a wagonyard and livery at the corner of the second block.

"We can leave the boys there…Twelve hours in the saddle, my tired is hanging out."

Fiona nodded. "Mine too, and the animals are dragging their feet a little also." She looked over at the cat asleep in the middle of Spot's saddle and chuckled. "Even Smoky looks dead to the world."

The reined up in front of the big red barn. A middle-aged smallish man was sitting in a ladderback chair to the side of the big open double doors. He was whittling on a small wooden horse with his jackknife.

The man looked up at the two law officers. "Howdo."

"Howdy," replied Bill. "Need to put our guys up for the night."

"Well, that's gonna work out jest fine…That's why I'm in business. Bertram's Livery Emporium…Such as it is."

"Been a bit slow lately?" asked Fiona.

"Naw…jest ain't been real heavy, if you know what I mean." He held up the wooden horse. "Almost finished with this toy fer my daughter."

"That's really good…How old is she?" inquired Bill.

"Eight…Goin' on twenty." He laughed. "Think she loves horses mor'n me."

Fiona grinned. "I can relate to that. Was the same way growing up."

"Fine lookin' paloose you got there. Never seen a black one with a white blanket like 'im 'fore…er the colored mule neither,

187

fer that matter. Mind if I let her brush 'em down fer ya?...No charge. She loves to do it. Made her a special stool to stand on fer the big 'uns."

She shook her head. "No, can't do that."

Bertram's face fell.

"But I will pay her fifty cents each for grooming...If she does a good job." Fiona grinned.

The man jumped up. "Hot dang. I'll go in the office and fetch her. She's doin' her homework...stays up here at the livery after school. I'm a widower, don't you see? Don't like her bein' at the house by herself."

He laughed again. "She'd rather be up here with all the horses anyways...Yer stock will shine like new dollars." He spun on his heels and went inside through the big doors.

In a moment, he came back out with a with a freckled-faced girl with long blond pigtails wearing a red and green calico dress.

"Well, hello," said Fiona as she stepped down. "What's your name?"

She grinned big, looked at Bill, and then Fiona and replied, "My name's Becky Waller...Pleased ta meetcha." She curtsied.

"I'm Fiona and his name is Bill." She nodded at Roberts as he too was dismounting.

"Hello there, missy."

The little girl looked him directly in the eye. "It's Becky, not Missy."

Bill grinned, glanced over at Fiona. "My error…Becky. Fiona here is the same way about being called Ma'am."

"I am indeed…and I don't blame you. Becky is a beautiful name."

She curtsied again. "Thank you. It's short for Rebecca."

"Did you know that originally it was from the Bible and was spelled R-e-b-e-k-a-h…It means captivating," said Fiona.

She blushed, and then asked a question to change the subject, "What's your horse's name? He's really pretty."

"His name's Diablo, which means devil…But, he's a real sweetheart. I've had him since he was a foal…Actually helped birth him."

Becky reached up and rubbed the horse on his forehead just under his forelock and below the browband of his headstall. Diablo dropped his head and his eyes closed halfway in pleasure.

She looked over at Fiona. "I like him." Her eyes focused on the badge pinned to her vest. "My goodness, are you a law officer?"

"I'm a Deputy United States Marshal." She glanced over at Bill. "We both are."

"I never heard of a lady marshal before…Can I touch your badge?"

Fiona leaned over and Becky rubbed the shiny crescent and star with the words 'Deputy Marshal' across the top and US in the center of the star.

"It's made from a Liberty silver dollar," commented Bill. "Both of ours are."

"Are ya'll married?"

They both chuckled and simultaneously answered, "No!…We're just partners."

Becky turned to her grinning father. "That's what I want to be when I grow up…a United States Marshal."

Fiona handed her Diablo's reins. "Well, this is America, Becky. I'm sure you can be anything you set your mind to…If you work hard."

"I don't mind workin' hard…Startin' with givin' Diablo and the others a good brushing…I would have done it for free." She turned to Bill. "What's your horse's name? I like him, too."

"Tippy. Had him a long time…He's my best friend."

"And the mule?"

"His name is Spot," said Bill.

Becky giggled. "That fits…Oh! Oh! That's a kitty! Can I pet him?"

Fiona smiled. "I imagine he would like that. He loves attention…Name's Smoky."

The little girl reached way up and gathered the cat from Spot's saddle and held it to her chest. "I like kitties almost as much as horses."

Smoky reached up and stroked her cheek softly with his paw, and then butted her chin.

"Well, he likes you. Doesn't take to just anybody…You must be special."

Becky blushed once again.

"They say cats is good luck fer horse barns," commented Bertram.

"Are you superstitious?" asked Bill.

"Naw…It's bad luck to be superstitious."

Fiona ducked her head, grinned, and then said, "Becky, if you and your dad will take care of our critters. We're going down the street and have some supper."

"That's Aunt Nell's place…Well, she's not really′my aunt. But, everybody calls her that…Her special today is meat loaf and gravy with smashed potatoes…It's yummy, oh, and be sure to have her buttermilk pie…Tell her I said so."

Fiona grinned. "I'll do that…I don't suppose you know if the boarding house across the street has a bath?"

"Oh, that Aunt Nell's too, and yes, she has a Chinese lady that takes care of the bathhouse in the back…There are really two, one for men and one for ladies…Ming Lu won't let men and women bathe in the same room. I read they do that in China…Or maybe it was Japan. One or the other."

Bill and Fiona both grinned.

"That's a good thing," Roberts said under his breath.

They untied their bags from Spot's saddle, pulled their Winchesters and headed off in the general direction of Aunt Nell's.

"I am so looking forward to a hot bath…I don't care who's in the room," commented Fiona.

"I'm looking forward to something besides the cold, hard ground to sleep on."

"That, too."

AUNT NELL'S CAFE

Fiona pushed back a little from the table and took a sip of her after dinner coffee. "Well, I must say little Becky was right. That buttermilk pie was almost decadent."

Bill grinned and shook his head. "It was…It was indeed." He wiped his mouth with his napkin. "Now, my dear…It's your turn."

"My turn? I got the last check."

"No, no…Nice try. Your story."

"Oh…That."

She paused and looked out the big front window. "Well, I was raised at a little hamlet just outside of Tahlequah called Moodys…all three buildings of it. When I was eighteen, I met a man named Frank Miller. He was five years older than me and was a deacon in our church…His grandmother came over *Nunna daul Tsuny*…"

Bill interrupted, "The Trail of Tears."

She nodded. "He was half Cherokee…Anyway we had been married for a little over four years and had saved up enough money to open a general store…Miller's Merchantile."

"In Tahlequah?"

Fiona nodded. "After a slow start, the store was really doing well…Our motto was, 'If we don't have it…you don't need it.' It was coming up on Thanksgiving and business was booming when this big, long-haired Cherokee came in the store." She paused again and looked at her hands twisting her napkin.

"I'm sure you know that the large majority of the Indians in the Nations cut their hair short and wear white man's clothing. That's one reason the five nations, Creek, Seminole, Chickasaw, Chocktaw and the Cherokee are called the 'Civilized Tribes'."

"Trying to fit into the white man's world."

"Something like that…Those few men who wear their hair long are known as renegades…and resist the white ways…Definitely atavistic.

"You see, this one was on the scout…ugly as sin, long dirty hair and with a white scar from his left ear to his chin…looked like a knife or saber cut. He came in and robbed us of all our cash…over two hundred dollars."

Fiona took a deep breath and softly sighed. "As he was leaving, he stopped at the door, turned…and shot Frank in the heart…right in front of me…" She choked back a sob. "…and said, 'Hate half-breeds.' He spat on the floor, went out, mounted his claybank horse and rode out of town like nothing had ever happened."

"When did you find out who he was?"

"I was over at the sheriff's office looking through his wanted dodgers and saw his face. There was no question…he was a full-blood Cherokee wanted for murder, larceny, rape and arson…His name was Cal Mankiller…An appropriate name, don't you agree?"

"I'd say so," commented Bill.

"The sheriff said the Cherokee Lighthorse had been after him for over five years. He commits a crime and disappears…Nobody can find him."

"And that's when you decided to become a peace officer."

She nodded. "I sold the store…after I had picked out some guns I liked…a matched set of .38-40 Peacemakers with ivory-grips…" She patted the both of them she carried in cross-draw. "…and an '86 Winchester chambered in .45-70 for long-range shooting. I went back out to our farm and practiced for over a year until I felt I was good enough…"

"Wow, no question about that. I've never seen anyone as fast as you…and I guess I'll finally have to include me."

"It seemed to come naturally…with either hand…I caught the train to Fort Smith and finally convinced Judge Parker to give me a commission…Never told him why. I knew he didn't sanction revenge hunts…Anyway, he assigned me to Marshal Cantrel at McAlister.

"I served felony warrants…murder, arson, whiskey peddling, larceny, you name it, all over the Choctaw Nation…Then a little over a year later, the Judge assigned me to Bass when Jack broke his leg…And now you know the rest of the story."

§§§

CHAPTER TEN

VELMA, IT

Bill reached around the paper for his white ceramic coffee cup, blew across the top, took a sip and set it back on the table. He had purchased a four-page weekly Saturday newspaper before they came into Aunt Nell's for breakfast. He folded it in half and perused the two-inch column headlines on the front page.

Fiona finished her pancakes and sausage, pushed the plate away and motioned to Aunt Nell for a refresher on her coffee by holding her cup up and grinning. She turned to Bill.

"Anything interesting?"

He folded the paper once again to a quarter of its original size. "Oh, not much. Lot of local stuff, obituaries, marriages and…Uh, oh, what's this?"

"See something?"

"Could say that."

"Well?"

"Bank robbery up at Chickasha, IT." He looked across the table at her over the top of the paper. "It's on the Chicago, Rock Island and Pacific Railway line, a couple of miles south of the Washita."

"And?"

"Hang on. Just give me a moment…" He continued to read. "Wow!"

"I'm going to hit you."

"All right, all right…It seems that eight Indians, tribes unknown, robbed the local bank. They killed the bank president and four customers in cold blood. The two tellers escaped injury by ducking down and hiding behind their counter after they filled the bags for the outlaws.

"They thought at least four of the robbers were either Apache or Comanche, maybe even Kiowa, because of the knee-high moccasins they wore…They said the five inside also wore several different types of cloth headbands.

"Other witnesses on the street saw three others minding the horses outside the bank and they too wore headbands…All eight had long hair." He glanced up and cocked an eyebrow.

197

"Do you think?" asked Fiona.

"Like Bass always said, 'Never put much stock in coincidences'."

She nodded. "He does say that and I have to agree…Same direction…I'm for riding over to Duncan…it's only about ten miles, right?"

"It is."

"Let's catch the train up to Chickasha. It'll be a lot faster and not near as tough on the stock than trailing them up there."

"Agreed…It's better than sixty miles overland."

They tightened the girths on the horses outside the front of Bertram's Livery Emporium.

"You really did a fine job on the boys, Becky. I've never seen them look so good…I'll bet they enjoyed it too." Fiona handed her two Morgan silver dollars.

"Oh! This is too much Marshal," she said as she shifted Smoky to her shoulder and looked at the coins.

"Nonsense. You even cleaned and oiled our tack…I'd say you earned it."

Becky shyly ducked her head. "It needed it."

Her father grinned, took out a plug of Brown's Mule and cut a chaw with his pocket knife. "That's the way she is. Don't have to tell her anythin'. Her mama, God rest her soul, always tol' her to 'make work'."

Bill wrinkled his forehead. "Make work?"

"Yeah, if'n you run out of somethin' to do, then find somethin' else…you know?…Make work."

He chuckled. "Well, I'll have to remember that one."

Becky lifted Smoky up and tried to hand her to Fiona, but he struggled to get back to her shoulder.

"Well, looks like he likes it here." She leaned over and looked in his green eyes. "Traitor."

He reached out and brushed the tip of her nose with his paw.

"Well, I guess that means you still love me…But you are better off here with Becky than on the trail with us."

"I'll take good care of him. He already likes sleeping at the foot of my bed next to my feet…Maybe you can come back for a visit?"

Fiona bent over and hugged the little girl, and then scratched Smoky under his chin. "Count on it, sweetheart." She turned, stuck her toe in the stirrup and swung easily into the saddle.

Becky and her dad waved at them as they rode out of town, heading west.

**RAILROAD DEPOT
DUNCAN, IT**

Fiona and Bill stepped down the four iron steps from the passenger car to the red brick platform between the depot and the tracks and glanced around.

"You know, I think that was the first train ride we've taken that somebody didn't try to rob it," commented Bill.

"You want to get back on and keep going?"

"No, no, I'm good. Just making an observation."

"Well, as you once said, some knucklehead tries to rob one out of four trains in the Nations…The odds were on our side."

"Guess so."

They headed down the train toward the livestock car to get their horses and Spot.

"What's first?" asked Bill.

"Need to talk to some actual witnesses…and the local sheriff, Lighthorse or town marshal."

"We do."

An hour later, they sat in the sheriff's office talking with the two surviving tellers from the robbery.

"What can you tell us about the Indians who were inside the bank, gentlemen?" asked Bill.

The youngest of the men, Jared Smith, looked at the other teller, Marston Bell, and then back to Roberts. "It was hard to tell, I mean I…" He looked at his coworker again. "…we were scared for our lives, Marshal, and were just trying to do what we were told…"

"Four of them wore those knee-high moccasins, you know, like Apaches wear," said Bell.

"What about the fifth?" inquired Fiona.

Marston continued, "That's the thing, now he had a red cloth headband like the others, but he was wearing brogans...pretty worn ones, at that."

Bill and Fiona exchanged glances.

"Was there anything else particularly noticeable about him?" asked Bill.

Jared looked at Marston again. "Well, he was big."

"Yeah, real big...an' some kind of ugly," added Bell.

Jared nodded. "Make the south end of a northbound mule look good...beg pardon, Ma'am."

"Let's lose the 'Ma'am', shall we?...Marshal Miller will do."

"Can you be more specific?" Roberts pushed.

"Oh...Well, say, he had a big scar from his..." Marston paused to think. "...his left ear all the way down to his chin...Nasty lookin' one, too."

Fiona turned to the resident Chickasaw Lighthorse, *Issoba Chola*. "Yellow Horse, which direction did they go when they rode out of town?"

"Me and Sheriff Tucker track eight renegades to sunset. They run horses, slow to walk after two miles, then stop an' palaver...Go to three winds." He motioned with his hands.

"Different directions...Did you see a bar shoe in the tracks?" she asked.

"Unnn, me see. That one go into Oklahoma Territory, toward Wichita." He swept his hand to the north.

"Split up to throw any posse off their trail. They'll come back together further out," said Bill.

"Agreed. I say we follow Mankiller's buckskin…"

"Mankiller?" asked Sheriff Tucker, sitting up in his chair behind his desk. "Got a federal dodger from Fort Smith on a Cal Mankiller…Two thousand dollar re-ward…One mean son of a gun…'cordin' to the warrant."

"That's him. Been on his trail for some time. Went on a real killing spree down in northern Pickens County…Men, women, children…Six adults, a boy and two young girls…Butchered and scalped," offered Fiona.

"God…Hope you get him," said Tucker.

"We will…His string is running out." Fiona set her jaw.

"He shot down the bank president in cold blood…No reason…no reason atall," added the sheriff.

"He had a reason," said Bill.

"What?"

"The banker was a white man."

CADDO COUNTY, OT

Bill and Fiona waded their horses across the belly-deep Wichita. The river was a little over one hundred yards wide at this point.

"When we get to the other side, we'll split. You go east, I'll go west till we pick up his trail again," she said.

"He hasn't made much effort in hiding his tracks so far...Even I can follow them and I'm not nearly a good as you."

"Sometimes I've known him to get a little overconfident or just plain careless...Don't think he's real familiar with this part of the country."

"Probably why he hooked up with those other renegades who are," commented Bill.

"This part of the Territory is pretty loamy and rolling. It would be next to impossible to hide his tracks anyway."

They waded out of the shallows and up the sandy bank on the north side a little to the west of a thick grove of willows.

Fiona turned Diablo to her left. "I'll take this direction, you go around that copse of willows...Never mind." She leaned to her right and studied the ground. "Got him...Heading north."

"It's a good thing there hasn't been any rain since before the holdup."

"It is." She nudged her Appaloosa into a smooth single-foot. "I'll follow these three-day old tracks...You've got your spyglass, don't you?"

"Of course."

"I suspect it would be a good idea for you to scan ahead and to the sides for possible ambush sites."

"Good idea. Not many good places in this country except for the occasional creek bottom."

She pointed at the crest of a hill a couple of hundred yards away. "He could lay down in the prairie grass at the top of that rise…Be pretty hard to see."

"Right again, Marshal, right again." Bill reached back into his saddle bags and pulled out the leather-bound tube, extended it fully, and started slowly sweeping the horizon to both sides and ahead.

"Actually, considering his sign is three days old, I doubt he would still be watching his back trail…but, it's the wise person that is prudent ten times rather than to be killed once."

"I'm not familiar with that quote…who said it?"

She grinned. "I did."

A little over a mile along the trail, the tracks curved back to the west.

"Well, well, I'd say you were right, Marshal Roberts."

"About what?"

"I do believe he's heading back to a rendezvous…most likely back across the river."

A peal of thunder rolled across the prairie.

They both glanced up at the dark bank laying off to the southwest.

"Uh, oh…Think we're about to get wet," said Fiona.

"Not to say anything about washing out the tracks."

"Don't think it's going to matter much."

"How so?"

"As usual, Bass is right…They're meeting back up and heading for the Wichita Mountains…How far are they?"

Bill pulled out his map again. "Uh, twenty miles…as the crow flies…southwest of Anadarko."

"How far is Anadarko?"

He glanced down. "Umm…'Bout three or four miles. On the other side of Sugar Creek…that tree-lined bottom right up there." He pointed ahead of them less than a hundred yards.

"Well, if we pick up the pace, we just might make town ahead of that storm."

"If we're lucky," Bill added as he sniffed the air. "Definitely rain coming."

"Hear that?"

"What?"

They both listened and heard the loud throaty chuck-chuck-chuck sound of a bird coming from the trees ahead.

"What kind of bird is that?" asked Bill.

"We call it a rain crow. It's a raven-sized brown bird you only hear when it's going to rain."

"Huh…Didn't have those in New Mexico or Arizona."

"'Course not. You don't get enough rain…The poor creatures wouldn't have anything to do."

"Point taken, Marshal."

They squeezed their mounts into a mile-eating road trot.

ANADARKO, OT

Fiona and Bill dismounted in front of Redskin Livery as a bespeckled elderly man in tattered bib overalls and an even more tattered once-gray fedora got up from a calf-hide bottomed chair leaning against the wall.

Rain was beginning to fall in dime-sized drops, creating small craters in the dust of the street.

The proprietor had a wad of tobacco larger than a baseball in the right side of his mouth. He spat what looked like a quart of brown juice in the dirt to the side. "What kin I do you fer?"

"You the owner?" asked Bill.

"Am today…was yesterd'y, reckon I will be t'mora…Lord willin'. Need to stable yer stock?"

"Could say that."

"Could er do?"

Bill grinned. "Do." He looked up again, got a raindrop in his eye, blinked and rubbed it with the back of his hand. "If we don't get drowned first."

"What 'er you doin' standin' 'round out here fer, then?"

The rain was coming down heavier.

"Good idea," said Fiona as she led Diablo and Spot inside the big barn ahead of Bill and Tippy.

"You got a name?" asked Bill.

"Yep, had one since I was little…My daddy always called me, 'While yer up', but my momma said I had a Bible name…Aminadab. The back name is Muffleshaw. Now ain't

206

that a moniker?…Aminadab Muffleshaw, haw." He spat to the side again. "Nobody liked it but her, so everbody else jest called me Dab…You know, Dab of this er Dab of that?" He spat once again and chuckled…It stuck."

"I can believe it," said Bill.

"Jest git yer traps, ol' Dab'll take care of the rest. They's a hotel 'cross the street from the Sandbar Saloon right down yonder." He pointed to the west.

"Sandbar?" asked Fiona. "That's an odd name."

"Well, not so's you'd notice…The owner, a Caddo named *Kiwat Lesh*…everbody calls him Big Dog…man could go bar huntin' with a willow switch."

He spat another long stream of the viscous fluid. "Built the back side stickin' out over the river, he did…Easy way to handle the drunks, ya see. Good place to put his indoor privy, too."

"Interesting."

"Some say so."

Fiona whispered to Bill as they pulled out their slicker and poncho and threw them over their heads, "Remind me not to fill our canteens down river from here."

He grimaced. "Uh, oh."

She glanced at him as they took out at a brisk walk the three blocks down to the Sandbar.

They ducked inside the batwing doors, shook the water from their rain gear and hung it on some handy hooks crafted from old horseshoes nailed against the wall.

The room was dim, lit only by six kerosene lanterns mounted on a wagon wheel seven feet overhead. A slight haze of tobacco smoke hung in the air.

"Come in, 'fore you git wet," said Big Dog from behind the thirty-foot polished hickory bar, decorated with mule deer antlers on each corner.

Bill smiled. "Too late."

"Come in anyways…What'll you have?"

"Coffee for me," said Fiona.

"Good hot coffee sounds great to me, too…I'm a bit chilled," added Roberts.

"Don't know how good it is, but, it is hot."

They set their carpet bags on the floor, leaned their Winchesters against the bar and quickly glanced around the room. There were three cowboys at the other end of the bar, four men playing poker at a table and two Indians at another table against the back wall, drinking beer.

Bill leaned over and whispered in Fiona's ear. "Follow my lead. I'm going to see if I can get a reaction from some of these folks."

She nodded.

Big Dog set two steaming mugs of black coffee in front of them. "Anythin' else?" he asked as he scooped up the dime Bill had placed on the bar.

"Some information?"

"Depends," the bartender said as he glanced at their badges.

"You had a big Cherokee with a scar on his face come in here in the last week or so?"

"Might have," *Lesh* said as he wiped a nonexistent stain from the bar. "What's he done?"

"He kills men, women and babies and we got paper on him...Name's Cal Mankiller," he raised his voice slightly.

The two Potawatomi at the back table got to their feet.

"I'd sit back down, boys," ordered Fiona as she turned their way.

Maumksuck drew his Colt from his belt. He never got a shot off as there was an earsplitting roar in the room and a hole appeared in the center his forehead, just below his red headband. A thin rivulet of blood oozed out and trickled down the side of his nose before his knees buckled and he fell backward to the floor.

Smoke curled from the barrel of one of Fiona's Peacemakers.

Michicaba Pokagon, nearest the exit, ducked her second shot, sprinted down the hallway, burst through the back screen door and dove headfirst into the river.

Fiona and Bill followed to the rear balcony and tried to peer through the driving rain to the water ten feet below.

"No good…Can't see anything," he said before they turned and went back into the saloon.

"Guess that answers that," Fiona commented as she brushed the water from her jacket.

"Who were they?" Bill asked Big Dog.

"Couple of renegade Potawatomi. Called themselves Big Foot and Snapping Turtle. That's Big Foot on the floor over there."

"Potawatomi? I had figured them to be Apache or Comanch," offered Fiona. "With the knee moccasins, long hair and headbands."

Lesh shook his head. "Kiowa, Apache, Comanch, Potawatomi, even some Caddo dress thataway round here…Especially the renegade types. Call it their silent protest to the *magaanii* presence."

"But not you?" asked Bill.

The big man shook his head again, swinging his single braid from side to side. "I'm a business man, Marshal. Been to the white man's school back east, called Yale College…We Caddo all have long hair…it's a spiritual thing. I try to git along with everybody, if you know what I mean…Feller tends to live longer thataway."

"He does."

"It was obvious those two knew Mankiller," Fiona commented.

"Yep, introduced 'em myself when he came in last week...Didn't know at the time he was such a malefactor."

"You wouldn't believe...He and seven other renegades killed five people, including one woman and one old man in cold blood over in Chickasha three days ago. They split up...Tracked him across the Washita, and then back this direction. Figured they were going to get back together south of here...maybe in the Wichitas," Fiona replied.

"That's some snaky, treacherous country. Caves, canyons, big rock territory...If that's where they are, be tough to find," said *Lesh*. "Lots of folks go in there an' are never seen again...Even soldiers and law."

WICHITA MOUNTAINS, OT

"I have got to get me a set of those made," said Bill as he appraised Fiona's light tan buckskins.

There were Cherokee beaded spiritual images and patterns over the top of her shoulders and part of the way down the front. Four-inch fringe hung from the back of her sleeves. The bottom of the butter-soft doeskin shirt, left naturally uneven, came a little below her rear and over the top of her pants The top had four cut-deer antler buttons holding it together in the front.

Her cross-draw gunbelt and holsters hung around her shapely hips over the top of the shirt. An eight-inch bone-handled Bowie in a custom beaded sheath was slipped under the belt in the middle of her back.

Her newly acquired knee-high moccasins from Bass finished her trail outfit.

"Learned from Marshal Reeves that buckskins are much better than my split skirt and morning coat, when the need for some wood lore and foot travel is necessary…"

"I can certainly see that," Bill said as he looked at the towering gray granite tor-thrust outcroppings and rugged canyons ahead—made even more spectacular by the rolling plains surrounding them.

"My late husband's grandmother made these for me to go with my moccasins the last time I visited home."

The rounded top of Mount Scott—the second highest peak in the range lay to the east—with the balance of the Wichitas extending further west some fifty miles.

"You realize we have two chances of finding those renegades in there, don't you?" asked Bill.

"I know…slim and none…But, like Bass says, 'gotta think like the miscreants do'."

"All right, Outlaw Queen…Where first?"

Fiona pinched her face in thought. "Let's follow Medicine Creek northwest along the foothills and cut for sign heading into the North Mountain wilderness area."

"Whatever you say, Belle."

Fiona cut her eyes sharply at him. "You're pushing it, Marshal Roberts." She turned Diablo to her right and eased him into an easy trot as she studied the ground. "Same routine, I cut, you scan the hills with your spyglass."

He grinned as he pulled out the three-draw tube from his saddlebags. "As you wish."

They worked their way along the creek near the north side bank, knowing any tracks would be easier to spot in the softer ground. After covering three fruitless miles and approaching Saddle Mountain, Fiona pulled rein.

"Hah!" A huge grin spread across her face. "Same tracks we found when we first left Anadarko this morning…My guess is that it's Snapping Turtle, the other Potawatomi that dove in the river yesterday afternoon."

"Well, don't look so gruntled…All we know is that one of them is headed into the mountains."

"Better than none, don't you agree?"

He nodded. "I do." Bill glanced at the sun setting behind the mountains. "We should make camp down in the creek bottom. Goin' to be dark fair soon."

"Agreed. Need to find a vertical bank on the opposite side to hide a small fire. No reason to advertise our presence…just yet."

"True words, Marshal." He looked up and down the creek. "See that big juniper down there about thirty yards? Should be a

213

place underneath it to build our campfire. There's enough green in the boughs to disperse what little smoke dry wood will create."

Fiona nodded, eased Diablo down the sloping bank, into the dark knee-deep water and let him drink his fill. Bill followed suit with Tippy and Spot. When they had finished, they waded across to the other side, up the bank and down toward the tree.

"If you'll pull our gear and picket the boys, think I see enough deadfall and dry drift wood to get our fire going," she said.

"Looks like there's enough flat ground between that cedar and the creek for a camp site...Say! I'll break out a hook and line, cut a willow branch and see if I can catch us some fresh supper."

"What are you going to use for bait?"

"Cut some thin strips of bacon rind."

"That should work." She dismounted, untied the poke sack from Spot's saddle and headed over toward the tree. "Have the coffee on in a short...I'll go ahead and fry up some salt pork to cook the fish and some cornbread in...assuming you catch a mess, that is."

"Never fear, they'll look up, see it's me and fight one another to grab hold of my hook."

"Now you sound like Bass."

"Where do you think I got it?" He grinned, unsaddled the horses and mule, led them up the bank to some green winter cheat grass and yellow-flowering lespedeza in a small open area behind the cedar and hobbled them for the night.

"There you go fellers, should be plenty of graze for you."

Bill worked his way back upstream to a copse of willow, cut a branch thick enough for a fishing pole, stripped the small twigs from it and attached the woven-linen line and hook.

He found a dry piece of cottonwood, broke a two-inch piece off and tied it to the line three feet above the hook for a bobber.

Fiona walked over to him and handed him four strips of bacon rind. "Saved you some trouble, Marshal."

"Well, thank you, m'lady…Supper coming up."

"Let's hope so…I'll bring you a cup of coffee as soon as it boils again."

"Oh, that sounds good," he said as he walked downstream about thirty feet, baited his hook and swung it out in the middle of the creek.

The hook and bobber had no more than hit the water when the piece of cottonwood disappeared under the surface. Bill allowed the fish to run a couple of feet, and then he set the hook.

The willow branch bent almost double, the water churned and the fish slapped the water several times with his tail. Bill was finally able to pull his catch out and over to the bank behind him.

"Blue cat! Gotta be at least two pounds," he yelled.

"This is a start," Fiona said with a smile as she held the flopping fish down with her foot and eased the hook from its mouth. "I'll clean this one. A couple more and we'll have a nice mess." She picked it up by the gills and headed back over toward the fire.

Bill checked his bait, added another piece of rind and threw it back out where it landed with a plop. "Told ya."

Fifteen minutes later he walked toward the campfire and held up a forked short piece of willow with four more catfish strung through the gills hanging from it. "This enough?"

Fiona looked up from filleting the large first cat on a flat slab of limestone. She sprinkled the last piece with some cornmeal mixed with scraped pink salt and ground pepper and laid it with several other fillets in the skillet of hot bacon grease.

"All right, give me two, I'll clean and prepare them, you clean the other two. We have enough for breakfast, too…Nice work, Marshal."

He pulled two from the wooden stringer, handed them over and walked down toward the water to clean his. "I know," he said over his shoulder.

She hit him in the back with a fish head…

§§§

CHAPTER ELEVEN

SKEANS BOARDING HOUSE
GAINESVILLE, TEXAS

Bodie slowly rocked in the slat-backed rocking chair on the wide verandah of the big Victorian house. There was a small patchwork quilt throw across his lap covering his legs. His face was still a little drawn, but his color was getting better everyday.

The white-framed gingerbread screen door opened and slammed shut as Annabel stepped out with a cup of tea.

"Well, you look right pert," he said as he looked up.

"Thank you…Enjoying the fresh air, my dear?"

"Yes, I am…I truly am."

"Good. Here's your tea."

He frowned as he took the cup and saucer from her hand. "Be glad when I don't have to drink this skunk cabbage and pleurisy root tea anymore. Gets harder to take every time."

"You can stop when Doctor Wellman says your lungs are completely clear...You almost died, you know."

He nodded. "I know."

"The only reason he and Doctor Ashalatubbi gave their permission for you to leave the hospital was that we promised that you would behave and take your medicine."

"The only good part is those oils you keep dripping on my neckerchief...I like 'em, smell good." He took a sip of the tea and wrinkled his nose. "Any word from Fiona and Bill?"

She reached in a slash pocket on the side of her dark green skirt and handed him a yellow flimsy. "Walt got a telegram this morning."

He took the thin missive and read through it. "Huh...Think Mankiller hooked up with some other renegades...They're headin' down into the Wichitas." He handed it back to Annabel. "Damnation! Wish I could help."

"Well, that hole in your chest is just now starting to heal, mister. You don't need another...I'm sure Fiona and Bill are quite capable."

"Yeah, but, now they're not only tanglin' with Mankiller, but Apaches, Comanch, Kiowa an' God knows who else..." He paused and shook his head. "They're fer sure goin' in harm's way…Plus that's some kinda nasty country. Ready made for an ambush." He stared out across the yard and clenched his teeth.

WICHITA MOUNTAINS, OT

Michicaba Pokagon tethered his lathered gelding to a wind-twisted scrub oak near the entrance. He walked into the large cave located in the western part of the mountains and south of Medicine Creek.

It was named Spanish Cave by early settlers because of the brass Morion style helmet believed to have been worn by the Spanish explorers and conquistadors found deep inside.

The cave was also thought to have been mined for gold back in the sixteenth century from the exposed veins of white quartz that streaked through the gray granite of the mountain—very little trace of the valuable metal remained.

Juh glanced up from where he sat cross-legged near the campfire as *Pokagon* squatted down and cut a chunk of meat with his knife from the sizzling venison haunch grilling on a water-soaked oak branch propped over the fire.

His strong white teeth tore a long strip of the half-cooked flesh that was charred on the outside. He chewed ravenously, allowing the aromatic juices to run down the side of his chin.

"Where Big Foot?" asked the Apache.

The Potawatomi finished chewing and swallowed. "Dead." He bit off another piece.

"Where?"

"Big Dog's saloon, Anadarko."

The six other Indians around the fire exchanged glances.

"Who kill?" questioned *Juh*.

"White woman law dog marshal." He unslung the strap to his gourd water bottle from over his shoulder, pulled the plug and took a long drink. "Wear two guns...Fast, like *tl'iish* striking." He held up one hand and jabbed it forward in the imitation of a snake.

Mankiller jumped to his feet. "What woman look like?"

"Much tall, like warrior. Long shiny hair like raven or Indian...with small man. He also wear badge."

"Paugh!" The Cherokee spat into the fire. "*Ageyv Tvs-gina!*"

"What *Ageyv Tvs-gina*, Black Fox?" asked *Nacoma*, the Comanche.

"Is Cherokee for She Devil...Follow Mankiller for over three seasons."

"Snapping Turtle fool! Lead law woman to Wichitas," snapped *Juh*.

Pokagon sliced another chunk from the haunch with his Green River knife. "No white track Potawatomi."

"Snapping Turtle not know *Ageyv Tvs-gina*. She learn much from Bass Reeves...meby track shadow through dark room," said Mankiller.

Juh got to his feet, walked over to their saddles and bedrolls and grabbed his well-used '66 Yellow Boy and pitched it to the

Potawatomi. "Snapping Turtle go back along trail...You find. You kill."

The Cherokee snatched the rifle from the other Indian's hands. "Mankiller go. *Ageyv Tvs-gina* is his to kill...No other."

Juh whipped his Old Hickory butcher knife from his belt and held the point against the Cherokee's throat drawing a small trace of blood that trickled down his neck. "*Juh* say Potawatomi go. He lead *magaanii* to mountains...He must regain honor...*Inoli* wish to fight *Juh*?"

Mankiller glared at the fierce-looking Apache for a long moment, released his grip on the Winchester, and slowly sat back down.

Michicaba Pokagon cut one more piece of venison, turned and headed back to his horse.

MEDICINE CREEK
WICHITA MOUNTAINS

The sun was peeking over the crest of Mount Scott as Fiona stirred the fire to life. The morning was frosty, but clear.

She threw several handfuls of fresh ground coffee in the pot already three-quarters filled with creek water.

Bill walked back into camp with an armload of dry deadfall he had gathered after taking care of his morning constitution. "Definitely got to get me a set of buckskins. Have to be warmer than town clothes...Like to have froze to death last night."

"I have to agree, they are warmer than cloth, especially over a union suit...Why didn't you get up and add some more wood to the fire?"

He piled the armload near the fire pit. "Did...Burned almost all our wood up and still froze. That's why I had to go foraging this morning."

She glanced around. "Thought something looked different. There was just enough wood left to get the coffee going."

Fiona set the skillet across the same three rocks she had used last night to fry the fish and hot water cornbread. She added some more sliced salt pork for the grease and placed the filets she had saved from supper in the pan.

Bill grabbed one of his gloves from his gunbelt and picked up the coffee pot to keep it from boiling over. He waited a moment, and then set it back next to the fire for the second boiling.

"Thanks, I couldn't get to it in time," said Fiona.

Forty-five minutes later, they had cleaned up the camp site, packed, mounted and headed toward Mount Scott in the distance. It didn't take long for Fiona to locate the Potawatomi's tracks on the west side of the creek.

The tracks ended after two miles, when the sandy loam soil gave way to rounded granite massifs flush with the surface as they neared the base of the mountain. The entire area of the Wichita

Mountains was a type of igneous intrusion formed during the Cambrian some five hundred and forty million years ago. They were exposed and rounded by weathering during the Permian, almost three hundred million years ago.

"Now what, O' Bandit Queen?" Bill said as he crossed his arms over his saddle horn.

Her steel-gray eyes flashed momentarily at her partner. "'Ye of little faith,' said Jesus to his disciples."

He grinned. "I know, Matthew 8-26."

"Step down," she said as she dismounted and dropped to one knee. "Don't you remember Bass telling us about the nail heads that stick out just a little from the bottom of a horseshoe?"

"Uh…vaguely."

She pointed. "You do have to look closely. See those tiny light marks?"

"Yeah."

"Even granite will show scratches from steel…Just have to know what to look for. We're lucky that he must have stolen the horse from a white man…It's shod. Should eventually be able to find Mankiller's tracks, because his horse is shod, too."

"Ah, ye of great wisdom."

"No, I just paid attention when Bass was talking."

Fiona turned, grabbed the saddlehorn and stuck her toe in her stirrup. There was a loud thump of a bullet striking flesh followed a half second later by the echoing boom of a rifle.

Diablo screamed and grunted. He staggered, fell to his knees, and then lay over on his side.

Instinctively, Bill jerked his Winchester from the boot on his saddle and levered off four rounds as rapidly as he could at the cloud of gunsmoke halfway up the mountain side almost two hundred yards away.

He fired the first two at the center of the smoke and the second two one foot to the right. The nimble lawman hit the ground, rolled over and fired two more, one foot to the left.

There was a brief silence as the smoke from Bill's rifle slowly drifted away. It was followed by Fiona's sobs as she held Diablo's head in her arms. Blood ran freely to the ground from a finger-sized hole in the center of his chest while he vainly tried to breathe.

"Oh, Diablo, my Diablo…I'm so sorry…Please forgive me, please." She buried her face in his mane as he shuddered, sighed his last breath and the light left his deep brown eyes forever.

After a long moment, she raised her tear-streaked face and looked toward the remnants of the smoke at the mountain. She turned to Bill who was just getting to his feet.

"I was there and helped birth him…and…now…now I got to hold him while…while he died," she whispered through her sobs.

"You know that shot was meant for you?"

She slowly nodded. "I know."

"If it means anything...I think I got the shooter." He took a deep breath. "Can't help but think it's my fault...I wasn't doing my job scanning up ahead...I'm so sorry."

Fiona shook her head. "No, I told you to get down so I could show you the tracks...It's nobody's fault...He gave his life for me."

She buried her face in his mane again for a long moment, raised up and gently closed his eyes with her fingertips. Then Fiona got to her feet, stared down at her faithful mount, and then stepped around to his hips. Reaching behind her, she pulled her razor-sharp Bowie from its sheath in her belt and cut a thick lock from Diablo's flowing black tail.

"I'm going to braid a bracelet." She sniffed, rolled the hair around three fingers, tied a single knot to hold it together temporarily and placed the hair carefully in her beaded parfleche pouch hanging at her side. "I'll always have part of him with me." She looked at Bill. "He will forever be my best friend...He never quit on me and I'll never quit on him."

"I know, I feel the same about Tippy." He handed her his handkerchief.

"Thank you." Fiona took a deep breath, looked down again and dried her eyes. "Run well over the rainbow, my friend...Run well." She glanced back at Bill. "Let's put my gear on Spot and go check your marksmanship."

Bill and Fiona slowly coaxed their mounts up the side of the mountain, picking their way around the larger rocks and boulders. They dismounted near the body lying next to a stagecoach-sized boulder. A trace of sulfur from his black powder gunsmoke hung in the still air.

"Two rounds…one in his chest, one in his throat. Nice shooting, Marshal…Looks like the other Potawatomi, Snapping Turtle."

Bill nodded. "Had to be luck. I just shot everywhere I thought he could be on the other side of the smoke…He couldn't have been waiting all this time on us. I'd say the leader sent him to check his back trail."

"I agree." Fiona glanced over at a shallow draw nearby. "There's his horse…Looks about done in."

"Let's strip his gear. Let him run free. Plenty of winter grass around."

"I don't think so. It's a white man's horse…used to being cared for. He would die sure…We can use him for a pack horse after he recovers."

"Probably a good idea…Amazing he's still alive. You know the western plains Indians don't treat their horses like we do. A white man will ride one until it's worn out, and then walk…An Indian'll come along, get the horse up, ride it twenty more miles and then eat him."

"A bit short sighted, don't you think?" Fiona suggested.

"Depends on where you're trying to go or who you're trying to get away from...and how hungry you are."

She shook her head. "Hard to fathom...But, I suppose it's a culture thing."

"I'd say." Bill bent down, removed the Indian's gun and gunbelt and picked up the Yellow Boy. "Pretty worn, but you never know when you'll need an extra gun and ammunition out here." He also went through his pockets and got six silver dollars and one double eagle gold piece. "Huh...Probably from that bank robbery in Chickasha."

"I suspect the leader is still carrying the bulk," she said over her shoulder as she untied the gainted bay gelding. "At least he doesn't appear to be wind broke."

She loosened the cinch a little so the animal could breathe better.

"That's good," said Bill as he put the gunbelt in the saddlebags and slid the Winchester in the empty boot.

Fiona took the horses' lead, they mounted and headed back down the mountain, backtracking Snapping Turtle.

At the base, they discovered a game trail that led into the interior of the mountains.

"Knew there had to be trails through all these upthrusts and boulders made by the elk, deer and buffalo...Like water or really anything else, they take the path of least resistance to go somewhere," said Fiona as she followed the Potawatomi's tracks.

Bill carefully scanned the sides and tops of the surrounding mountains with his glass as he followed immediately behind her. "Apparently, including the recently deceased…We don't want to ride unawares into the renegade's camp."

"Don't think there's much chance of that, especially if they heard that gunfire echoing through these canyons and passes…My guess is they'll be relocating."

"Gotta start somewhere."

"True…I think our advantage is this isn't their native country."

"Meaning?" asked Bill.

"They don't know it any better than we do."

"Wonder if they have a government map like we do?"

"Could be…Maybe one of them walked into the Fort Sill victualer or suttler's store and asked for one?"

He grinned. "Not likely…They probably used the by-gosh-and-by-golly method that Myra Maybelle Shirley did."

"Come again?" asked Fiona, turning in her saddle to look at Bill.

"Better known as Belle Starr…You don't know the story?"

"I guess not."

"Well, as it goes…Belle and her gang robbed a military train of gold headed to Denver to be minted into coins."

"They know how much?"

"Not exactly, but it's thought to be well over a million dollars in bullion."

"Goodness." Fiona continued to follow the Indian's sign along the trail. "He must have been pretty confident...Made no effort to cover his tracks."

"Yeah," Bill commented as he scanned the sides of the pass ahead. "Anyway, they took the iron door off the express car and drug it behind them into the Wichitas, somewhere in the general vicinity of Elk Mountain in the Charon Gardens area."

"The outlaws drug a iron door through this stuff?" She pointed at all the rocks, boulders and scrub brush around.

"Probably found a better trail than this one."

"You think?"

"I do...They either found a cave or an old mine, stashed the gold in the back, and then fitted that door in the entrance. Belle is said to have designed some kind of an intricate locking system, and then they covered it the whole thing over with rock and brush."

"The outlaws didn't go back and get it?" asked Fiona.

Bill chuckled. "It seems her gang tried to pull another military train robbery and the soldiers who were guarding the payroll shot 'em to doll rags...Every one of them."

"But Belle wasn't along?"

"Nope, she had gone back to her home near Eufala in the Cherokee Nation and got herself shot from ambush in '89...You know about that, of course?"

Fiona nodded. "I do…They never found out who did it."

"The upshot is, with her murder, there was nobody left alive who knew the location of the gold cache behind the iron door in the Wichitas."

"All of the southwest is rife with stories of lost treasure, from Sam Bass's in a cave somewhere in Montague County, Texas, to the lost Duchman mine in Arizona…Person could spend the rest of their lives just looking for hidden outlaw loot."

"There's even the story of the James gang hiding some stolen gold in the Wichitas, too."

"It's a wonder these mountains are not full of treasure hunters."

"True…It's a good thing it's not summer time."

"Because?"

"Rattlesnake heaven."

"Hate snakes." Fiona just shook her head as she reined Spot to the left and took a smaller trail that appeared to head up the mountain.

"How's he ride?" asked Bill.

"Smooth. Has a natural single-foot…Sure footed."

SPANISH CAVE

"We go," said *Juh* as he got to his feet. "Too many shots," he referenced the sounds that had echoed through the passes a few moments ago. "Snapping Turtle dead."

"Where go?" asked *Inoli*.

"What Cherokee care? He run from She Devil," snapped *Juh*.

"If Mankiller go back down Snapping Turtle trail, there be no reason to move. He kill, not be killed."

"Fah! Like before for three seasons…Woman chase? Mankiller soft," countered *Juh*. "Not like Apache…*Juh* catch, cut nose off and make slave."

The Cherokee glared at the Mescalero war chief, and then turned to pick up his bedroll and rifle.

"*Kuruk* see good place for camp on Cache Creek half-day ride from here. Good water, grass and place where big rocks fall from cliff to make shelter on three side," commented the other Apache.

They all looked up as they heard a rolling peal of thunder from the southwest.

"Rain come soon. Wash tracks from trails in canyons…is good," said *Nacoma,* one of the Comanche.

CHARON GARDENS WILDERNESS

"Uh, oh," murmured Bill.

"What?"

"Didn't you hear that?"

"Of course…Thunder. The rain crows have been churking all morning…We've been rained on before."

"Well, if this country is anything like New Mexico and Arizona, these passes and draws will become raging torrents in very short order...I suggest we find a place to get out before the rain starts."

Fiona looked up at the sky. "I don't see any clouds yet."

"They could be laying just over the crest of those mountains..." He pointed ahead to the southwest. "...and they could be on us before you could say scat..."

"And we would be in deep trouble down here."

"Now you have it."

The thunder rolled again, closer this time as Bill looked at the almost vertical walls on both sides. He turned in the saddle and checked behind them.

"Too far to try to go back...Can't climb the walls with the animals..."

Fiona interrupted him. "Only choice is to go forward and hope we find a way out ahead of the rain...Let's pick up the pace."

The horses and mule were already sensing the coming storm and were getting nervous. Their natural instincts were to seek higher ground.

They squeezed them up into as fast a lope as they could, considering the winding trail.

A lightening bolt struck the mountain top just to their left followed immediately by a tremendous clap of thunder. The smell of ozone permeated the air around them.

They looked up again and saw the edge of a black cloud boiling above the ridge. A fierce downburst of wind hit them in the face, followed by a wall of water from the cloud as it rolled over the top of the mountain.

Fiona and Bill grabbed their hats with one hand and leaned into the rain. She pulled out her slicker and donned it and he grabbed his oiled poncho.

"See anything?" yelled Bill from behind her.

"No," she screamed back. "Keep going!"

Water was already streaming down the sides of the canyon and gathering to form a small stream at the bottom. The water soon reached the knees of the animals and kept rising, further panicking them as the cold piercing rain fell in sheets.

Fiona leaned around in her saddle. "Up ahead, to the right. Looks like a low area. We have to climb there!"

She reined Spot to the right and bumped his ribs with her heels. The panicked animal didn't need much encouragement. His feet dug into the soft mud and he slipped to his knees. The mule struggled back to his feet and surged ahead.

Bill took two more dallies around his saddlehorn with the gelding's lead rope and literally pulled the weakened horse up the side of the mountain.

Twelve feet higher on a lesser-used trail, they were out of the dangerous churning water at the bottom. There was only three inches cascading down the trail they were on, making their footing slippery, but manageable.

Fiona glanced to her left and saw a monstrous ten foot high wall of branches, uprooted trees, dirt, small boulders and other debris being pushed like a living thing by the water along the bottom of the arroyo they had just vacated.

"Higher," shouted Bill, just as Snapping Turtle's horse's hindquarters were knocked out from under him.

The gelding screamed and tried to scramble to his feet in the slippery mud. Roberts kicked Tippy hard in the side with both heels. "Come on, son, you can make it."

The powerful, thick-chested Morgan dug all four feet into the mud, lunged once, slid back, scrambled—then lunged again, making a little headway.

The loop from Fiona's rawhide reata sailed through the driving rain to settle around Tippy's neck. She dallied off and added Spot's awesome pulling power to aid the pair behind her.

Slowly, but surely, the mule and Bill's horse made headway up the hill. The exhausted pony was finally able to get his back feet under him and the three worked their way to a small flat area on the side of the hill, a scant six feet above the muddy churning flash flood below.

She lifted the loop from Tippy's neck, recoiled the braided rawhide and tied it back to her saddle. "Glad I decided to put my gear on Spot. We'd have been in deep trouble without it."

"I'd say." He wiped the water from his eyes and looked up past Fiona. "Hey, is that a cave there behind that big boulder?" He squinted through the splattering rain.

She turned and looked. "Think you're right...or an old mine." With a slight nudge, she bumped Spot toward the dark shadow, partially hidden by a wagon-sized rock.

Fiona eased around the boulder and into the entrance. "It's big enough for us and the animals."

She dismounted, led the painted mule deep within and turned him around.

Bill stepped Tippy just inside the opening and also dismounted to lead his charges out of the blinding rain.

"I've heard of fortuitous things, but this...Guess it's like Mark Twain said, 'All you need in this life is ignorance and confidence, and then success is sure'."

"Which do we have?" asked Bill.

She grinned. "Apparently both, because someone else has taken shelter in this cave in the past. There's a fire pit and a stack of dried wood left."

Fiona took some of the loose twigs, built a tiny teepee over some punk from her parfleche pouch—knowing her matches probably wouldn't strike—lit it with a spark from a piece of flint and a small steel bar she always carried in the pouch.

"If you'll pull the gear from the boys and get the fixings out of the poke, I'll have us some hot coffee in just a bit."

"Sounds good...Where's the smoke going?"

Fiona leaned over and looked up. "Crack in the rock overhead. Must go all the way outside, because that's where what little smoke there is heading…But even that won't matter, what with the rain."

He handed her the pot, coffee and canteen. "I'll rub the boys down with their saddle blankets while you do that."

Twenty minutes later, they were leaning against their saddles, sipping on the hot coffee. Fiona had cut some salt pork and dumped a can of beans over it in a skillet to cook.

"Sure glad we found this cave. Looks like the rain is setting in for a spell," said Bill.

"We may be in here for a while even after it quits…until the water goes down," added Fiona.

"Yep…Shhhh. Hear that?" Bill looked back into the inky depths of the cave.

"Something's back there…Don't suppose we've usurped a bear or mountain lion's lair, do you?"

"I think we would have known. Both bear and lion den's have an odor you can't mistake."

"Look," she whispered. "I see the glow of a light back there. What in the world?" Fiona got to her feet, drew one of her pistols, cocking it with the characteristic soft double click.

Bill did the same with his Thunderer…

§§§

CHAPTER TWELVE

CACHE CREEK
WITCHITA MOUNTAINS

The six renegade Indians led their horses against the driving rain up the side of the canyon away from the tumultuous, churning Cache Creek below.

Nacoma, the Comanche, guided the way to the semi-shelter of the giant granite boulders that had tumbled down the cliff face eons ago forming a type of pocket. They had barely escaped from the game trail that ran along the normally placid pool in Cache Creek formed by the same landslide when the flash flood roared down the mountainside.

A house-sized boulder had fallen on top of several others of almost equal size, creating a roof of sorts. Water from the pouring rain dripped down the back side and created a small pool in the rear before running on down the mountain side to the creek.

Out of the direct rain, the Indians hobbled their mounts, removed their gear and piled it on the driest side of the shelter against one of the supporting boulders.

"*Nacoma*, could have found better…many caves around." The Apache glanced around the area. "No dry wood under rocks to build fire."

"If *Juh* wanted better camp, *Juh* should have found one himself. Mighty war chief of Apache…Paugh!"

CAVE
CHARON GARDENS WILDERNESS

"Settle down, pilgrims. No need fer shootin' irons."

The light grew brighter as it came around a bend twenty feet back into the stygian depths of the cave. A small, grizzled, white-bearded old prospector in grimy buckskins with a lantern in one hand and leading a pack-laden burro stepped into the main chamber.

"Ol' Pike ain't agonna hurtcha none...Coffee smells right good. Could tell you had some aboilin' all the way to the other end...Hope you didn't use up all my wood."

Fiona and Bill uncocked their weapons and slipped them back in their holsters.

"We're sorry, didn't know the cave was occupied...Just trying to get in out of the rain," said Fiona.

"Don't blame you none there. This is a real frog strangler...an' the cave wadn't occupied when you come in."

"How so?" asked Bill.

"I come in the back door...Shaft goes all the way through this here hill. Ain't a straight shot though...Kindly meanders about like a creek.

"Them Spaniards knowed what they was adoin' back in the day when it come to minin' gold. They had the Injun slaves foller the quartz vein wherever it led...Took a right smart of the yeller stuff outta this here mountain. Still some left though...'long with some other treasure...You gonna let me have some of that there coffee er not?"

"Got a cup in your poke?" asked Bill.

"Well, a 'course...Feller wouldn't be worth a jot er a tittle if'n he didn't have a cup to hold his coffee in."

"I'd say," commented Roberts.

"You'd say what?"

"That a man always should have a cup, if he's a coffee drinker."

The old timer squinted one eye at Bill. "Thought I jest said that." He looked over at the fire pit and sniffed the air. "Is that salt pork an' beans a cookin' there?" Pike pointed at the skillet.

"It is. Would you like some?" asked Fiona.

"Why, thought I's gonna dry up and blow away 'fore you asked." He chuckled.

"Don't suppose you've got a plate to go along with your cup?" inquired Bill.

Pike cocked one eyebrow. "Now there you go ag'in, pilgrim." He pulled the gear from the donkey's back and piled it next to Fiona and Bill's. "Awright Lulabelle you kin go lay down now."

"That's a nice jenny," said Fiona.

"That she is, lass, that she is…By the by, I'm a guessin' yore momma and daddy's give you names, did they?"

"I'm Brushy Bill Roberts and this is Fiona Mae Miller."

"Not hitched?"

They simultaneously answered firmly, "No!"

"We're both Deputy US Marshals," said Fiona as she took the crescent and star badge out of her pouch and held it up.

Bill pulled his coat aside to show his.

"Well, dang ol' Andy's hide…A lady law. Next thang you know you'll be a runnin' fer office er a votin'."

"Would that be so bad?" she asked.

Pike thought a moment and then laughed. "Well, meby not. Might straighten some of them crooked Whigs and Democrats out...If there's anything corrupt in a person, electin' them to office will normally bring it out...an' a woman is usually the first to spot it."

He laughed again. "Never git on the angry side of a woman, I always say."

"You got a point there, old timer," said Bill.

"I do, don't I?...Figgered out some time ago how to tell what mood a woman is in."

"Oh, that might be something worth knowing." He winked at Fiona.

"It's a sure sign she's angry when she's holdin' a shootin' iron." Pike slapped his thigh and giggled.

He handed his tin cup to Fiona. "No offense, lass. I was jest a funnin'. Been a spell since I had somebody to talk to 'sides Lulabelle...She don't keep her side of the conversation agoin' very well."

She filled his cup and handed it back to him.

"Don't suppose you got'ny sugar?"

"We do." Bill handed him a cloth bag. "Grab you a pinch or two."

Pike pulled open the top, reached in, got a fistful and dumped it in the steaming cup. He gave the bag back to Roberts, and then licked the palm of his hand. He unsheathed an Arkansas Toothpick from his belt and gave the coffee a stir.

"Like a little coffee in your sugar, do you?" She smiled.

"Only when I kin git it, lass….He said yer name's Fiona? That's Scottish."

She nodded. "It is."

"A cousin of mine, James Macpherson…he's a poet, used that name in one of his poems."

"Macpherson…Your last name too?"

"Aye, that it is…Pahdraig Macpherson is the full moniker, but it's too much of a mouthful. They started callin' me Pike when I was a conscripted bosun's mate on HMS Audacious.

"She was a three-masted, seventy-four gun warship of the line servin' the English crown…I managed to jump ship when she docked in Boston durin' the French and Indian war. I headed west from there."

"Interesting," said Bill.

"I do believe the salt pork and beans are ready. Hand me your plates, gentlemen."

After supper, Fiona brewed a fresh pot of coffee and filled everyone's cup.

"By the Lord Harry, but you make a cracker of a cup of coffee," said Pike.

"Thank you, kind sir." She curtseyed slightly.

Bill took out a cigar from his saddlebag, bit the end off and lit it with a burning branch from the fire. He blew a blue cloud of smoke over his head.

"Don't reckon you mayhaps have another one of those...er a chaw?"

"No chaw, old timer, but do have some more of these Virginia cigars." He pulled out another and passed it to Pike.

"Shame you don't have Cubans. They is somethin' else...Got some when we docked in Havana onct."

Bill stuck his hand back out. "Well, let me have it back, then."

"No, no. This is fine, I'm sure."

"Thought so." He leaned forward and lit the old man's cigar from the same branch.

Pike took a long draw, blew it out and turned to Fiona. "Take it you don't hold with smokin' cigars. lassie?"

"Oh, I do on occasion...But I prefer Cubans."

Pike guffawed and looked at Bill. "Ain't she a hat full of fire?...I like you, lass." He took another draw. "Tell me, what brings you to the Wichitas? Don't look like yer a prospectin' er treasure huntin'."

"Got paper on a Cherokee renegade for multiple murders and a plethora of lessor crimes. We believe he's hooked up with some other renegades from various tribes in the Territory," Fiona said.

"Yep, that bunch's been raisin' hob fer a spell...Sorry as they come. Been campin' over to Spanish Cave and leavin' their trash around, spoilin' my mountains...Ain't like the redskins used to be. They worshiped Mother Earth…Leave no sign upon the ground you were here, was their mantra."

"You've seen them?" asked Bill.

"Shore…Was eight of 'em…Now they ain't but six."

"We've killed two of them. Both were Potawatomi…But how did you know? I shot one in Anadarko and Bill only shot the one called Snapping Turtle this morning after he took down my horse trying to shoot me," said Fiona.

Pike took a sip of his coffee. "I know…Ain't much ol' Pike don't know about when it comes to these here mountains."

"Could you lead us to Spanish Cave?" Bill inquired.

"Could."

"But?"

"Won't do you no good."

"How so?" asked Fiona.

"Ain't there no more…Pulled up traps an' left after you put that Potawatomi's lights out."

"And I suppose you know where they went?" questioned Bill.

"Shore." He held his cup toward Fiona. "Mind if'n I have a little warm up?"

"Noticed you don't carry a gun," said Bill.

"Don't need one…Ain't sceered of no redhide, ner 'ny other critter in these here mountains." He chuckled. "Why they don't know ol' Pike's even around."

"But you can take us where the renegades are?" asked Fiona.

He nodded. "We'll go when she finishes rainin'." He glanced at the water dripping past the opening of the cave. "Be over sometime after midnight...You folks best git some sleep. We'll be headin' out 'bout light-thirty of a mornin'."

"Won't there still be water in the canyons?"

"Lassie, once it quits rainin', the water runs off 'bout as quick as she comes."

"What about you? Aren't you going to get some sleep?" inquired Bill.

"Oh, I'll be along. Gonna sit up a while an' finish this here ceegar and this fine coffee, the lassie made...been out of it since bully was a pup."

They grabbed their soogans and unrolled them against the far wall of the cave, but near enough to benefit from the warmth of the fire.

Fiona laid down with her head pillowed against her saddle and looked one last time at the quirky old prospector, sitting cross-legged on the other side of the fire, smiling as he smoked his cigar and nursed his coffee.

The gray light of early morning filtered in the cave from the entrance along with the song of a mockingbird going through his extensive repertoire.

Fiona blinked and rubbed the sleep from her eyes. She looked across the cave at Pike sitting next to the fire, slowly adding sticks to the coals creating a cheery blaze.

He glanced over at the movement. "Well, see you survived the night, lassie."

She pushed her blanket back and sat up. "I don't suppose there's anyplace around here a lady..."

"Shore. Take this here lantern an' go back around the bend in the back. They's a side shaft on the left, bout thirty-feet deep where you kin take keer of yer business. There's a short-handled shovel back there too, fer..."

"I get the idea." She got to her feet, walked over, picked up the lantern and turned the wick up. "Be back in a bit, then I'll start the coffee and get some breakfast on."

"Them's mighty purty words," he said as Fiona headed toward the back of the cave.

"Ya'll sure do make a lot of racket," Bill said as he sat up. "Coffee on?"

"Not yet, pilgrim. The lassie said she'd start it soon as she gets back."

"Where'd she...Never mind." He grabbed his boots, turned them over and shook them in case any spiders or scorpions had decided to take up residence during the night. Finding them clear, he slipped his feet in.

Both men turned as Fiona walked silently back in. Pike noticed the knee high moccasins.

"Smart to wear moccasins in the mountains, lass...You should take the hint, Marshal Roberts. Them slick-soled boots kin git you hurt…Shoulda taken those that Injun you kilt was a wearin'."

"A dead man's moccasins?"

"Shore, who's to know the difference?"

"Me."

"That kinda thinkin' kin sometimes bite you in the butt."

"You took his gun and gunbelt didn't you?" asked Fiona.

"That's different…Took his horse, too."

"An' jest how is it different, pilgrim?"

Bill hesitated. "Well…danged if I know. Just sounded right when I said it."

"I'd say you was on the wrong side of right then," said Pike as he got to his feet and walked over to his gear.

In a short moment, he walked back and pitched a set of tall moccasins in Bill's lap. "I went down an' got these after ya'll rode off. Figgered they might come in handy fer some ignorant pilgrim."

Bill blushed, pulled off his boots, slipped on the rabbit fur lined elk skin moccasins and laced them up the side of his calf. "I'll be…they fit." He got to his feet. "Ooo, that's nice."

"I think some people call that a lesson learned, Marshal," said Fiona. "It would be interesting to know what you were like as a child."

Bill looked at her and grinned. "Shorter."

After breakfast, they loaded up and led their mounts out the front of the cave and into the bright sunlight.

"Mmm, the sun feels good," said Fiona as she blinked and allowed her eyes to adjust to the change.

"I'd lead your steeds down to the main trail. Still gonna be a tad slick up here…We'll be a headin' to the west."

They nodded and followed the old man down to the main trail. There was still a small three-foot wide muddy stream flowing along the bottom of the draw. The path was relatively clear save the occasional debris they had to step over left by the flood.

They passed a stove-sized boulder that was on the downside of the trail. Fiona glanced over as something glinted in the sunlight.

"Hold it," she said and knelt down beside a small depression on the downstream side of the rock caused by an eddy. She pushed some of the loose material away and picked up the items that had caught her eye. "Look! Gold coins."

Bill and Pike turned around to see what Fiona had found. She held her hand out with the two coins in her palm.

"Great jubilee! Spanish doubloons!" Pike reached over, picked up one and studied it. "Minted in Mexico City…eight escudos."

"What does that mean?" asked Bill.

"Doubloon is from the Latin word *duplus* meaning double, it's a reference to the denomination of the coin. They minted two, four and eight escudos," said Fiona. "See the image on this side is the coat of arms of the Hapsburg royal family and on the reverse is the Crusaders Cross...Also on the back is a lion, representing the Spanish province of Leon and a castle, the symbol of the province of Castile, the historical capital of Spain."

"She's speakin' the truth. They's a lot of treasure hidden in these mountains. Figgerin' what the outlaws like Belle Starr brought in an' the James boys...But they was pikers considerin' what the Spaniards left...Been lookin' fer these long as I kin remember."

Pike looked up the mountain where the main rush of water had came from and pointed. "Up there...these come from somewheres up there."

"Where did the gold come from originally?" asked Bill

"Well, see back in the 1500s, the Spaniards enslaved the Tawehash an' the Wichitas an' made 'em mine gold. They shipped it down to Mexico City in long trains of burros a loaded down with the stuff after they busted it out of the quartz an' melted it down into ingots...Even heered tell they was at least one train of gold what didn't make it through Texas...The Injuns of the Atakapan Tejas tribe of the Caddos supposedly got it.

"Anyways, the Spanish rulers would send the donkeys back with supplies plus bags and bags of coins to pay the soldiers."

"How many were there?" asked Fiona.

"Some say several thousand was here to keep the Injuns under control. Nobody really knows."

"I don't understand why they left it here," said Bill.

"Story goes they was an earthquake 'round the year 1550 er so like the one in 18 and 11…"

"The New Madrid quake," interrupted Fiona. "The Mississippi actually reversed its flow and ran backward for a time."

"Yep, that one…Well, seems there was what's called a five hunerd year storm 'bout the same time, so the Spaniards had jest received a shipment of coins an' were agonna ship down some more bullion. They got sceered 'bout the weather an' put everthang into a couple of their mines high upon one of these here mountains an' they got inside too…you know, gittin' outta the storm…All the Spaniards, the burros and everthang was buried by the quake…The Injuns, though, was smart, they felt that Earth Mother was angry, an' they stayed out in the open…Rather face the rain than be eaten by the ground."

"So it's all still there?"

"What they say…An' what most of these treasure hunters an' such don't realize is these mountains still move a bit on occasion…Somebody kin find somethin', go to town to git supplies…an' then cain't find their spot again…" He chuckled. "Mountains don't want 'em too."

"May have to look into this a bit after we take care of business with those renegades," said Bill.

"I don't 'spect how it's agoin' no place 'ny time soon."

"How far to where the Indians are camped?" asked Fiona.

"Half-day…Should be there 'bout noon."

"Where is *there*?" Bill inquired.

"Cache Creek."

CACHE CREEK
WITCHITA MOUNTAINS

"*Kadar*, go back along trail and be lookout for *pindah-lickyoee*," *Juh* told his brother Apache. "*Nacoma*, you go downstream, find back way out….*Kuruk* and White Horse set up camp. Black Fox build fire and put rest of venison over to cook."

"Mankiller is not woman to build fire and cook meat."

"Black Fox will do what *Juh* say. He bring woman law into our country."

Nacoma worked his way downstream along the game trail beside the creek a little over six hundred yards. The mountains on both sides got steeper and more narrow until the water was the only passageway between two vertical walls. It was a little over fifty feet wide from cliff to cliff.

The water had slowed substantially, but was still muddy with some flotsam drifting on the surface. The Comanche waded out into the creek up almost to his waist. He continued downstream in the middle around a bend to the left where the cliff walls narrowed even more and were completely vertical. Some junipers grew from tiny crevices a hundred feet up the cliff.

The creek was only about thirty feet wide at this point. He looked almost straight overhead over three hundred feet to the tops of the unclimbable cliffs on both sides.

Nacoma continued downstream another two hundred yards until he came to a confluence. Cache Creek was joined by another stream from the north. The larger combined creek meandered its way on south.

The east bank on the far side fell to a series of low rolling hills with granite surface outcroppings. The Comanche turned around and waded back west upstream to where the bank with the trail had ended. He stepped out and completed his return to the camp.

The fire was burning at the front of the shelter. Mankiller had put what venison they had left on a thick green willow branch and propped it out over the flames.

Nacoma sat down and extended his feet with his wet moccasins close to the heat to dry them.

Juh sat down across the fire and stared at *Nacoma* for a moment.

Finally the Comanche spoke, "Creek joined by another, half mile downstream, go south. Tall cliffs go away. Low ground on east side of bigger creek. Water only belly deep on horses. Good way out."

Juh grunted and got to his feet. "Always good to have back way out." He turned and walked down toward the creek.

BOULDER MOUNTAIN

"Best leave our stock down here. Lulabelle might could make it, but she don't like it none," said Pike

They hobbled the animals on some winter grass down in the pass and started up the rugged mountain on foot.

"Some folks call this Eagle Mountain, but the Injuns always called it Boulder Mountain…fer obvious reasons." The old prospector moved up the hillside, over and around the numerous boulders like a mountain goat.

"How does he do that?" Bill whispered to Fiona.

"Practice…God only knows how long he's been roaming these mountains."

Pike looked back over his shoulder. "Come along, children. Cain't see nothin' till we git to the top."

"Right behind, you," said Bill. "Damn, glad he gave me these moccasins. I'd never be able to climb over this granite in boots."

"Uh, huh." Fiona grinned as she moved past him.

As they reached the rounded summit, Pike dropped to his stomach and arm crawled the final ten feet to the crest. Fiona and Bill took the hint, figuring the Indians would be in sight from the top. If they could see them, then the renegades could return the favor.

They wormed their way forward until they could see over the edge down into the canyon.

"Yep, jest like I said...there they be." He looked off to the left and spotted *Kadar* crouching next to a boulder above the trail. "Got a lookout on their back trail...see 'im yonder?"

The two law officers glanced back to the north and nodded.

"You kin pick off one er two with yer long guns 'fore they know yer up here."

Fiona shook her head. "Unh, uhh, that's not the way we work. Got paper on at least one. Need to try to take them alive, if possible."

Pike glanced over at her. "That ain't agonna happen, lassie, but it's yer funeral...Wuz me, I'd take 'em out 'ny way I could...Jest a word to the wise, them redhides don't play by no rules...Ol' Andy learnt that in the Florida swamps a fightin' with the Seminoles...Wait! What's happenin'?"

"That's Mankiller," said Fiona. "Looks like he's arguing with one of the others."

"Black Fox tires of *Juh*. War chief...Paugh!" He spat on the ground. "He is squaw."

Juh slapped the Cherokee across the face.

"We fight Indian style." Mankiller whipped the wild rag from around his neck, wrapped one end around his left hand, and then held the faded red cloth out to *Juh*.

The Apache did the same. They both drew their knives and began to move in a tight circle.

"You will die today, *Inoli*."

"Mankiller may die today...but not at hand of dog-eating Apache. He is coward who runs from woman." He spat in the dirt again and flicked his blade at *Juh's* midsection.

Juh leaned away from the sharp point and countered with his own blade at the Cherokee's forward leg, slicing a shallow cut across his thigh.

It was a matter of honor to not only maintain a grip on the cloth between them, but also to not strike the left arm of either. There was nothing in the code about not using it for leverage though.

The larger Mankiller lunged back, jerking the Apache forward. He dropped, thrust his foot in *Juh's* midsection and flipped him over his head behind him. He swept his knife above him as the renegade leader was in the air, cutting a gash across his chest.

They both twisted around and jumped to their feet at the same time. The front of the Apache's shirt was rapidly soaking with blood.

Juh lunged forward, catching Black Fox in the side, laying the flesh open to the ribs. The Cherokee twisted away and with a backhanded jab, buried his ten-inch Bowie under the Apache's armpit to the hilt, and then twisted. The twist wasn't necessary as the tip of the blade had pierced *Juh's* heart.

The Apache looked at Mankiller's face, confusion and disbelief showing in his eyes. The Cherokee jerked his knife free as *Juh* collapsed to the dirt. He released his grip on the rag and grabbed the front of the Apache's hair and sliced quickly, removing the man's scalplock. He held the bloody trophy high over his head and screamed the Cherokee war cry.

"Oh, my God," Fiona whispered as she looked away.

"Well, pilgrims, that's one less to deal with…Wonder who that big man is?" asked Pike.

"Calvin Mankiller, the Cherokee…The one we've been chasing," she answered.

"A formidable foe, I'd say."

"Don't intend to knife fight him," she hissed.

The Cherokee spun around facing the others, his bloody knife in one hand, *Juh's* scalp in the other. The normally long white scar on his face had turned blood red. His ebon eyes glared in defiance. "Anyone challenge Mankiller?"

The other renegades looked away in acquiescence of Mankiller's dominance. He bent down and wiped his blade clean on what was left of *Juh's* hair.

"We not wait on *Ageyv Tvs-gina* to find…Indian no longer the hunted…We the hunter. We find her…She die."

§§§

CHAPTER THIRTEEN

BOULDER MOUNTAIN

"Wonder what he's telling them?" asked Bill.

"He's showin' that he's now the leader er the chief. See how the others avoid eye contact? Jest like a pack of wolves...When a new leader comes to dominance...the others look away in acceptance. Makin' eye contact with any wild critter is a form of challenge."

"Well, this bunch is definitely wild...and vicious," added Fiona.

The three worked their way back down from the crest far enough to stand.

"What's yer plan now, children?"

Fiona tilted her head to the north. "We take the lookout first."

"I'd say you got it well in hand. Ol' Pike's gonna git on about his bidness. Don't fergit what I said...take 'em out 'ny way you kin...they is without honor." He turned and headed back down to where Lulabelle was hobbled.

"Interesting man," commented Bill.

"More to him than meets the eye," added Fiona as she watched him disappear around some boulders at the bottom of the mountain.

"How do you want to do it?" asked Bill.

"Best way I know how...Head on."

Roberts nodded. "My favorite too...I'd say on foot. The boys would make too much noise. No need in lettin' them know we're coming that far ahead."

"Agreed, Marshal...Shall we?" Fiona nodded toward a point in the trail between the lookout and the renegade's camp.

When they reached the referenced point, Bill and Fiona headed to the left toward the lookout's hiding place. The Indian's focus was back up the trail and he wasn't aware of their presence until he heard a voice from behind him.

"I'd turn around real slow if I were you," said Fiona softly. Her Peacemakers were still in her holsters.

The Apache froze, and then turned, his Winchester in his hands.

"Drop it," said Bill, fifteen feet to Fiona's right. He had his Thunderer pointed at the Indian.

The Apache glanced his way, and then back to her. "You be *Ageyv Tvs-gina*...She Devil."

She grinned. "Good a name as any. You're Apache I take it?"

He nodded. "*Kadar,* mean Powerful in our tongue." He slapped his chest with his left hand. "No surrender to *pindah-lickyoee.*"

He spat on the ground.

"Your choice," she said.

Kadar rapidly levered a round into the chamber as he raised the rifle to his shoulder. His finger never tightened before Fiona's pistol roared and a .38-40 ball from her right hand pistol thudded into his chest. He looked down at the hole just as the blood started trickling out.

The renegade screamed the Apache war cry, took one step toward her when a slug from her left Peacemaker impacted his forehead. His head snapped back, he staggered against the boulder and collapsed like a sack of wet grain—dead before he hit the ground.

"Damn, woman, you drew and fired before I could squeeze my trigger…and my finger was on it," said Bill as he shook his head. "I think you're gettin' faster."

"I wasn't thinking about it…you were. Thinking slows you down."

"I'll remember that."

"I expect they know we're coming now."

"I expect so."

The Cherokee and the other three remaining renegades looked in the direction of the two shots as they echoed and reverberated up and down the canyon.

"She comes…Is good." He hand motioned the Comanche and the two Kiowa to different places to fire from. He took a position beside one of the support boulders for the cave.

Nacoma climbed almost fifty feet above the creek while *Kuruk* and White Horse positioned themselves closer to the trail entrance to the campsite, one on each side—they waited.

Bill and Fiona split up and took opposite sides of the trail, working their way through the boulders part way up the sides of the canyon.

Nacoma saw Fiona creeping in his direction. He was above her and not in her line of sight. He eased the lever down and back up on his Henry, quietly chambering a round.

She cautiously slipped around a chifforobe-sized rock, flattened her back against it and peeked around the side.

The Comanche snapped off a shot when he saw her white face momentarily appear not thirty feet away. His .44-40 round ricocheted from the granite and whined off down the canyon with a mournful sound.

Fiona jerked back after being showered with glasslike rock fragments and sharp splinters. One piece cut a gash over her left eye and another small one imbedded down on her jaw line. Both bled freely.

She grabbed the kerchief from her neck and quickly tied it around her head and over the cut to keep the blood from running down into her eye.

"I know where you are now," she mumbled when she saw the cloud of black powder smoke.

She stepped out from the rock, snapped off four quick rounds, two from her left and two from her right pistols at the boulder directly behind where the Indian had shot from, and then ducked back to cover.

Fiona was rewarded with a scream of pain from the shooter as he fell from his hide and tumbled down the mountainside. The Indian lodged limply against a small gnarled juniper beside the trail.

"More than one way to use a ricochet." She flipped open the gate, ejected the spent shells and replaced them with four rounds from her belt.

Fiona watched the body for any movement for a couple of beats—there was none. "Not breathing and not Mankiller...three more...Come out, come out, where ever you are," she said to no one in particular.

Bill crept up on top of a large boulder and looked over the edge at one of the Kiowas, White Horse. The Indian carefully watched the back trail, and then was distracted by the gunfire.

Bill took that as a cue, scrunched his hat down, drew his Bowie and launched his body at the renegade below. At only one hundred and fifty pounds, Roberts was not a big man. But, hurtling down eight feet through the air created a force that took the larger Indian from his feet, momentarily stunning him.

White Horse staggered erect while Bill bounced up, sweeping a leg under the Kiowa and sending him down again. Roberts dove on top, buried his knife up to the hilt in the man's chest and held it there until his last spasm. He raised up from the dead Indian and whistled sharply once.

"That makes two." Fiona worked her way forward until she was no more than fifty feet from the wide open area in front of the cave. She tried to make out Bill's position across the trail and finally saw the top of his gray Homburg on the other side of a boulder. At the same time she heard the pounding of horses' hooves, and then the splashing as they entered the water.

She stepped out from her cover to see two Indians on horseback sloshing in the middle of the creek, sending white spray high into the air, and then disappearing around the far bend through the narrows. One of them was unquestionably Cal Mankiller.

"Dammit to hell!"

Across the trail, Bill raised up and saw them disappear also. He made his way over to her position.

"And our horses are a half-mile back there."

"Might as well be a hundred," she answered.

Bill looked at the blood on her face, pulled out a clean handkerchief and handed it to her. "You get hit?"

"Just rock splinters…ricochet." She dabbed at the small cut on her chin. "Ow, I think a piece is still in there."

Fiona tilted her head up for him to take a look. He leaned in, took the kerchief from her hand and cleaned the rest of the blood away.

"Yep." He took out his small pocket knife, unfolded the long master blade, flicked the sharp piece of granite loose and removed it with the cloth. "Here you go." Bill handed it to her.

"Thanks, but I don't want it…Don't keep souvenirs."

"Right." He shook the splinter free from the handkerchief, and then handed it back to her. "Still bleeding. Hold this on there till we get to the horses. Got a styptic stick in my shaving kit…I'll check that one under your headband there."

They turned and headed back up the trail.

"Might as well fix a bite of lunch and boil up some coffee before we set out after them," Fiona said after Bill cleaned the larger wound above her eye.

He stopped the bleeding and gave her a clean bandana to wrap around her head.

"Should be able find their sign after we go through that narrow canyon. Be like shootin' turtles in a barrel if they caught us coming through there."

"Good thinkin'. Let 'em settle down and think we're not on their tail. Maybe they'll think we got wounded in the exchange with the others."

She nodded. "Wonder were Ol' Pike got off to? Figured he'd come back after the shooting stopped."

"No telling. He's an odd one, all right."

After their coffee and cold corn dodgers, they tightened their cinches and rode back down to the camp area until they ran out of trail.

"They apparently checked the depth of the creek well before we got here," said Bill as they were splashing through the water.

He nervously scanned the tall cliffs above their heads.

"Good hard rock bottom, too. It was an ideal place to camp."

They rounded the last bend and came to the conjunction of Panther Creek from the north and West Cache Creek. The combined creek flowed in the direction of Fort Sill. They waded their mounts out of the water on the east side.

"Well, don't think they would go south. That goes to the fort," said Fiona as she cut for sign to the north along the bank. "Here we go." She reined Spot to a halt and studied the tracks that came out of the water. "No question, Mankiller's horse…They're headed north."

Bill took out his map and studied the area for a moment, and then looked over at Fiona. "Anadarko?"

She sidepassed the mule until he was next to Robert's Tippy and looked over at the map, too. "Fort Sill to the south, nothing but prairie to the east until the Nations. Then back to Elk Mountain to the west and eighty miles to Cloudchief to the northwest…Anadarko less than thirty miles to the northeast."

Fiona paused for a moment in thought. "To quote Arthur Conan Doyle's great detective, Sherlock Holmes, '…when you have eliminated all which is impossible, then whatever remains, however improbable, must be the truth.' I think Bass would say Anadarko." She glanced off to the south. "Well, looks like a cavalry patrol coming our way…Must have heard the gunfire."

"The echoes travel a long way in hard rock mountains." Bill looked over at the ten-man patrol, as the officer to the left of the right guide held up a gauntleted hand.

"Detail…Halt." The officer nudged his mount forward.

"Good afternoon, I'm Captain Bryan, please state your business here," said the handsome thirty-three year old soldier.

"Captain. I'm Deputy US Marshal Bill Roberts." He pulled his coat back to show his badge. "And this is Deputy US Marshal F.M. Miller."

She held up her badge from her pouch.

He noticed the blood on the bandana around her head and the fresh scab on her chin. "Do you require medical assistance, Ma'am?"

"They're just scratches and I'm fine."

"We're tracking some renegade Indians. We had a skirmish back down in the canyon there." Bill indicated behind them. "Two of them got away."

"We'll take over from here Marshal. If they're the renegades we've had reports on, it's our job to capture them and take them back to the reservation."

"I'm afraid not, Captain."

His deep blue eyes snapped over to Fiona. "I beg your pardon, Ma'am."

"One, it's not Ma'am, it's Marshal or Fiona…and two, we have jurisdiction. These particular renegades have committed multiple felonies over in the Nations and we've tracked them here.

"You may, if you so choose, recover the bodies behind us. Three may be found a little over a half mile back up Cache Creek."

"That's called The Narrows, Marshal."

"An apt description, Captain…Marshal Roberts and I killed two there. The third was a result of an argument between two of the Indians over leadership and a fourth is a half-day's ride to the north, just this side of Medicine Creek…He was dispatched by Marshal Roberts yesterday."

She pulled out the warrant from her pouch. "We're tracking the last two…This is the warrant from the Ninth Judicial District Court in Fort Smith, Arkansas, on one Calvin Mankiller…A full blood Cherokee. He's wanted for multiple counts of murder, arson, rape, larceny of horses and kidnapping…The other Indian with him is Apache or possibly Kiowa, we believe."

The officer took the paper, scanned it and handed it back. "Appears to be in order, Ma'am, uh…Marshal. Is there anything we can do to help?…I would be happy to split the patrol. Send half on body detail and I could bring the other half and assist you and Marshal Roberts."

"Not necessary, Captain Bryan…No offense intended, but, we work better alone…If you know what I mean. There are only two of them and we believe them to be heading to Anadarko."

"Yes, Ma'am, I mean Marshal. It is kind of difficult to keep a cavalry patrol quiet." He grinned as he appraised Fiona's unique attractiveness.

"Exactly…But we appreciate the offer." She flashed a big smile at the officer as her steel-gray eyes twinkled.

He blushed slightly, looked away momentarily, and then touched the brim of his olive drab slouch hat with the crossed sabers on the front and nodded.

"Detail, left wheel at the trot...Ho." He swept his right gauntleted hand over his head and pointed west.

The unit splashed forward into the water by twos behind the Captain and the right guide and headed up the canyon.

The sun was setting as Fiona and Bill trotted along to the north. The newly acquired pack horse from the Potawatomi had almost completely recovered and was easily keeping up with Tippy and Spot.

"I do believe that Captain Bryan was smitten," Bill said with a grin.

"Oh, I think he was just being polite."

He chuckled. "Not likely."

"You really think so?"

"Unh, huh...It's another ten miles or so to Anadarko, what say we camp over there by Tonkawa Creek?" commented Bill.

"I'm for that. Don't know about you, but I'm a bit worn."

"So am I...Climbing up and down mountains can do that to a body."

They reined down into the creek bottom and found an open area surrounded by trees. After pulling their tack and letting them drink their fill, they picketed the animals on some good graze.

Bill built a firepit while Fiona was over behind some cedars, changing from her buckskins to her traveling clothes. She stepped out, pulling her sheepskin coat on against the cold north wind that had sprung up.

"Hope we don't get hit by sleet again," she commented.

Bill turned, stood up from adding some larger deadfall limbs he had broken up to the growing fire and looked to the north. "Don't think so. No cloud bank…Feels like just a dry norther."

"Well, whatever…That wind can cut right through you."

"I noticed," he said as he pulled out his sheepskin coat from his carpet bag, slipped it on and wrapped a thick green wool scarf around his neck. "If you'll start the coffee and supper, I'll go gather enough driftwood and deadfall to last the night."

"Deal."

Bill dropped his third armful of wood near the firepit. He grabbed his cup and using one of his black leather gloves as a hotpad, picked up the pot filled it with Fiona's hot, stout, trail brew. "Ready?"

"I am. Everything is on and should be ready in fifteen or twenty minutes." She held out her cup.

He filled it and set the pot back on a flat rock next to the fire. "Saw what looked to be a campfire couple miles or so to the north while I was gathering wood."

"Think it was them?"

"My guess."

"Want to try to slip up to their camp?"

Bill shook his head. "No way we could sneak up on them in this country...Flat as a pancake between them and us. Nothing else, their horses would hear ours coming and alert them."

"Rather that didn't happen...Don't intend on letting them get set."

"Yep. Noticed that about you." Bill sat down on a large log he had pulled up next to the fire. "Heat feels good...Glad we're down here in the bottom. They can't see the glow and dry wood doesn't smoke much." He sniffed. "Stew smells good, too."

She grinned. "It's amazing what you can make with jerky, potatoes, wild onions, some spices and a little creativity."

The morning dawned clear and cold. A thin layer of ice crystals had formed along the edge of the bank.

Fiona filled the coffee pot and walked back to the fire as Bill was adding some more sticks and bigger branches to the coals. The dry wood almost instantly burst into flame.

Fiona opened the bag of ground coffee, added two handfuls to the water and set the blue-speckled graniteware pot on the rock at the edge of the fire. She sliced some salt pork into one skillet and poured some cornmeal and flour mush in dollops into the hot grease in another for fry bread.

Bill held his hands out to the flames and rubbed them together. He had led the boys downstream to drink, and then took them back up to their picket area and slipped nose bags on each with a bait of grain.

"We probably should lunge the guys around a bit after putting the saddles on. Expect they'll have a hump in their backs this morning."

Fiona grinned and nodded her head. "That's probably a capital idea, Marshal Roberts. This is not the kind of morning I would choose to get bucked off...Actually I wouldn't want to get bucked off anytime...If you know what I mean?"

"I do, Marshal Miller, I do indeed...Back in my younger and dumber days when I worked for Mister Chisum, that's what my job was...busting broncs. I can really tell it on mornings like this...Takes a while after I get up to get everything workin'."

"I could tell." She laughed and started forking the fry bread out of the skillet and onto a plate next to the thick slices of salt pork. "Come and get it, Mister Roberts."

He raked some of the bread and pork into his tin plate. "Now, if we just had some fresh buttermilk to go with this sumptuous meal."

"You'll have to settle for trail coffee, sir."

"It'll do m'lady, it'll do." He held out his cup for a refill.

Tippy and Spot had been lunged, brushed and saddled before Bill and Fiona mounted.

"It was a good idea to warm them up. I got to thinking, how would I feel if somebody jumped on my back first thing on a cold morning," commented Bill.

"Spot seems to be very comfortable and smooth, but, he's always smooth. He just glides, never seen a natural single foot like his."

"I can agree to that. Bet he can jump too."

"Jump?" Fiona asked as they headed out to the north at a jog trot.

"Yeah, in New Mexico they have contests for jumpin' mules. They are especially good at a standing jump...You know, what we would call a flatfoot jump?"

"No. I have no idea what you're talking about."

"I'll have to show you some time."

"How far do you think that fire you saw last night was?"

Bill rubbed the back of his neck. "Hard to tell at night. Depends on how big it was. If it was the Injuns, they don't build any bigger fire than they need to cook their dinner...so, might have been two or three miles."

"That's what I thought." She pulled her .45-70 Winchester from its boot, checked the chamber for a round, uncocked the hammer and laid it across her thighs.

"Think they're still there?" asked Bill.

"Probably not...Never known Mankiller to keep to camp much past daybreak...just like to be prepared. Remember when he shot your hat off down by the Red?"

He shucked his Winchester too. "I do, I do indeed."

"Be a good idea to scan ahead with your spyglass, too."

"Right, as usual." He reached back to his saddlebags and fished out the nine-inch three-stage glass.

"Where did you come by that anyway? Looks like a good one."

"Met a mariner once. Did him a favor and he gave it to me. I think he said it was a nine-power glass, extended all the way out."

"Nine power?"

"That means things look nine times closer than they really are."

"I know what it means. I've just never heard of a spyglass that powerful…A seven, yes."

He handed it across to her. "Give a look."

Fiona pulled all three sections out, making the tube a little over twenty inches long and put the small end up to her right eye. "Ow."

"What's the matter?"

"My eyebrow is still a bit sore from that cut." She held it up again and panned across the horizon ahead. "Oh, my. That's wonderful."

"See anything?"

"Just a coyote cutting out of a plum thicket and chasing a cottontail through the buffalo grass…a male coyote."

"You could tell that through the glass?"

"No, I was just funning you."

He shook his head and held out his hand. "Gimme that. I might have known…You do the trackin', I'll scout."

She grinned. "Let's check that coolie over there that runs down to the creek. I'd say it's between two or three miles from our campsite."

"Looks like a good spot to start."

Fiona's mule turned one of his long ears back toward Bill. She laughed. "I think he thought you were talking to him."

"Smart mule."

"I could've told you that."

They pulled rein at the edge of the shallow draw. "Ah, hah, ashes…They're not even trying to hide their tracks. Either they're overconfident or they're wanting us to follow them."

"Follow them?"

"Confrontation time. I think he's tired of running and wants to get his revenge for me shooting him…He's trying to make it on his terms…That's not going to happen."

Two miles closer to Anadarko, Fiona was first to notice a spiral of smoke ahead and to the east over a slight rise.

"Smoke? Too big to be a campfire."

"I think it's a house or barn fire," commented Bill.

"Oh, no!" She nudged Spot into a gallop.

Bill urged Tippy and the pack horse to keep up.

They topped the low hill to see a small white board and batt house fully engulfed in flames. There were three bodies in the yard scattered between the house and a small shed.

She dismounted from Spot before he was completely stopped and ran to the smallest body that was nearest the house. It was a young girl around three years old in a faded calico dress. Her throat was cut—and she had been scalped.

Fiona slumped to her knees as her body shook with sobs. "Damn him, damn him, damn him," she whispered through gritted teeth and her tears while gently closing the sightless eyes with her finger tips.

Bill dismounted, checked the woman, and then the man closer to the shed. Both were dead, shot and scalped.

The farmer was unarmed. Bill walked over to Fiona and helped the crying woman to her feet. He held her against his chest.

"Let it go, Fiona, let it go."

"Why is God doing this? Why? Why? Why?"

"It's not God, this is Lucifer's doings. That Cherokee is the messenger and personification of evil…the archenemy of all humankind."

She leaned back, tears streaming down her face. "Then I am God's sword of justice and will see him cast into the lake of fire."

They buried the family near an apple tree at the side of the ashes of their home.

Fiona took her King James Bible from her saddlebags and read over the graves, "'To every thing there is a season, and a time to every purpose under the heaven: A time to be born, and a time to die; a time to plant, and a time to pluck up that which is planted; A time to kill, and a time to heal…When thou passest through the waters, I will be with thee; and through the rivers, they shall not overflow thee: when thou walkest through the fire, thou shalt not be burned; neither shall the flame kindle upon thee.'"

She closed her small leather-bound Bible and held it close to her breast and with tears still streaming down her face, she looked heavenward. "Take these innocent souls, Lord, and hold them to thy bosom. These things we ask in Jesus name…Amen."

"Amen," added Bill.

"We'll have the undertaker from Anadarko come out and erect markers. Surly someone in town will know this family's name."

"Let's hope so."

Fiona stopped and looked at the ground before she mounted Spot. "There are two more sets of tracks that joined Mankiller and the other renegade."

"Looks like reinforcements."

§§§

CHAPTER FOURTEEN

ANADARKO, OT

They pulled rein in front of the Redskin Livery at the end of the main street. Dab Muffleshaw, the elderly proprietor, stepped out, his cheek bulging with his customary wad of tobacco. He let go a long stream of the obnoxious brown fluid in the dirt.

"Well, looky here, looky here. It's Marshals Miller and Roberts. Back from yer trek to the mountains I see...Where's your paloose?"

A dark cloud came over Fiona's face. "One of those renegades shot him out from under me."

"Damnation! Sorry to hear that. He was a fine animal."

"He was."

"Did you get the scoundrel what done it?"

"Marshal Roberts did."

Dab spat another stream in the dirt, splattering some on his worn Jefferson boondockers. "Damn."

He wiped the dribble on his chin with the sleeve of his once white boiled shirt, lifted his battered old gray fedora and cleaned the inside band with a grimy blue kerchief, and then put it back on his balding head.

"Seen two of that original bunch come into town couple of hours ago, they was two more with 'em I ain't seen afore…Took 'em to be Apache. Tied their horses in front of Big Dog's saloon, they did."

They looked down the street and saw four animals standing hip-shot at the hitching rails…the dried lather on their shoulders glistened in the sun. There were six additional horses tied on the other side.

"Need to get them outside, Marshal," said Bill. "Looks like *Lesh* is getting a crowd in there…too dangerous. Some citizens are gonna get hurt."

"You're right. I don't see Mankiller coming peaceable or any of the others, most likely…I suspect the reason he recruited some help is he's ready for a confrontation." Fiona set her jaw. "But, he wants the numbers in his favor."

"Well, he's got that. It's four to me and you…Guess he doesn't realize how much trouble he's in."

Fiona noticed a teenaged boy in faded bib overalls over a tattered pullover long sleeved shirt inside the livery, cleaning stalls. "Who's the young man you have working in there, Dab?"

"Oh, that's a local boy, Willie McFee. The school marm, let's him out jest after lunch so's he can come down here and work for me…Family needs the money, if you know what I mean?"

She smiled. "Oh, I do, I do indeed…Call him out here, would you please?"

He nodded and turned to the open doorway. "Willie! Put yer rake down an' come out here fer a minute."

The redheaded lad looked up, leaned his rake against a stall and shuffled out the front. He jerked his battered Melon hat from his head and held it in front of him, nervously twisting it in his hands. "Yessir."

"Willie, this here is Marshals Miller and Roberts."

"Howdo…Did I do somethin' wrong?"

His apprehension was obvious as he nodded at the two law officers.

Fiona took a a short pencil and a small spiral notebook from her inside coat pocket, opened it and jotted down something on the first page. She ripped it out and folded it over.

"No, nothing like that…Willie, we need you to take this note in to Mister *Lesh* down at the saloon…If you can do that, I've got two silver dollars for you."

"Golly gee, Marshal! That's more'n I make in a week." He grinned from ear to ear and his eyes lit up.

"Can you do it?"

"Yessum, I shore can." He jammed his hat back on his head as she handed him the note. "Now, you tell Big Dog that Marshals Miller and Roberts gave you this note and he's to read it to some Indians inside. Understand?…He'll know who."

He nodded.

"Then you skeedaddle on out of there. Don't dawdle…All right?"

"Yessum, I'm more'n pleased to take care of this for you. Mister *Lesh* is my friend. He lets me sweep up ever Sunday mornin' 'fore church…Place kin git purty tore up on Saturday nights, you know?"

"I can imagine…Now scoot."

Willie took off at a dead run toward the Sandbar Saloon at the opposite end of the street.

"Hope he does what I told him and gets right on out of there. I don't trust Mankiller as far as I can throw him."

"Hear tell he's a real miscreant an' evildoer," commented Dab.

"That doesn't even start telling it with him," said Bill.

Willie slipped in the saloon by crawling under the batwing doors instead of pushing through them. He quickly walked over to the end of the bar nearest the door.

Kiwat Lesh, serving a cowboy at the opposite end, noticed the young man motioning. He strolled over to him and pretended to wipe the top of the bar.

"What can I help you with Willie? You look a little out of breath."

"Yessir, I ran all the way from down to the livery. Got a message fer ya." He handed him the note. "This is from Marshals Miller and Roberts. The lady law said to tell you this was from them an' to read the note to some Injuns."

He looked around the saloon and noticed the four renegades against the far wall, drinking beer. "Said you'd know who an' then fer me to git."

"I understand, Willie. Now you hightail it….Go, go," he whispered and nodded toward the door.

"Yessir." He turned, scooted back under the door and took off running back down the street to the livery.

Lesh unfolded the note and looked up at the four Indians across the room. He reached down under the bar and brought up his sawed-off double-barreled Remington shotgun and laid it on top. "Mankiller! Got a message for you," the big man raised his voice so the renegades could hear—but so could everyone else in the saloon.

The Cherokee's gaze moved to the bartender. "What?" he replied with no small degree of irritation.

"There's two marshals down the street...one of them is a lady. Says you call her, *Ageyv Tvs-gina*...She Devil. The other is *pindah-lickyoee*. Sent you a note: 'Black Fox, whose Cherokee name should be *Asgaihv Tsisdu* or Frightened Rabbit, brings much shame upon his people. Killer of women and children doesn't have the courage to meet She Devil outside. He should bring his cowardly Apache friends for help. We wait'." He laid his hand on top of the deadly ten gauge.

His action was noted by Mankiller. "*Inoli* does not fear any woman. He kill," he said as he got to his feet.

The Cherokee motioned to the other three at the table—they also rose. He leaned over and whispered in *Kuruk's* ear.

The Apache nodded, grabbed his Winchester leaning against the wall, turned and headed down the hallway to the back deck that extended out over the Wichita River.

Kuruk pushed open the screen door at the back, walked to the west end of the deck and climbed up a wooden ladder built against the side of the building to the roof. He crawled on top, slipped over and knelt down behind the four-foot high false front that extended above the roof.

The Apache levered a round into the chamber of his rifle and peeked over the top of the facade. From his vantage point, he could see the entire length of the street—he waited.

Willie ran back up to the marshals and Dab. They had stepped just inside the aisleway of the livery.

"I done jest like you said, Marshal Miller."

She reached in her coat pocket and pulled out three shiny Morgan silver dollars and handed two of them to the teenager. "Thank you, young man. Now here's another if you'll stall our stock, give them a good brushing and a bait of your best grain." She gave him the third dollar. "You stay inside here, no matter what, you hear me?"

"Yessum." He stared at the three ounces of silver in the palm of his hand. "I'll spend the whole night in here, if'n you want me too."

Fiona patted his shoulder. "I really don't think that will be necessary, Willie, but thank you."

"Unh, huh, thank you, Marshal." He grinned as he led Spot and the two horses toward their stalls.

"Just a minute, Willie."

The young man stopped and turned. "Yessum?"

"I need to get something." She stepped over to Spot and pulled her '86 .45-70 long-barreled Winchester from its boot. "Now you can go ahead."

She headed back to Bill and Dab. "Two to one Mankiller is putting one of the Indians on the roof of the saloon as we speak. He'll spread out the other two on each side of the street…Then the treacherous bastard will claim he wants to meet me, one on one."

"Marshals, if'n you don't mind, I'd like to help."

She and Bill both shook their heads.

"Too dangerous, Dab. We appreciate it, though."

"Don't mean to brag, but I made a livin' shootin' buffler back in the day...Learn't the trade bein' a sharpshooter fer the Confederates with a .451 Whitworth...She was accurate up to 600 yards."

Fiona and Bill exchanged glances.

Dab looked out the big double doors of the livery and pointed. "I could git atop of Gibson's Drygoods 'cross the street. Good view of the saloon from there...Ain't but two hunderd yards...Hell, I kin purtnear spit that fer." He chuckled.

Fiona grinned and handed him her rifle. "All right...I know this isn't a Whitworth, but it'll hold seven rounds. Shouldn't have to reload."

"If'n they's only one Injun on top of the Sandbar...won't need but one round...bring you six back." He spat into the loose straw in the aisleway. "I'll slip out the back, circle around to the west an' go in the rear of Gibson's...Percy's got a inside ladder to the roof fer patchin' leaks an' such."

"We'll wait till we see you wave from the top, before we head out. If Mankiller did put somebody up there, he'll wait till we're about fifty feet or so from the saloon. Then he'll raise up to take his shot, thinking he's got us dead to rights, so to speak," said Bill.

"It'll be the last thang that redhide'll ever do…Ol' Dab'll cut him loose from his pockets."

Mankiller waited until he heard *Kuruk* on the roof. "*Taza* go across street to water trough down in front of store that sells food. *Delshay* stay on this side. Go to alley one block before livery…hide other side of barrels. Wait till law dogs pass. You be behind…Mankiller wait in street. We kill *liga haasti'*."

Dab settled in on Gibson's roof, checked down the street and briefly saw the top of the Apache's head above the facade. The renegade wasn't looking his way yet. He waved at Bill watching from inside the alleyway.

He and Fiona stepped out into the street, but then they split up. Bill got on the boardwalk on the north side and Fiona on the south—both stayed in the shadow of the canopies.

Dab chuckled. "Yep, never do what they expect."

He looked down at his target above the saloon. The Apache had poked his head up three times like a turkey, and then ducked back down.

Delshay got to his feet from behind the trash barrels in the alley, stepped out a couple of steps and pulled the hammer back on his Henry. He took a bead on Fiona's back after she passed.

A shot rang out, followed by the thud of a bullet striking flesh. Another shot discharged into the dirt of the alleyway as the Apache's finger spasmed on his trigger. He collapsed and fell forward, mortally wounded with a hole in the middle of his chest from Bill's Thunderer from across the street.

Taza looked up from his hiding place behind the water trough and saw *Delshay* fall. He turned to fire at the source of the smoke on his side of the street and took a bullet through his ribs from one of Fiona's .38-40s. He staggered forward and Bill put a round in the middle of his forehead.

Mankiller was confused. He stood in the middle of the street, looking first at the gunsmoke on one side, and then on the other. He saw both Apaches fall, but could not see either of the marshals in the shadows. Sweat began to bead on his upper lip as his soulless black eyes flicked about.

Fiona replaced the spent round in her pistol and holstered it. As if on cue, she and Bill stepped out into the street walking slowly toward the Cherokee.

Behind the false front above the Sandbar, *Kuruk* saw his chance, raised up and aimed down into the street. A large chunk of wood was torn from the top of the facade to the left of his face. The Apache jerked his shot in reaction and the bullet meant for Fiona caught Bill in the thigh.

Kuruk's head exploded into a massive cloud of pink mist as the second boom of the big bore .45-70 echoed up and down the street. He collapsed to his knees, fell over the facade, tumbled to the top of the porch canopy, and then rolled off into the street. His body landed ten feet to Mankiller's right.

"You hit, Bill?" she asked.

"Only in the leg," he replied. "Too far from my heart."

Fiona continued her inexorable march toward the Cherokee. She finally stopped thirty feet in front of him.

She had removed her black morning coat down at the livery and was down to her red paisley bustier over a white blouse with mutton sleeves and her dark gray split riding skirt.

Her Deputy US Marshal's badge was pinned on the left side just below the top of the bustier. Her ivory-gripped twin Peacemakers she carried in a black concho studded cross-draw belt and holsters, shone in the sunshine.

Mankiller shook from both anger and confusion.

"Do you want to turn yourself in Calvin Mankiller?" she said softly.

"Cherokee die first," he hissed.

"Suits me."

"But take *Ageyv Tvs-gina* with him."

Fiona grinned. "Not likely."

His left hand flicked and in the blink of an eye, his ten inch bone-handled Bowie buried itself in her left shoulder. It struck below her clavicle with a loud thunk. He had hidden the deadly weapon in his hand folded up behind his arm. The Cherokee reached for his revolver.

Fiona staggered back one step, simultaneously palmed her right hand Peacemaker. It roared as she shot Mankiller in the arm before he could clear leather with his Remington pistol. He yelled in pain, grabbed his upper arm with his off hand and dropped the gun to the street. The Indian tried to reach down and pick it up.

She took a step forward, cocked her pistol again and shot him in the left kneecap. He screamed and dropped to that knee. "That was for the Histree family in Pickens County."

Her pistol roared again as she shot his right ear off. He screamed once more and tried to grab the bleeding side of his head.

"That was for the Butlers and their two children you killed and scalped, you worthless scum."

Fiona cocked her pistol again and shot his left foot. "That's for the Farquhars and their three year old daughter whose throat you cut, and then you scalped."

The air around her was permeated with the sulfuric smell and haze of blackpowder smoke.

She shot his right kneecap. He collapsed to the dirt and raised up on his elbow.

"That was for the four people you killed at Ashalintubbi's Merchantile, including a seven year old girl," she said through gritted teeth.

"No, *Ageyv Tvs-gina*…Stop!"

"How many of your victims asked and pleaded for you to stop? How many?...Tell me, you evil bastard!"

She shot his left ear off, holstered that Peacemaker, reached over and drew the other and cocked it. Her left arm hung uselessly at her side. "That was for the Hancocks in Cooke County that you gutted in front of their children."

He held up his right hand, tears of pain were rolling down his brown face. "Stop...Stop, Mankiller surrender."

She shot him through that hand. "That's for my friend Faye Skeens, that you kidnapped and raped."

Fiona cocked her pistol again. This time she gut shot him. "And that's for the family and a scalped little three year old blond-headed child we buried right outside of town this morning." Tears were running down her cheeks.

Mankiller lifted his face from the dirt and held up his bloody hand again. "Please!"

"All right, if you insist...This is for my husband...Welcome to your first day in hell!" she hissed.

Fiona shot him between the eyes and holstered her Peacemaker as Mankiller flopped over on his back. His left heel drummed briefly in the dirt—and then was still.

Bill hobbled up beside her and was quickly joined by a wide-eyed Dab. "My God in Heaven, Fiona. I thought you were going to bring him to justice."

"I just did." Her eyes rolled back up into her head and she collapsed to the street.

"Get a doctor," Bill yelled.

Big Dog had come out of his saloon and watched her ceremoniously dispatch Mankiller. "Don't have one."

He turned as he heard hooves pounding from down the street. "Look, here comes Captain Bryan and his cavalry patrol. He'll have a doctor with him."

"Detail...halt." He held up his hand and quickly assessed the situation. "Medical Officer, front and center." He dismounted and handed his reins to the right guide.

A US Army Major in the second rank behind the captain, dismounted, unbuckled his medical kit from behind the cantle of the McCellan saddle, rushed forward and removed his gauntlets. He knelt beside Fiona, and felt her pulse.

"We've got to get this woman inside somewhere. That knife has to come out...plus she's in shock."

"Corporals Smith and Tyree, Privates Barber and Rigler, front and center with a blanket, on the double...Place Marshal Miller in the center, be particular with her now, and carry her..." ordered the Captain. "...where, Mister *Lesh*?"

"This way, men, I have an empty bedroom in the back...it's mine," said Big Dog.

He led the four troopers carrying Fiona into the saloon and to his room in the back.

The doctor noticed Bill's blood-soaked pant leg as he hobbled toward the batwing doors of the saloon. "It appears you are in need of medical attention also, Marshal."

"It'll keep. Tend to her first."

"I'm Major George Williford. Take this strap and wrap it above the wound as a tourniquet. It doesn't appear that the bullet hit your artery and with you walking…it didn't hit the femur either." He handed Bill a one inch wide woven canvas strap with a brass buckle from his bag.

"No, sir. I guess if it had I'd already be dead."

"That's probably true, Marshal…?"

"Roberts, Brushy Bill Roberts."

"Just sit down inside and prop that leg up, Marshal Roberts. I'll take care of it later."

"All right if I have a drink?"

"Can't see that it could hurt at this stage. Might help deaden the pain."

He motioned to the two remaining troopers as they were finishing tying the patrol's mounts to the hitching rails. "Give this man a hand, gentlemen."

"Yessir," the two soldiers responded.

Bill draped his arms over each man's shoulders and they proceeded into the saloon.

Thirty minutes later, the Major came out of *Lesh's* bedroom drying his hands on a clean towel. He had removed his blouse, rolled up the sleeves to his dark blue center-button shirt and opened his collar.

"How's Fiona?" asked Bill.

"She's going to be fine, no major damage and she's out of danger from shock, now. Her scapula prevented the knife from going all the way through, so, only had one wound to disinfect and sew up…She'll be pretty sore for a few weeks…Glad she didn't wake up until I finished the stitches…Don't have any ether with me." He looked down at Robert's blood-soaked pant leg again.

"Sorry, Marshal, I'm going to have to cut your trousers to get to that wound."

"That's fine Major. They're already torn in a few places from crawling over your mountains down south…plus the bullet hole." He tried to chuckle, but the increasing pain wouldn't let him.

The doctor, took out his scissors and split Bill's pants from knee to hip. "Big Dog, I need some more hot water for the good marshal here."

"Comin' right up, Doc," said *Lesh*.

"Here, Marshal, drink this…I've got to dig that bullet out."

Bill looked at the dark green bottle. "Laudanum?"

"It is…Two big swallows, if you would."

"Wonderful. Hate this stuff."

"Beats the alternative," said the doctor.

"It does that. I've been there a few times…Actually I have some twenty-five bullet and knife scars at last count…Well, I guess I'll have twenty-six when you're finished."

He took his two swallows of the bitter, cocaine-laced pain killer and wrinkled his face.

"Great stars, man! How did you get all that many?"

Bill shook his head and grinned. "Been on both sides of this badge since I was about seventeen…Gotta learn to duck more."

Kiwat Lesh set a pan of hot water on a table. "Anything else, Doc?"

"Yes, need to pull a couple of these tables together so I can stretch Marshal Roberts out. Easier to work on his leg."

"Dab, wanta to give me a hand?"

"Shore, Big Dog."

The two men pulled the tables together. *Lesh* got a cloth from under the bar and covered them, and then he and Dab helped Roberts up and laid him down across the tops.

"Be back in a moment with a pillow, Marshal."

"Would appreciate it, Dog." Bill smiled a lopsided grin.

"Looks like my patient is about ready," said the doctor.

Thirty minutes later, the doctor finished tying off a clean white bandage around a semiconscious Bill Roberts' thigh. "I had no idea there were that many verses to *Lily of the West*," Major Williford said with grin.

A bloody pair of forceps and a .44-40 slug lay in a wash pan on a table behind him.

Bill looked up at him, his eyes were still a little dilated. "Are you done, Doc?"

"I am, Marshal."

"Damn good thing…Felt like you were grubbing for potatoes in there."

"Mister Muffleshaw went across the street to get you a set of crutches from the mercantile."

He sat up on one elbow. "Who?"

"Dab…Dab Muffleshaw."

"Oh, hell, why didn't you just say so." He laid back down on the table. "I think I need another shot of your sour mash, Mister *Lesh*.

Kiwat looked at the doctor.

He nodded. "Think I'll have one too. That all right with you, Captain?"

"Let's say you're officially off duty, Doctor…Actually let's say we're all officially off duty."

"Drinks are on the house, then," announced Big Dog.

Dab came back in the front door with a set of brand new crutches and leaned them against the tables Bill was lying on.

He sat up, grabbed the crutches and balanced on one leg until he got them under each arm. "Whew, glad to get off that table. It's worse than sleeping on the ground…Gotta go check on Fiona." Bill worked his way toward *Kiwat Lesh's* room where she was and eased the door open.

Dab, Captain Bryan, the doctor and Big Dog followed him inside.

She was propped up in the bed on some pillows and looked over as the group entered. "Well, I know this isn't a wake, so it must be the welcome back committee."

"Ha, she lives," said Bill. He glanced over and saw Mankiller's knife on the bedside stand. "Thought you didn't keep souvenirs?"

She glanced at the big knife too. "Decided to make an exception…Gonna hang it on my wall. If I ever get one."

"Hell of a knife," Bill commented. "Damn lucky, I'd say."

Fiona looked down at the bandages and her left arm in a new white cotton sling, and then up at Bill and *his* bandages. "I see you've also been the recipient of the good Doctor Williford's ministrations."

"I have." Bill swung the crutches aside, sat down in a bow chair next to the bed and held out his hand to Dab for his shot glass of whisky. "Thank you, sir."

"If that's sour mash, where's mine?" inquired Fiona.

"Coming right up, Marshal," said *Lesh* as he left the room.

She looked over at Dab. "One shot, huh, Mister Muffleshaw? I heard two from my Winchester."

Dab looked down at the floor. "Sorry, Marshal, she shoots a tad to the left. The first shot told me that." He grinned. "I put the second one in his melon." He reached in his pocket and pulled out some of the big rounds. "Here's five back."

She smiled. "Good enough. I'll get them later...Sights must have gotten knocked off when my sweet Diablo went down...You're forgiven."

"Oh, I took them renegade's horses and tack down to the livery. You won't believe what I found in one set of the saddlebags."

The corners of Fiona's eyes turned down. "Scalps."

"Stinkin' to high Heaven."

"Bury them, if you would. Three of them, including one that would be blond with ring curls, belong to the family just outside of town."

Dab nodded. "The Patterson family. The little girl was named Kathrine...I'll see that the undertaker gets 'em. I'm gonna sell the horses and tack and have him bury them proper, in caskets and all...They were friends of mine," his voice broke slightly.

"Thank you," Fiona whispered to him.

Lesh came back with a glass of whisky in one hand and the bottle in the other. "Your sour mash, Marshal...I brought the bottle in case anybody needs a refill."

She held the glass up with her good right hand. "Here's to the elimination of another scourge of the west...In a country that becomes too civilized to administer exact justice to evil...barbarians will rule."

"Another quote I don't recognize, Miz Miller. Who said that one?" asked Bill

Fiona looked at him with a wry grin. "Whose lips were moving when you heard it, Marshal Roberts?"

§§§

EPILOGUE

SANDBAR SALOON
ANADARKO, OT

Fiona and Bill sat at a table near the bar having snifters of a special liquor with Captain Bryan. Roberts had his crutches propped against a nearby chair.

"Excellent brandy, *Kiwat*," said Bryan.

"Just a little somethin' I keep in the back for special people, except it's not really brandy."

"What is it?"

"This is called Courvoisier VS, Captain, a brand of cognac made in France. It was a favorite of Napoleon," said Fiona.

"Unbelievably smooth," commented Bill. "What does the VS stand for?"

"Very Special," replied *Lesh.*

"And very special it is too. Never had anything quite like it...I'm afraid you may have spoiled me, *Kiwat,*" said the Captain. He glanced over at Fiona with her white cotton sling. "How's that shoulder, Marshal?"

Her steel-gray eyes looked at the tall cavalry officer from under the brim of her hat. "Sore...But Doctor Williford did a nice job stitching it up. Just glad we can ride the train back to Gainesville. Don't think horseback, or in my case muleback would do it a lot of good."

"Captain, I've heard there's some trouble brewing down in Cuba...I'm considering coming down to Fort Sill and enlisting soon as my leg heals up."

"Interesting you bring that up, Bill. President McKinley has called for 1,250 cavalry volunteers to assist in the war efforts. Assistant Secretary of the Navy, Theodore Roosevelt, has been pushing for American involvement in the Cuban War of Independence since it started. It just so happens that Fort Sill is one of the recruitment stations for the 2nd Cavalry Brigade."

"Bill! This is the first I've heard of this."

He ducked his head and grinned. "Well, you know me, Fiona, I haven't been in one place more than two years since I left New Mexico in '81." He glanced over at Bryan. "I've always admired the cavalry, Captain."

"Call me Jim...for now. Of course, after you enlist it will be 'Sir'."

Roberts laughed. "Sounds good to me."

"Your name is Jim, short for James?"

"That's what my mama said. 'Course she only called me James...with my middle name, when I was in trouble."

She smiled. "What's your middle name?"

"Reese...James Reese Bryan...I can still hear her, 'James Reese, you get out of there. I'll take a peach switch to your bohunkas.'...And the funny thing was, she didn't even have to see me to know what I was doing."

"Mothers are like that." Her eyes twinkled.

He raised his glass in a toast. "To mothers everywhere."

They each took a sip of the Courvoisier.

"Well, here's to the United States Cavalry," said Bill holding his glass up.

"Here, here," said Bryan.

They each took another sip.

"May have to keep thinking of things to toast."

"I've got several more bottles, Captain," commented *Lesh*.

Bryan turned to Fiona. "I took it on myself to wire your friend in Gainesville, Town Marshal Walt Durbin, to bring him up to date on you, Bill and Mankiller. He told me there was a two thousand dollar reward on the Cherokee, now...It would be waiting for you when you get back."

She glanced at Bill. "I want to tell him to give it to the Hancock children there in Cooke County...That all right with you, Bill?"

"Absolutely...Don't think I'll be needing it anyway."

"Well...I'm considering resigning my commission."

"Do what?" Bill almost shouted. "Why?"

"One, I took care of the main reason I became a marshal in the first place, and two...I feel like I pushed the ethics envelope when I took him down...but, in my heart, I felt like just hanging wasn't enough punishment for all the inhuman atrocities he committed...I wanted him to suffer like he made his victims suffer."

"And not counting the fact that Judge Parker's no longer around to see justice done...I can't help but remember one of his expressions the preacher used at his funeral, 'It is not the severity of the punishment that is the deterrent...but the certainty of it'...No telling what philosophy the new judge is going to have...What do you think you'll do?" asked Bill.

"I've developed some pretty good skills and bounty hunters don't have to answer to anyone...I'm sure there are others out there in the same category as Mankiller...murderers, rapists, pedophiles...I would go after the worst, they always have dead or alive conditions to their bounty."

Bill nodded. "Yeah...A lot more profitable, too."

"I just didn't think I could handle it if somehow that beast got off."

Roberts grinned slightly. "I think you took care of that situation, quite well...But, I understand what you're saying."

"You know, I'm still amazed you and Bill took out that entire gang of renegades. Wish we could have participated. They were some of the baddest of the bad."

"Oh, believe me, you're preaching to the choir, Jim. I had been after the Cherokee for three years...Thought I killed him once. I was making sure this time...I'm just glad we had some help from Dab in taking them out here in town. Chances are that Apache could have shot us both from that roof top...I wouldn't mind having him watch my back anytime."

"It was a great shot, once he zeroed in." Bill chuckled.

"But the biggest problem was locating them." She took a sip of her cognac. "Without Pike, we might still be hunting them."

Lesh looked up from drying a shot glass. "Who did you say, Marshal?"

Fiona looked over at the big bartender. "We met an old white-haired prospector in buckskins. Knew the mountains like the back of his hand. Actually we found him by accident, or he found us when we took shelter in his cave. He came in the back way with his burro, Lulabelle...Quirky old fellow. Led us right to where the renegades were camping."

"What was his name?" Big Dog cautiously asked again.

"He was Scottish. Said his name was Pahdraig Macpherson, but they called him Pike when he was in the English navy…said it stuck."

Lesh cleared his throat. "Uh, Marshal, don't really know how to tell you this, but…Ol' Pike Macpherson has been dead for nigh on to fifty years."

"That can't be," exclaimed Bill. "We ate with him. He drank our coffee and smoked one of my Virginia cigars…said he preferred Cuban though."

"Well, I have to tell you, you're not the first that's seen him…Tell me, did he talk about Andrew Jackson?"

"Yes, several times," said Bill.

"Jackson was president when Pike was roaming the Wichitas…Did you, uh, happen to find any Spanish coins?"

Fiona pulled out the two gold doubloons from her coat pocket and placed them on the bar.

Lesh and the Captain both leaned over to look at them.

"It means he wants you to come back."

"You're telling us that we spent more than twenty hours with a ghost?"

"I don't know, Marshal…I'll ask you one more question…Where was the cave where you encountered him?"

"On the south side of Elk Mountain. He said it was an old Spanish dig and went all the way through the mountain…It's where we went to get out of the storm."

Big Dog shook his head. "There is no cave in Elk Mountain...not any more. They say it collapsed in 1846 during an earthquake...Buried Pike and his donkey. Nobody knows where it even was anymore."

Bill and Fiona exchanged glances.

She picked up the coins. "And these?"

"The story goes he found the lost Spanish treasure, but never showed anybody where it was."

"May have to check that out one day. He pointed to where it was when we found these."

"I do hope you'll look me up when you come back, Marshal."

"And I do hope you'll quit calling me Marshal. How about Fiona?"

He gave her a big smile. "Make you a deal, you call me Jim and I'll call you Fiona...and to repeat, I do hope you'll look me up when you come back...Fiona."

"I think you can count on it, Jim...and, of course there's nothing to prohibit you from coming down to Texas on your next furlough...Is there?" She gave him an equally big smile, too.

The Captain looked out the batwing doors for a moment, and then back to Fiona. "There is one thing you should know."

"And?"

"I have a daughter...she's nine. Her mother died in childbirth...She goes with me to where ever my duty post is."

Fiona put her hand on his arm. "I'm so sorry that you lost your wife...I guess that's something we have in common...What's your daughter's name?"

"Ruth Ann." He smiled as he thought about her. "She's my life...I think you'll like her."

"If she's anything like her father...I'm sure I will. Can't wait to meet her."

They clinked, interlocked their arms and sipped their Courvoisier.

§§§§

TIMBER CREEK PRESS

PREVIEW OF THE NEXT
EXCITING NOVEL
IN THE NATIONS SERIES

Featuring
Fiona Miller

BLUE WATER WOMAN

by

KEN FARMER

CHAPTER ONE

RED RIVER BOTTOM
COOKE COUNTY, TEXAS

"Oh, God, run!" encouraged Billy.

"I can't," Rita said breathlessly as she staggered and fell on the game trail through the woods.

The young man came back, grabbed her arm and helped her back to her feet. "Yes, you can…Now move."

He pushed his seventeen-year old girlfriend along in front of him. Her long sandy hair waved in the slight breeze as they started running again through the dense river bottom.

Billy ran past her a short distance to clear the way through the branches and briars.

Rita tripped over an exposed root and fell again. She looked back down the trail behind her and screamed.

Her boyfriend stopped and turned. "No!"

He sprinted back around a small bend in the trail to help Rita.

Billy's death scream abruptly stopped…

SHERIFF'S OFFICE
GAINESVILLE, TEXAS

Brothers Burton and Dwight Haywood stood in front of Walt Durbin's desk, both nervously fidgeting with their short-billed caps.

The former Texas Ranger, and newly elected Sheriff of Cooke County, held up his hands to the two young men. Burton was twenty and Dwight was seventeen.

"Now slow down, boys, slow down. One at a time…Burton, you go first."

The older brother glanced over at former Deputy US Marshal Fiona Miller sitting in a straight-backed oak chair to the right of Walt's desk and then back to Sheriff Durbin. "Uh, well, you see…me an' Dee wuz squirrel huntin' along Frog Bottom, you know? 'Tween Wolf Run Ridge an' the Red?" He looked at his brother. "Anyways we come upon these two bodies…"

Dee interrupted. "It was a boy an' a girl. We knowed 'em, it was Tunk Merrill and Lucy Mae Carter...they was sweet on each other..."

"I'm tellin' this, Dee. The Sheriff tol' me to do the talkin'."

"You wuz leavin' stuff out, nimrod."

"Don't you nimrod me, you jaywacker. I'll kick yer butt from here to next week."

"Like hell..."

"Hey!" Walt snapped at them. "I said one at a time...Dee, you can talk when yer brother finishes. Understand?...I'll put one or the other of you upstairs in the hoosegow." The Sheriff nodded at Burton to continue.

The older Haywood glared at his younger sibling for a short moment, and then back to Walt. "Like I wuz sayin', we come upon Tunk and Lucy Mae's bodies an' they wuz tore up somethin' fierce..."

"Only their throats..."

He snapped at Dee. "I'm gittin' to that! Shut yer pie hole." He turned back to Walt. "Their throats wuz tore completely out like a bear er somethin' got ahold of 'em...but, they wuzn't touched no where's else that we could see."

"We hunt the Red River bottom from Montague to Grayson Counties an' we ain't never seen no bear, nor even 'ny bear sign." Dee looked at his brother. "Ain't that right, Burton?"

He nodded. "Uh, huh. Seen some panther sign couple times, though."

312

"Heard 'em, too," added Dee. "Sound like a woman a screamin'."

"Did you touch the bodies?" asked Fiona as she squinted her steel-gray eyes at the two boys.

"Uh, uh, no way, no day...Blood wuz fresh. Didn't know but what, who...er whatever done it was still close by...We run like turpentined cats," said Burton.

Fiona tried to hide a smile at their alliteration.

"Alright, boys, that'll do...for now. Believe I got the location down good enough we kin find it...Why don't you hunt on the east side of the river fer a while?"

"Yessir, don't have to tell us twict 'bout that. Ain't no way we're goin' back down to Frog Bottom," commented Dee.

He and Burton got to their feet, nodded at Fiona, and then at Walt before they turned and headed out the office door.

"What do you think?" He looked at the attractive, raven-haired former law officer, turned bounty hunter, after the door closed.

"They saw something that scared the pee out of them, that's for sure...I have to pick up Captain Bryan and his daughter, Ruth Ann, at the depot at eleven and then I can go out there for you...I'm sure he'll want to go with me. We'll leave Ruthie at Faye's... Definitely don't want to take her out there."

"How long is his furlough?"

"Two weeks."

"If I didn't have that meetin' with the new mayor and county commissioners court…"

"That's why I suggested that I go."

"How about I deputize you, to make everything legal?"

"Against my better judgment, but, just this once. You know why I resigned my marshal's commission."

"I do, but, this is a horse of a different color."

Walt opened a desk drawer and removed a brass deputy sheriff's badge, walked around his desk and started to pin it to Fiona's bustier.

"Uh, maybe you'd better do this." He handed the badge to her. "Repeat after me…"

GAINESVILLE DEPOT

The big 4x4x2 coal-fired steam locomotive released her pressure shortly after braking to a stop at the platform. Huge clouds of steam boiled out on each side and was rapidly cleared away by the morning breeze.

White-jacket clad porters pushed the four-wheel luggage dollies across the red bricks close to the tracks as passengers disembarked.

Fiona eyed the stairs at the ends of three passenger cars, and then saw a tall dark-haired man with a nine year old girl holding on to his hand. They stepped down the four steel steps to the platform and glanced around.

"Jim, Ruth Ann! Over here," Fiona waved from down the platform and walked their way.

The young girl released her father's hand, waved excitedly at the tall statuesque brunette and headed toward her. Her blonde ring curls bounced as she ran.

"Fiona, Fiona!" She wrapped her arms around the woman's tiny waist and hugged her tight.

"Ruthie, it's so good to see you again." She looked down at the big blue eyes and hugged the little girl back as her father walked up carrying two large carpet bags.

"I almost didn't recognize you without your uniform," Fiona said.

They hugged.

"That's one of the nice things about my annual furlough…I get to wear civilian clothes for a while."

"Fiona!"

They turned toward the voice and saw Doctor Winchester Ashalatubbi stepping down from the third passenger car down the platform. The white-haired Chickasaw practitioner in the dark three-piece suit and tall, uncreased black Stetson with a Red Tailed Hawk feather in the band waved.

"Who's that?" asked Ruth Ann.

"A very good friend," Fiona answered.

"Doctor Ashalatubbi. I didn't know you were coming down."

"I had a little break and thought I'd come to Gainesville and check on Bodie…and who are these lovely people?" He set his bag and physician's black valise down.

"Jim, Ruth Ann, I want you to meet a very special person…Doctor Winchester Ashalatubbi. He also goes by his Chickasaw tribal name of *Anompoli Lawa*. It means 'He Who Talks to Many'. He's a physician as well as the tribal shaman…Doctor, this is Captain Jim Bryan of the 2nd Cavalry Brigade at Fort Sill. He's on furlough…and this is his daughter, Ruth Ann."

Winchester shook Jim's hand. "Captain." He bent over, took Ruthie's hand in his and lightly kissed her fingers. "My dear it's a pleasure."

She blushed and curtsied to the elderly man. "Thank you, sir. It's an honor."

"And please call me Jim," her father said.

"Are you staying at Faye's?" asked Fiona.

"I am indeed," replied Winchester.

"I have a buggy, you're welcome to ride with us."

"Very good, I thought I was going to have to take the trolley."

"It's over this way." She led them off toward the street side of the depot.

"How's that shoulder, Fiona?" asked Ashalatubbi.

"It's still a little stiff…Finally got rid of the sling, though."

Winchester nodded. "Do plenty of stretching and range of motion exercises. It will help break down the adhesions...I'll give you some wormwood salve to rub on the scar, too."

"What are adhesions?" inquired Ruth Ann.

"Mostly scar tissue, my child...The entire shoulder has to be worked to restore full use...Takes a little time." Winchester noted the badge she was wearing. "You working for Walt now?"

"Temporarily."

"I was going to ask you about that," said Jim.

"There was a double murder up in the Red River bottom this morning. Walt has a meeting with the new mayor and the county commissioners, so I volunteered to check out the crime scene for him...It seems it's a bit unusual."

"Oh, in what way?" asked the doctor.

"The victims, a young man and woman, had their throats torn out, but no other visible signs of trauma...according to the hunters that found them...I need to go right out there." She turned to Bryan. "If you don't mind, Jim."

"No, no problem...Ruthie, do you mind staying with Missus Skeens...and maybe helping Annabel with the twins?"

She squealed. "Oh, no, daddy. I've so been looking forward to meeting Annabel and her babies."

Fiona grinned. "They're a handful."

"I should probably go out there with you after I do a quick check on Bodie. Doctor Wellman told me he was fairly covered

317

up. I'm sure he would appreciate it if I filled out the death certificates and bring the bodies in."

"Oh, wonderful. We can't take the buggy, the woods are too thick in the bottom. We'll have to pick up some horses from Clark's Livery for you and Jim…and a couple of mules for the deceased."

"Glad I brought some trail clothes," commented Bryan.

SKEENS BOARDING HOUSE

"Maybe I could go with ya'll," Bodie suggested.

Annabel looked over at Winchester. "Doctor?"

He looked up from listening to Bodie's chest with his custom-made elk antler stethoscope and scratched the back of his neck. "Well, actually, a little activity would do you some good…as long as we don't get into a hell-bent-for-leather chase with a gang of outlaws."

"Hot dang!" Bodie got up from the green velvet couch. "Let me go get my boots and gunbelt."

"What do you need your gunbelt for?" asked his wife, Annabel.

"I've decided after that run-in with Mankiller, I'm not going anywhere without it…Period. End of discussion."

"Probably not a bad idea. I feel naked without mine," said Fiona.

Bodie headed upstairs.

In a short moment, he came back down, buckling his Colt around his trim hips.

Fiona looked at Jim, the doctor and Bodie. "Shall we go, gentlemen?"

FROG BOTTOM

The horses, pack mules and even Fiona's mule, Spot, showed signs of nervousness as they neared the area of the crime scene. They snorted and danced with their ears erect and forward, their eyes focused on the dark woods up the bank from the sandbar that ran along the side of the river.

"I'd say we need to leave the stock here. All their dancing around will destroy what tracks there might be," said Fiona as she dismounted. "Let's hobble them instead of trying to tie them up to a limb or something…If they panic for some reason, we don't want to be afoot."

"Good idea," said Bodie.

The three men also stepped down and hobbled the animals.

They walked deeper up into the woods toward where the hunters said they found the bodies. Both were sprawled in grotesque positions on the game trail.

"Everyone, watch where you step," cautioned Fiona as she bent over and studied the victims. Noticing their hands, she lifted one of the young man's to look at the fresh dirt on his palms and under his fingernails.

She shuddered as a vision of an all-blue Indian woman, wearing an ornate cowrie shell and lapis lazuli necklace, swam briefly before her eyes, and just as quickly disappeared.

Winchester went directly to the bodies, knelt down beside her and examined the horrific wounds to their throats with a magnifying glass he pulled from his coat pocket. "Sweet Jesus."

He stiffened as brief vision of a giant golden-eyed white wolf flashed in his mind. The shaman shook his head, and then quickly looked the couple over for additional wounds—there were none.

"Holy Mother of God...Fiona, come over here," said Bodie from the edge of the trail.

She walked over to the Texas Ranger. "What did you find?

"Only the largest wolf track I've ever seen...The animal has got to be well over two hundred pounds."

"Can't be. Even Timber Wolves don't get that big and the only wolves we have in this part of the country are Red wolves...They're not much bigger than coyotes." Fiona knelt down to study the track.

"Damn, no question, that's a wolf track. It's as big as the fossilized tracks of Dire Wolves I've seen...They went extinct over ten thousand years ago."

Winchester stepped over from the bodies to look at the tracks. "Maybe...maybe not." He glanced around at the dense woods on both sides of the trail.

"Lord, I'd hate to meet whatever made this," commented Jim.

Fiona unconsciously loosened her right-hand Peacemaker in its holster. She still wasn't comfortable drawing with her left. "Doc, if you want to get the bodies ready to load, I'm going to backtrack them...Jim, you and Bodie see if you can follow the wolf tracks."

The two men exchanged glances.

"Right. It looks like there are more than one, maybe as many as four," agreed Bodie

"I'd say two are females," added *Anompoli Lawa*.

"Watch yourself," cautioned Fiona.

"You, too," answered Jim.

The Captain and Bodie headed off in one direction—she in another.

Fiona followed the tracks of the couple back along the game trail, stopped and knelt down. "Running," she continued, a little faster than before, and then stopped again. "The girl fell the first time. Her boyfriend came back and helped her to her feet," she mumbled.

Miller's eyes scanned the brush on both sides of the trail. She spotted a clearing through the woods ahead about thirty yards.

The two men followed the wolf tracks down to a small creek where they disappeared into the water. They crossed and walked up and down in both directions, studying the creek bank.

"I got nothing. You, Jim?"

"Nope."

"They either stayed in the creek or disappeared into thin air…There's somethin' spooky about this…Feel like we're bein' watched," said Bodie.

"You, too?"

"The hair on the back of my neck is standin' straight up…Let's see if we can catch up to Fiona."

"Agreed," said Captain Bryan.

They turned and headed back the way they had come.

Fiona broke into the small clearing, saw two shovels, two canteens and a set of large canvas saddlebags.

There were several freshly dug holes. One was at the side of a twenty-foot diameter, five-foot high earthen mound near an oak tree.

She opened one side of the bags and pulled out a map of the river bottom and a handwritten list of Indian artifacts.

Bodie and Jim reentered the part of the trail where Doctor Ashalatubbi was securing the bodies with a ball of heavy twine from his medical valise and the canvas tarps from the pack mules. He looked up as they came out of the woods.

"Any luck?"

Bodie shook his head. "Disappeared in the creek..." He looked around. "What was that?"

"What?" asked Jim.

"I heard something."

"So did I," added Winchester.

The three men looked around nervously.

"There!" said Bodie.

"Where?" inquired Jim.

Ashalatubbi pointed. "Thought I saw something move through the brush that way."

Hickman and Bryan looked in that direction.

"I don't see anything," said Jim.

"What do you hear?" asked the Chickasaw shaman.

Bodie replied, "Nothin', why?"

Anompoli Lawa looked at the two younger men. "That's the problem...There's no sound at all, no birds, no insects...Nothing."

Hickman and the cavalry officer both drew their .45s and glanced apprehensively at the dense river bottom forest around them.

A pair of gold eyes surrounded by white fur looked out from the shadows.

Fiona studied the map and noticed that the location of the mound was marked, as well as several other sites. She opened the other side of the saddlebags.

There were a number of Indian artifacts: pottery shards, some bones, a dirt-covered skull, and an ornate necklace wrapped in a linen handkerchief. It was made of cowrie shells, obsidian beads and a polished two-inch diameter lapis lazuli stone in the center, with gold flecks and filaments running through it. It was the same necklace the blue Indian woman was wearing in her vision.

Fiona held the necklace up and saw the vision once again. Chills ran down her back.

Ten minutes later she walked back into the crime scene, carrying the saddlebags and joined the three men.

"What did you find?" asked Winchester.

She set the bags down, pulled out the map and the necklace she had wrapped back in the cloth.

Ashalatubbi took the map, looked at it, and then unwrapped the necklace and held it up. "Oh, dear Jesus."

"What is it?" Bodie inquired.

The shaman looked at each of the other three, and then around at the surrounding woods. "We're on sacred land...It once belonged to the Atakapan Tejas Indian tribe…part of the Caddos…They date back many hundreds of years in this area."

"I saw a vision when I picked up the necklace of an Indian woman…She was all blue and there were several giant white wolves with her," said Fiona.

"Blue?" questioned Jim.

She nodded. "Everything. Hair, clothes…Even her skin had a light azure hue."

Jim and Bodie looked at her, and then at each other.

"As did I, Fiona," said *Anompoli Lawa*. "What we saw was an acolyte of St. Maria de Jesus de Agreda los Azule les agua Dios le Santos…the sacred spirit of the Atakapan Tejas Indian tribes…The Atakapan Tejas were also mound builders, like their relatives, the Caddo.

"Mary of Jesus' was a member of the Order of the Immaculate Conception and was widely known for the reports of her ability to bilocate between the Abby in Spain and its colonies in Texas. She was dubbed the Lady in Blue, or the Blue Nun, after the color of her order's habit…The natives called her acolyte, the Blue Water Woman."

"Bilocate?" asked Bodie.

"It was said that she never physically left Spain, but was transported by the aid of the angels to the settlements of the Indians. Her Atakapan acolyte was almost as revered as she was…The tribal Holy Shaman, if you will."

She wrinkled her forehead. "How do you know all that?"

The Chickasaw shaman cocked his head and grinned. "It's a gift…" He paused. "Like I said, this is sacred ground…and it has been violated."

Fiona frowned. "In my vision of the Blue Water Woman…she was wearing that necklace. I think they have disinterred her remains." She glanced around. "And we're being watched. I sense a presence."

"You're not the only one," said Bodie.

Several sets of gold eyes watched from the dark shadows.

"The spirit of the Blue Water Woman is disturbed. She and her Guardian Spirits are still a force to deal with," said Ashalatubbi.

"Guardian Spirits?" asked Fiona.

"Yes, they are very powerful and are able to transcend between the spirit world and our world."

"The wolves?"

Anompoli Lawa nodded. "Legend has it that the Atakapan were known to be able to shapeshift..."

"Shapeshift?" exclaimed Jim.

The old shaman looked at him. "The ability to change shape from human, or spirit, into an animal for protection or retribution."

"Like a wolf?"

"Like a wolf, Fiona…or eagles, hawk and even bear."

"Why are you and I seeing the visions?" she asked.

"For me, I'm a shaman and, as such, am in tune with the spirit world of the Indian. The Muskogean tribes...Choctaws, Chickasaws, Cherokees, Seminoles, Yamases and others of the North American continent are descended from the great mound builders. They ranged from Minnesota to Louisiana along the Mississippi basin over a thousand years ago."

"What about me? Why am I seeing them?"

"I don't know, Fiona. Something in your aura, I suppose...or possibly one of your progenitors...Now, someway, we must return her remains to her burial mound and sanctify this spot once again."

"How do we do that?" asked Bodie.

"We have to wash her remains in pure, blessed water and pray to the great spirit, *Chihoa*, to protect her as she protects others."

"Anybody got any water?"

"Not that easy, Bodie," said *Anompoli Lawa*.

Four sets of gold eyes back in the shadows surrounded the group...

SUGAR HILL SALOON
DEXTER, TEXAS

"The kids never showed back up," said Chaney, one of the four rough-looking cowboys at a round table in the dimly lit and smoky saloon.

"What do you mean,' never showed back up'?" asked Posey Sitterly, a short, stocky man, with a full mustache.

"Want me to draw you a damn picture? They didn't show up at the meeting place north of Gainesville…Me and Gifford waited till purtnear three, an' nothin'." He looked at the rail-thin man to his left. "Ain't that right, Giff?"

The pock-faced man, downed the rest of his bourbon and set the glass back on the table. "Chaney's tellin' it straight, Posey." He motioned to the portly bartender. "Owen, needin' a refill, while yer a restin'."

"Bossman's gonna be pissed," said Monte Wheeler. "Ain't real high on my list to be the one to tell him."

"What in hell's he want with all that old Injun junk fer, anyways?" asked the youngest of the group, Hayden Chaney.

"Well, damnation, Hayden, guess he plumb fergot to consult me on that," snapped Wheeler. "What do you care, long as his money's good?"

The young man looked up as the bartender filled his shot glass. "Nuthin', jest curious, is all."

"'Member what happened to Ames, when he started askin' questions?" asked Wheeler.

Chaney shook his head. "Went back to Austin, didn't he?"

The leader of the gang looked at Haden from under the brim of his worn and dirty slouch hat from his cavalry days for a long moment. "Did he?…An' leave all his gear in his hotel room?"

328

Wheeler spat at a spittoon against the wall next to their table and missed. "Shit."

RED RIVER BOTTOM
COOKE COUNTY, TEXAS

"What do you mean, Doc?" asked Bodie.

"I mean, the only place I know to get pure water is Eureka Springs in northern Arkansas."

"Excuse me?" questioned Captain Bryan.

"There's a bottomless spring there over one hundred feet across...It forms the headwaters of the White River...They say it's from melting glaciers all the way up in Canada.

"The water is purified by filtering through over three thousand miles of rock until it flows out of the ground at Eureka Springs...still ice cold. Our people camped there during *Nunna daul Tsuny.*"

"What's that?" asked Bodie.

"The Trail of Tears," responded *Anompoli Lawa.*

§§§

HISTORICAL FICTION WESTERN
THE NATIONS by Ken Farmer and Buck Stienke
HAUNTED FALLS by Ken Farmer and Buck Stienke
HELL HOLE by Ken Farmer
ACROSS the RED by Ken Farmer and Buck Stienke
BASS and the LADY by Ken Farmer and Buck Stienke
DEVIL'S CANYON by Buck Stienke

SY/FY
LEGEND of AURORA by Ken Farmer & Buck Stienke
AURORA: INVASION by Ken Farmer & Buck Stienke

HISTORICAL FICTION ROMANCE
THE TEMPLAR TRILOGY
MYSTERIOUS TEMPLAR by Adriana Girolami
THE CRIMSON AMULET by Adriana Girolami

Coming Soon

HISTORICAL FICTION WESTERN
BLUE WATER WOMAN by Ken Farmer

Coming Soon

HISTORICAL FICTION ROMANCE
TEMPLAR REDEMPTION by Adriana Girolami

TIMBER CREEK PRESS